Dragon Ops

DRAGONS VS. ROBOTS

Dragon Ops

Dragons vs. Robots

Mari Mancusi

LITTLE, BROWN AND COMPANY

NEW YORK BOSTON

Little, Brown and Company
Hachette Book Group
1290 Avenue of the Americas, New York, NY 10104
Visit us at LBYR.com

First Edition: June 2021

Little, Brown and Company is a division of Hachette Book Group, Inc. The Little, Brown name and logo are trademarks of Hachette Book Group, Inc.

The publisher is not responsible for websites (or their content) that are not owned by the publisher.

Library of Congress Cataloging-in-Publication Data
Names: Mancusi, Mari, author.
Title: Dragon Ops : dragons vs. robots / Mari Mancusi.
Other titles: Dragons vs. robots
Description: First edition. | New York : Little, Brown and Company, 2021. | Series: Dragon Ops ; 2 | Audience: Ages 8-12 | Summary: "When their friend Ikumi goes missing, Ian and Lilli must enter another dangerous digital world to save her and defeat Atreus" —Provided by publisher.
Identifiers: LCCN 2020048432 | ISBN 9780759555181 (hardcover) | ISBN 9780759555174 (ebook) | ISBN 9780759555198 (ebook)
Subjects: CYAC: Adventure and adventurers—Fiction. | Virtual reality—Fiction. | Video games—Fiction. | Dragons—Fiction.
Classification: LCC PZ7.M312178 Drg 2021 | DDC [Fic] —dc23
LC record available at https://lccn.loc.gov/2020048432

ISBNs: 978-0-7595-5518-1 (hardcover), 978-0-7595-5517-4 (ebook)

Printed in the United States of America

LSC-C

Printing 1, 2021

To Peral and Rubystar and the rest of the BPA guild.
For the transmog!!!

THE BLACK CARNIVAL

CHAT ROOM 143254

DragonOpzRumors:

Hey gamers! Check it out! I've got a NEW SCOOP straight from the vault. Something HUGE that the mainstream media is COMPLETELY IGNORING!

WhateverSauce:

This oughta be good. 🍿 🍿 🍿 🍿 🍿

DragonOpzRumors:

You know how the world's very first video game theme park, Dragon Ops, was supposed to open a month ago and never did?

DragonOpzRumors:

Well…I found out the REAL REASON it's kept its doors locked.

FieldsOfFantasyForever:

Uh, everyone knows that. They had technical difficulties. Couldn't get things to smell right.

WhateverSauce:

💩 💩 !!!

DragonOpzRumors:

YEAH. That's what THEY want you to think. But do you really believe they'd delay the opening of the biggest, most advanced, most EXPENSIVE mixed-reality theme park EVER built for SIX MONTHS because of some silly smell?

DragonOpzRumors:

It's WAY bigger than that. Like super conspiracy level big!

WhateverSauce:

😮 😮 😮

FieldsOfFantasyForever:

So what then? 🧐

DragonOpzRumors:

Turns out, they got sabotaged! By the Camelot's Honor game company.

WhateverSauce:

😮 😮 😮

DragonOpzRumors:

You know Camelot's Honor is making a similar gaming park, right? But they're way behind. So they got one of their guys to pretend to be a Dragon Ops employee. He hacked the game and trapped three kids inside—all alone!

GamingIsLife:

Trapped in a video game? What a dream come true! 😍 😍 😍 😍 😍 😍

DragonOpzRumors:

More like a nightmare! The only way out was for these kids to play through the entire game and beat the final boss—this crazy, artificially intelligent, super powered-up dragon. And if they didn't? They'd die. Like real life die.

FieldsOfFantasyForever:

Wait, DRAGON? Was it Atreus? The big bad guy in the original Fields of Fantasy game? PLEASE tell me it was Atreus! 🙏 🙏 🙏 🙏 🙏

DragonOpzRumors:

Yup. And he almost killed them, too! THAT'S why they had to delay the park opening. LITERAL ALMOST MURDER of their very first players!

WhateverSauce:

I'm not sure *literal* almost murder is a thing . . .

FieldsOfFantasyForever:

Why don't I *literally* almost murder you to find out?

WhateverSauce:

I'd LITERALLY almost like to see you try. 😂 😂 😂 😂 😂

GamingIsLife:

So wait! Who are these kids? Did they kill the dragon? Did they make it out alive? Where are they now?

GamingIsLife:

SO MANY QUESTIONS!!! 🪦 🪦 🪦 🪦 🪦

DragonOpzRumors:

Who knows? They totally disappeared off the face of the earth.

Clearly they were paid off to keep their story quiet. Otherwise no one would EVER go to Dragon Ops when it finally DOES open.

FieldsOfFantasyForever:

I would go. Anything to see Atreus in real life. Well, virtual real life anyway.

DragonOpzRumors:

Yeah, but you wouldn't. That's the craziest part!

FieldsOfFantasyForever:

⁉️ ⁉️ ⁉️ ⁉️

DragonOpzRumors:

Atreus escaped, too.

GamingIsLife:

WHAT?

DragonOpzRumors:

Yup. And they have NO IDEA where he went.

FieldsOfFantasyForever:

ATREUS IS OUT THERE? WHERE WE COULD MEET HIM? FOR FREE?

WhateverSauce:

🐉🔥🐉🔥🐉🔥🐉🔥🐉🔥🐉🔥🐉🔥🐉🔥🐉🔥🐉
🔥🐉🔥🐉🔥🐉🔥🐉🔥🐉🔥🐉🔥🐉🔥🐉🔥🐉🔥
🐉🔥🐉🔥🐉🔥🐉🔥🐉🔥🐉🔥🐉🔥🐉🔥🐉🔥🐉
🔥🐉🔥🐉🔥🐉🔥🐉🔥🐉🔥🐉🔥🐉🔥🐉🔥🐉🔥
🐉🔥🐉🔥🐉🔥🐉🔥💯💯💯💯💯💯💯

DragonOpzRumors:

It's not funny, dude. That thing is powerful. One of the most advanced AIs ever built. And now he's wandering the cloud. Who knows what he could do????

FieldsOfFantasyForever:

OMG! What if he tries to go after those kids who killed him! Like, REVENGE OF THE AI!

WhateverSauce:

🐉🔥🐉🔥🐉🔥🐉🔥🐉🔥🐉🔥🐉🔥🐉🔥🐉🔥🐉
🔥🐉🔥🐉🔥🐉🔥🐉🔥🐉🔥🐉🔥🐉🔥🐉🔥🐉🔥
🐉🔥🐉🔥🐉🔥🐉🔥🐉🔥🐉🔥🐉🔥🐉🔥🐉🔥🐉
🔥🐉🔥🐉🔥🐉🔥🐉🔥🐉🔥🐉🔥🐉🔥🐉🔥🐉🔥
🐉🔥🐉🔥🐉🔥🐉🔥💯💯💯💯💯💯💯

GamingIsLife:

Please. That's not going to happen. He's not a *real* bad guy. He's just a computer program. Computer programs don't have emotions. They don't seek revenge.

DragonOpzRumors:

But they DO follow their programming...

GamingIsLife:

What's that supposed to mean? 😱😱😱

DragonOpzRumors:

What if Atreus still thinks he's playing—but now out here in real life? What if he's wandering the cloud, still looking for those kids?

DragonOpzRumors:

What if he won't stop... until he defeats them? This time in real life?

WhateverSauce:

🐻 🐻

CHAPTER ONE

The goalie was bigger than I remembered.

That was my first thought as I approached the net, dribbling the soccer ball between my feet. He stood there blocking my shot, looking fierce and mean and taller than any twelve-year-old kid had any right to be. His face was twisted into an ugly scowl, and his beady eyes locked on me. As if to say, *Just try to get past me, dork!*

But I had to. I had no choice. The clock was ticking away. We were down three to four. No one was close enough to pass to. And the other team's defenders were bearing down.

One wrong move, and it would be game over. And it would be all my fault.

"Go, Ian! You can do it!"

My eyes shot to my left—just for the briefest second. Lilli

was in the stands, whooping and cheering in the loudest voice ever. Geez. Could she *be* any more embarrassing? Of course, my athletic sister was the one who dragged me into this whole soccer thing in the first place. The one who said it'd be "good for me" to try something new.

Easy for her to say.

I turned my attention back to the goal, now definitely within kicking reach. This was it. There was no turning back now. Should I shoot it straight or try to cross it? My heart thudded in my chest. I drew back my foot as the defenders barreled toward me. Only seconds to make the decision...

Do you want to play again?

Suddenly, my vision blurred. My whole body went numb, ice trickling down my spine. When I looked up, the goalie was gone. And in his place stood a huge red dragon with massive jaws and diamond-sharp teeth. He leered at me, sparks dancing on his tongue. Fire warming in his belly. Smoke rose around him, obscuring the goal completely.

Do you want to play again? his deep, growling voice whispered in my ear. *Do you want to play again?*

"No," I begged. "Not now. Please not now!"

"Ian! Shoot!" Lilli's voice sounded a million miles away. "What are you waiting for?"

I shook my head, trying to force myself back to reality. Soccer. Game. Real life. *Come on, Ian. Snap out of it!*

But it was too late. The defenders reached me, trampling

me, easily stealing the ball away. I hit the ground hard, breath knocked from my lungs. For a moment, I saw stars.

Then the buzzer rang. The clock ticked to zero. Cheerleaders screamed and cartwheeled across the field. The other team's parents cheered from the bleachers.

Game over.

I looked up blearily. The dragon, of course, had disappeared. Replaced by the not-actually-all-that-giant goalie who was dancing with glee. "Nice try, nerd!" he jeered. "Maybe next time you won't choke."

I dropped my head back into the grass. Maybe I would sink right through.

No such luck. "Rivera! What were you thinking?" a voice demanded from above. "You totally had that!"

I lifted my head. Josh, the team's captain, was standing over me, his blond mop of curly hair falling into his eyes. His arms were crossed over his chest, and his lips set into a scowl. Which was pretty much his default expression when looking at me.

I considered sticking my head back into the grass, pretending I'd died or something. Maybe he'd give up and go away.

"If you weren't going to shoot, you could have passed it to me," he added, his voice thick with exasperation. "I was totally open."

Uh yeah. I was pretty sure he hadn't been. No team ever let Josh the Jock run around the field without at least two defenders trailing close behind. It was too dangerous. He was too good.

But I didn't have the energy to argue. And hey, I prob-ably *should* have passed it to him, even if half the team had been up in his grill at the time. People like Josh didn't choke under pressure.

Unlike, say, people like me.

I forced myself to my feet. I could feel the cold stares of the other players, not to mention their parents, as I trudged off the field trying desperately not to cry. They wouldn't say anything to me—they weren't *those* kind of parents. But I knew what they were thinking. *Eight-Bit Ian, hopeless nerd. Go back to your video games.*

Yeah. Believe me, I would if I could...

Ugh. I should have never listened to Lilli.

Just think of it as a real-life video game, she'd said. *You'll have so much fun. Meet new people.*

She hadn't mentioned they'd be people like Josh. Who were about as *fun* as mandatory standardized testing a week before Christmas. Josh lived, breathed, and probably ate soc-cer ball cereal for breakfast. He cared for nothing but the game. Well, besides *winning* the game, that was. And let's just say he didn't appreciate noobs like me messing up his chances.

⚡

"Ian!" Lilli cried now, rushing in my direction. She threw her arms around me, hugging me as if I was the hero of the game instead of the guy who caused everyone to lose. I shrugged her off, annoyed. I didn't need her brand of rah-rah-believe-in-yourself in my life right now. Not when I'd just made a fool of myself in front of everyone.

"Are you okay?" she asked, peering at me worriedly. "You just kind of froze out there. Like...you'd seen a ghost or something."

I winced, untangling myself from her hug. If only she knew how close she was. And yet totally off base at the same time. In fact, I only wished it were a ghost taunting me from the goal. Because ghosts weren't real.

Unlike AI dragons escaped from a certain video game...

Do you want to play again? Do you want to play AGAIN?

"I'm fine," I muttered. "Just...a brain fart or whatever."

She gave me a pitying look. "It was a tough shot," she assured me. "I bet I couldn't have gotten it in, either."

"Of course you could have," I groaned. Lilli was as soccer crazy as Josh these days. She practiced in the backyard every chance she got. "You probably could have done it with your eyes closed."

"Maybe one eye," she teased. Then she caught my look and sighed. "Come on, Ian. You just started playing. You're going to get better. You just need practice. I'll practice with you if you want. Just the two of us. It'll be fun."

"Yeah. As much fun as the stomach flu at a spelling bee."

Her face sank, and I immediately felt bad. She had been

nothing but supportive of me through this whole thing. Teaching me the rules, helping me practice. Coming along to every game. None of this was her fault.

"Look, Lilli, it just isn't my thing," I tried to plead. "I tried it. I'm no good."

"Only because you haven't played enough. I mean, it's like a video game. How awful were we in Dragon Ops when we first started playing?"

I froze, my stomach suddenly swimming with nausea. Lilli caught my look and snapped her mouth shut, her face pinkening as she realized she'd just said the *D-O* words—something we were never ever supposed to do. Especially not in public. In fact, the game company's legal team had made us and our parents sign a bazillion forms that threatened all sorts of bad legal stuff if we ever went public with our story. Even mentioning the game's name was strictly off-limits. Never mind talking about all the crazy stuff that had happened to us there.

Stuff that had almost cost us our lives.

They'd tried to make up for it, of course. Threw a ton of money at us for our "pain and suffering" until our college funds were stuffed to the brim. I'd gotten a brand-new laptop out of the deal, too. Which at the time had seemed really awesome. But since then, well, the gag order was getting to me.

And the pain and suffering? That seemed to be just getting started.

At least for me. Lilli seemed fine. Totally back to normal. She played soccer daily, won tons of meets with her gymnastics team. Had made a bunch of new friends. Life was good for Lilli. It was like she'd moved on. No big deal.

So why was I still stuck in this nightmare? Why couldn't I move on, too? It seemed almost every night I'd wake in a cold sweat, shaking like a leaf. Visions of killer dragons haunting my dreams. Even during the day I'd sometimes find myself completely paralyzed with fear—like today on the soccer field. My mind replaying the scenes from Dragon Ops over and over and over again. Until I wanted to scream or run or hide or puke.

I tried to tell myself I was being ridiculous. That it was all just in my head, my brain trying to work through all we'd gone through in the game.

But deep down, I knew it was more than that. Derek had told us Atreus had escaped the game shortly after we'd gotten back home. Which would have been creepy enough. But then I'd gotten this weird message on my computer, scrolling down the screen. A message that, no matter what anyone said, I knew could only have come from him.

Do you want to play again?

Do you want to play again?

Yes. Atreus was out there. Somewhere. Watching, waiting. And I had no clue what he was planning next.

CHAPTER TWO

After the soccer game we headed to Uncle Jack's house down the street, where we were staying for the night. Our parents had gone away to Vegas, Dad tagging along with Mom to her programmer's conference. Mom hadn't wanted to leave us; she was still being super overprotective after what had happened at Dragon Ops. Also, I was pretty sure she still didn't completely trust her brother, Uncle Jack, since he was the one who had brought us there to begin with. But in the end, Dad had talked her into it, saying we all needed some time to chill. And so they went, leaving us six different phone numbers to call if anything went even remotely wrong while they were away.

"Hey, guys!" Uncle Jack greeted us as he opened his front door. "How was the game?"

"Ian did great!" Lilli said cheerfully.

"I literally caused the team to lose," I reminded her, walking into the house and slumping down at the kitchen table. My mood had not changed on the walk home. If anything, I felt more depressed. What was wrong with me? Seeing dragons on the soccer field? If anyone had any idea of why I really missed that shot, I'd be the laughingstock of school.

"I doubt that," Uncle Jack said, slapping me on the back. He reached into the freezer and pulled out a half gallon of cookies-and-cream ice cream—my favorite flavor—and set it on the table. "Dessert for dinner?" he asked, waggling his eyebrows. "That always made me feel better after a sports game gone bad." He chuckled. "Which...let's just say... happened quite a bit back in the day."

I gave a half laugh, knowing he was trying to make me feel better. Uncle Jack was awesome like that. And I knew I was his favorite relative. When I was younger, we used to spend hours playing video games together. He worked in games, so he always had beta versions of all the new ones that hadn't even come out yet. And since his own son, Derek, didn't care about gaming? I was the one he called to test them out.

But not anymore. I hadn't played a video game in three months. Not since that fateful day I'd gotten the mysterious message while playing *Fields of Fantasy*. The message I was sure had come from *him*. Even now, if I closed my eyes, I could still picture that white star spinning across my screen. The terrifying words scrolling below.

Do you want to play again?
Do you want to play again?
Do you want to play again?

At first, Lilli had been freaked out, too. Especially after I told her how Atreus had escaped the game and no one knew where he went. But, in the end, she rationalized it all away. Even if he was out there, she reminded me, he couldn't hurt us anymore. We were no longer in a game. In real life, we were safe.

Which I knew, in my head anyway, was probably true. But it didn't make me feel any better when I turned on my computer the next day and saw the message again, scrolling endlessly down the screen. *His* message. He was out there. And what if he could someday figure out a way to get to me? He was a state-of-the-art AI, after all. Which meant he was always learning. And he had a whole world of information at his disposal now that he was out of his game. What if he was mining the web even now, looking for ways to get at me—in real life?

I closed my laptop that day. And I hadn't opened it since.

"Ice cream for dinner sounds great to me!" Lilli cried, grabbing the container and yanking off the lid. "The only question is, do I bother with a bowl or just scoop it straight from the tub?"

"Let's stick with bowls," Aunt Robin said, coming into the kitchen. She reached into the cabinet and pulled out a stack of blue plastic bowls. "We're sugar freaks here, not savages."

"Also," Uncle Jack added, "please don't tell your mother. She would kill me dead if she found out I made you a meal without a single leafy green involved."

I couldn't help but smile, feeling a little better at their joking. The humiliation of the soccer game was starting to fade as I grabbed a bowl and wrestled the ice cream tub away from Lilli, who had already helped herself to a gigantic scoop. After I scooped out a few oversized scoops of my own, Uncle Jack tossed me the chocolate syrup, which I generously applied, topping it all off with a mountain of whipped cream.

Ice cream made everything better.

Uncle Jack looked around, frowning. "Where's number one son?" he asked his wife, suddenly realizing Derek wasn't with us.

She rolled her eyes. "In his bedroom, of course. Sucking in the last few milliseconds of screen time before we cut him off for the night." She turned to me. "Do you mind going and getting him? Let him know about the ice cream?"

"Sure. No problem." I pushed away from my chair and rose to my feet. As I did, Uncle Jack's phone started to ring.

He glanced at the caller ID, frowning. "I've got to take this," he said. Then he shot us a scolding look. "Don't even think about finishing that off before I get back!"

We laughed, and he disappeared out of the kitchen, heading to his office down the hall. I took one more heaping bite of ice cream, then followed him down the same hall, toward my cousin's bedroom. Derek had his door shut, and music with a heavy bass sound was blaring from the speakers.

I banged on the door. "Hey!" I cried. "Your mom says to come eat."

There was no answer. I tried again. "It's ice cream for dinner night," I added, then tried the handle. The door was locked. Of course.

"I'll get some later," he called back. "I'm working on my music."

"Cool," I said. "Can't wait to hear."

After his adventures as a bard in Dragon Ops, Derek had learned to embrace his love for music and now spent most of his time in his room, playing his bass guitar. He was good, too. And sometimes he'd even ask me to jam with him. (I sorta, kinda could play drums, though not very well.) We still weren't besties or anything, but at least we weren't outright enemies like before Dragon Ops. One thing good that had come out of the game, I guess.

Sometimes I wondered if Derek still had nightmares, too. Probably not. He was way too cool.

I sighed, feeling depressed all over again. If only I could just talk to someone about all this. It was killing me, keeping it inside. Like there was this powder keg in my stomach waiting to blow. So bad, it literally hurt sometimes.

I left Derek's room and headed back down the hall, pausing at Uncle Jack's door, my hand instinctively reaching for the knob. Maybe I could talk to him about it. I mean, we'd always been close, bonding over video games. And he did work for Dragon Ops—so he already knew everything that had happened. He might think I was crazy, but at least I was pretty sure he wouldn't laugh at me.

My hand wrapped around the door handle. I swallowed hard, daring myself to push it open. To step inside. To confess all.

"Are you freaking kidding me right now?"

Uncle Jack's sudden exclamation startled me, and I leapt back from the door, jerking my hand away.

"Since when?" he barked. "Why didn't anyone contact me sooner?"

I frowned. His voice sounded anxious, tense—panicked even. Much different from the friendly teasing voice he'd been using in the kitchen only minutes before. Was something wrong?

I leaned back in, pressing my ear to the door. Yes, I knew I shouldn't eavesdrop. Especially since a lot of what my uncle discussed was supersecret, video-game-related, and totally off-limits to normal people. Though, to be honest, that was one of the best reasons *to* listen at his door. Once, he had revealed this amazing exploit for *Fields of Fantasy* that ended up giving me unlimited gold to spend with the merchants. The code worked for months before they installed a patch that shut it off, and by then I had pretty much bought out the game.

But this didn't sound like a video game hack. This sounded way more serious.

"Let me get this straight," I heard Uncle Jack say. "Dragon Ops is set to open next month, and you're telling me you can't find its game maker?"

Wait, what?

I stared at the closed door, my mind racing as his words sank in. Was he talking about Hiro? Hiro Takanama—the Dragon Ops creator? He was missing?

We'd met Hiro when we first arrived at the Dragon Ops theme park. He'd taken over the company from his father, Atsuo Takanama, who had started the Fields of Fantasy franchise back in the 1990s. Hiro was a computer genius, an expert in artificial intelligence and game design. A rising video game legend.

Also, a father.

We'd met Hiro's daughter, Mirai, who went by the name Ikumi when we were in the game. At first we assumed she was playing virtually from back in her home in California. It wasn't until much later that we learned the real Mirai had died at the age of twelve from an autoimmune disease.

And her father, in his grief, had made a digital copy of her brain and uploaded it to the game. Which left her alive—in a sense—but also trapped alone in a simulation she wasn't allowed to leave. When we found her, she was desperate to escape the prison her father had put her in.

Not that Hiro had meant to be cruel. He loved his daughter. He wanted to protect her. But in the end, we convinced him to let her go. She needed her freedom, too. Just like the rest of us. And so he'd let her out of the game, allowing her to roam the cloud, free.

I thought back to the last time I'd seen her. I was still playing games at the time, and she'd found me in *Fields of Fantasy*, thanks to our old AI guide, the little dragon Yano, who was now her full-time companion. She'd looked so happy. So content. It made me happy, too. To know at least something good had come out of the nightmare we'd lived through. At least she had found her happily-ever-after.

Now, if I could just find my own. Or at least a new normal I could live with.

I shook my head, trying to return to the present. Pressing my ear to the door, I strained to listen to my uncle. "Has he used his credit cards? Checked into any hotels?" Uncle Jack was asking. He paused, then added, "Have there been any ransom notes?"

I froze, a shiver tingling down my spine. Ransom notes? But that would mean...

Had Hiro been kidnapped? But that was crazy!

Or was it? After all, his company owned a lot of technology that other companies would kill to obtain—literally. Something we'd found out firsthand when the company who made *Camelot's Honor* sabotaged Dragon Ops and trapped us inside. They had wanted to make the park seem unsafe and delay its opening so they could catch up with their own augmented reality theme park. And they didn't care that they almost killed us in the process.

Was Hiro's life now in danger—as ours had once been?

I pushed away from the door, dashing down the hall. I had to find Lilli. Now.

CHAPTER THREE

"**W**hat's going on?" Lilli demanded as I dragged her outside into the backyard. "Is it really so important you had to interrupt me mid-dessert dinner? I'd just found a whole Oreo in my ice cream, I'll have you know. With the cream still in the middle and everything!"

I shot her a warning look. "Just pretend you're teaching me soccer, okay?"

"Um, okay." She looked around. "Though we don't have a soccer ball, so kinda tough."

"Football, then. Karate. Whatever. Just act casual!"

"You mean like the opposite of the way you're acting right now?"

I glanced back at the house, half expecting weird men in black with dark sunglasses to be peering out the window, ready to take us away because we knew too much. But, of course, there was no one there. Aunt Robin was still in the kitchen. Derek was still in his bedroom. Uncle Jack was still in his office, likely still discussing the disappearance of the most important person in the video game industry. No one was concerned with us.

"How's this? *Hi-yah!*"

Lilli struck what I assumed was meant to be a karate pose, though truthfully it looked more like the start of a Tik-Tok dance. I rolled my eyes and grabbed her hand, dragging her to the back of the yard. Once there, I sat down on one of the swings from Derek's old weather-beaten playscape. Lilli joined me, plopping into the next one over.

"So ...?" she asked, turning to me. "You going to spill or what?"

"It's about Hiro," I said, keeping my voice low, just in case. "Hiro Takanama."

She frowned, looking from left to right, as if afraid we'd be overheard. Talking about Hiro was just as forbidden as talking about Dragon Ops, after all. But in this case, it couldn't be helped.

"He's disappeared," I whispered. "I heard Uncle Jack talking about it on the phone."

Lilli's eyebrows rose. Now I had her full attention. "Are you serious?"

I quickly related what I'd overheard. She listened

attentively, her brow creasing more and more until I'd finished. "That's awful," she said. "Do you really think someone kidnapped him?"

"I don't know." I shrugged. "I mean, it's possible, right? He's kind of a big deal. Maybe they want his Dragon Ops secrets. You know, like more sabotage."

"Do you think Ikumi knows?" Lilli asked after a pause. "That her father is missing, I mean. Do you think someone would think to tell her?"

I frowned. I hadn't thought of that.

"Probably not," I said. "Especially since most people assume she's dead. After all, that's why Hiro kept her in the game in the first place, right? He was worried that if people knew about her digital life, it could put her in danger."

I trailed off, a horrible thought coming to me. What if that was the real reason someone had kidnapped Hiro? Not for Dragon Ops. But for his brain emulation tech—the process through which he gave his dying daughter eternal life online. How valuable would something like that be? It had to be worth billions. Maybe trillions. Basically we were talking immortality here. Priceless.

My stomach squirmed. This could be worse than we thought.

Lilli jumped off her swing. "She needs to know," she said, clearly following my line of thought. "I mean, she could be in danger, too. Even if not, it's her dad, after all. And maybe she can even help track him down. She has the entire internet at her disposal, right? She could hack security cameras, access facial recognition software. Data mine from his online profile. If anyone can help find him, it would be her."

I lay down on the slide, looking up at the sky. Heavy clouds had rolled in, darkening the horizon. It looked as if it was going to storm soon. "Yeah," I said. "Maybe we should talk to Uncle Jack?"

"I was thinking more of doing it ourselves."

"Oh." My heart flipped. I tried to keep my expression neutral. "I don't know…"

"Why not?" Lilli demanded. "I mean, she gave you her *Fields of Fantasy* contact info, right? In case you needed to get in touch with her? We could send her an in-game message. Let her know what's going on." She put her hands on her hips. "We can't rely on Uncle Jack. What if he doesn't think it's a good idea? What if he tells us not to get involved?"

"Then…maybe we shouldn't get involved?" I squeaked, knowing this was a losing battle. When Lilli got an idea like this, there was no talking her down. "Also, I don't know if she still checks those messages or even logs in to the game anymore. I mean, she's not exactly a video game superfan these days, after being trapped in one for two years."

Even as I said the words, I knew I was just making excuses. The truth was, I was afraid of going back online. Especially into the very game where Atreus had first tracked me down. What if he was still in there, still waiting for me to log back in?

On the other hand, what if Ikumi really *was* in danger? What if we were the only ones who could warn her before it was too late?

And what if I was too much of a wimp to do it—and something terrible happened because of it?

"Come on, Ian," Lilli pleaded. "It's not like we're going back into you-know-where. We're just logging on to a regular video game. Sending a message. No big deal."

I almost said no. I really did. But then my mind flashed back to the final fight in our Dragon Ops game. The moment where we had all but lost. We'd tried, we'd dared, and we'd been defeated. And we were about to become dragon dinner. Game over, forever.

Except not. Because Ikumi had grabbed my sword. Leapt in front of the dragon. Eyes blazing. Mouth set in a determined frown.

You will leave my friends alone! she'd shouted.

She'd been so brave. Now it was time for me to be brave, too. For her.

"Okay," I said, swallowing down my fear. "Let's go send the message."

CHAPTER FOUR

We didn't even make it inside before the rain started to come down. A true Texas storm, complete with flashes of lighting streaking the sky and thunder crashing so loud it nearly made me jump out of my skin. Aunt Robin hustled us in, closing the door behind us.

"That came on quick," she remarked, staring out the window. "It's not supposed to last."

As if on cue, the lights flickered.

"Ugh," Uncle Jack said, walking into the room. "I really hope we don't lose power. I have a ton of work to get through tonight." He said it casually, as if he was planning to file his taxes. But I thought I caught a flicker of worry in his eyes. And I wondered if this "work" was trying to track down his boss's whereabouts.

"Everything okay?" I tried, giving him what I hoped was a meaningful look.

He frowned. "Yeah. Why do you ask, Ian?"

"Um, n-no reason," I stammered. Lilli poked me in the side.

"Okay," he said, still looking a little suspicious. "I'd better get started. Good night, all." And with that, he disappeared into his office. Aunt Robin watched him go, then shrugged, walking back to the kitchen to clean up the dinner mess.

We went and helped her with the dishes; Mom would have murdered us herself if we weren't good houseguests. There weren't that many, thankfully, since we'd just eaten ice cream for dinner.

"Do you want to watch a movie or something?" Aunt Robin asked once we had finished.

Lilli and I exchanged looks. "Nah," my sister said. "I'm pretty beat, actually."

"Me too!" I agreed, faking a yawn. Not a very good fake, though, judging from the weird look Aunt Robin gave me. But to her credit, she said nothing, hugging us both and saying good night. Then she walked over to the TV and turned it on, settling down on the couch.

Now was our chance. We headed down the hall to the guest bedroom where we were both staying. It had two twin beds side by side and reminded me of a cleaner version of that bedroom we stayed at in Ghost Hollow back in Dragon Ops. As Lilli closed the door, another round of thunder crashed outside. It sounded as if the storm was right on top of us now, and I could feel the electricity prickle my skin, making the hairs on my arms stand up on end.

Lilli glanced out the window. "Let's hope we don't lose power like Uncle Jack said." She frowned. "Or worse, the Wi-Fi goes out."

"No kidding." I scrambled onto my bed. "That would be just my luck. I finally decide to go online, and online is like, nah."

Of course even as I made the joke, I realized deep down I was kind of hoping for just that. A good excuse not to be able to do what we were about to do. *Too bad, so sad. Can't say we didn't try...*

But the lights remained on. And Lilli joined me on the bed, grabbing her laptop and plopping it on my lap.

I swallowed hard, the familiar fear rising to my throat. My heart raced in my chest as I stared down at the log-in screen. My hands shook as they settled on the keyboard.

This was it. There was no turning back now.

"The password's Atreus-One-Two-Three," Lilli informed me. I gave her a look. She shrugged sheepishly. "Sorry. Never got around to changing it."

I slowly typed in the password. Letter by letter. Number by number. With each stroke of a key, my anxiety rose.

Higher and higher, my breath catching in my throat. When I reached the end of the sequence, my finger hovered over the Enter key as I dared myself to press it.

"Come on already!" Lilli groaned, reaching over and punching it herself.

I watched, heart pounding, as the computer revealed my desktop, which unfortunately wallpapered long ago with a huge close-up shot of Atreus. Guess she had never bothered to change *that*, either.

In the corner, the little Wi-Fi icon blinked, then turned solid.

We were online.

"All right," Lilli said. "Now load up *Fields of Fantasy*. Let's get this over with."

I nodded slowly, trying to keep my vision from going blurry as I guided the cursor over to the familiar game icon. I hadn't opened the game in three months. Was Atreus still there, still waiting for me? What would he do if he saw me online?

I paused at the icon. Tried to will myself to click on it.

"Are you okay, Ian?" Lilli asked, peering at me. Her expression morphed into pity when she caught my face. She reached out for the laptop. "I'm sorry. You don't have to do this. Just give me back the laptop, and you can go back to the kitchen. I'll log in and deliver the message to Ikumi."

I felt my cheeks flush with embarrassment. She must

have thought I was so pathetic. I mean, what was I afraid of? Some evil video game dragon lurching from the screen to devour me in real life?

"I got it," I muttered, brushing her hands away. I tried to remind myself of Ikumi, who might actually be in real danger. Unlike me, safe and sound in a spare bedroom, afraid of some pixelated monster coming to get me.

I clicked and typed in my user name and password when the game loaded to the screen. Then I moved my cursor over to the New Mail button and opened my mailbox. To my surprise, there was a letter from Ikumi.

A letter dated two days ago.

"Ooh! Open it," Lilli cried. "Maybe it's about her dad!"

I nodded grimly, hands shaking as I clicked Open. The envelope blinked, then expanded the message to full screen.

I gasped as I read the single word, slashing in bold letters across my screen.

HELP!

And suddenly the lights went out.

CHAPTER FIVE

I screamed. I couldn't help it. But Lilli screamed, too, so I didn't feel quite so ridiculous. A moment later, Aunt Robin poked her head into our room, freaking us out all over again.

"You guys okay?" she asked.

For a split second I thought maybe she'd seen the help message. But then I realized she was talking about the power outage. Duh.

"The lightning must have knocked out a transformer or something," she continued. "The whole neighborhood's out."

"We're fine," Lilli assured her. "Just...Do you have a flashlight or something?"

We could see the outline of Aunt Robin's head nod in the darkness. She disappeared for a moment, then returned with two bright flashlights, tossing one to each of us. "Hopefully it won't last long," she said. "Let me know if you need anything." And with that, she left the room.

Lilli and I exchanged glances. Then we dropped the flashlights, turning back to the computer screen. Since we were working off a battery-powered laptop, it was still on. But *Fields of Fantasy* had disconnected.

"Ugh." Lilli made a face. "The Wi-Fi must be out, too. Just our luck."

I nodded grimly, my mind racing. "What are we going to do?"

"There's not much we can do," Lilli said with a shrug. "Just...wait for it to come back on, I guess."

"But that could take all night!" I protested, closing the laptop and setting it on the bed. "You saw the message. Ikumi needs our help. We can't just sit around and wait!"

"You got a better idea?" Lilli asked.

I glanced out the window. It looked as if the rain had stopped. Though that didn't guarantee our electricity would come back on anytime soon. I remembered the last time we had an outage; it had taken half the day for them to fix the damaged transformer. It had been our first day of winter break, too, and I was bouncing off the walls with no TV, no games, no internet. Mom had finally gotten fed up and announced we were leaving the house. She was taking me to—

I shot up from the bed. "What if we went to Epic Fun Play?"

Epic Fun Play was this awesome old-school video arcade that had opened last year, not far from our house. It had this amazing two-floor laser tag room and all these old-school video games from back when our parents were kids. *Pac-Man, Dig Dug, Centipede.* It was like a *Wreck-It Ralph* movie come to life. I would go there sometimes to play games. Games that didn't need the internet to function.

But the place *did* have free Wi-Fi. I remembered seeing the signs.

Lilli glanced at her watch. "Do you think they're open still?"

"Even if not, I bet Maddy will let us in," I said. Maddy was the owner of the arcade and basically the second-coolest adult I'd ever met after Uncle Jack. Not only did she love video games, but she was also an artist who illustrated manga and other graphic novels. Like, real ones you found in bookstores. She lived in an apartment above the arcade, so I knew she'd be there, even after hours.

"Yeah, but she might be out of power, too," Lilli reminded me.

"Maybe. But she has a generator," I said. "Remember? That's why Mom took us there when the power went out over Christmas break. All the lights in the neighborhood were out except for hers."

"That's right!" Lilli remembered. "Good thinking, Ian!"

I smiled, feeling pleased. Except also feeling more

freaked out. Here I'd had a very good excuse not to go online. And I'd gone and blown it up.

For Ikumi, I reminded myself. *You're doing this for Ikumi.*

My sister glanced at the closed bedroom door. "Okay," she said. "We're going to need to sneak out. No way Uncle Jack and Aunt Robin are going to let us go out on our own at night."

I nodded, wrinkling my nose. She wasn't wrong. But still, what if Aunt Robin came to check on us again and we weren't there? She would totally freak. Uncle Jack would probably call out the National Guard. After all, he'd almost lost us once already in a video game theme park.

"We'll leave a note," I decided aloud. "In case anyone comes to check on us. They'll be mad, but at least they'll know where we are and that we're safe."

"Good idea," Lilli agreed, flicking on her flashlight and digging in the nightstand drawer for paper and pen. I watched as she scribbled an explanation, then set it down on her pillow.

Something inside me squirmed. No turning back now.

Thankfully, the bedroom was on the first floor, which meant we could easily pop out the screen and slip out the window. I felt a little like I was in a real-life video game as we climbed out into the dark night as quietly as we could, Lilli's laptop safely in a messenger bag. A real-life sneak mission that, while never one of my favorites in the game world, was actually kind of cool in real life.

Once outside and away from the house, I looked around, shining my flashlight onto the quiet street. Every house on the block was dark, completely without power. Even the streetlights were unlit. Kind of giving the normally safe suburban neighborhood a distinct horror movie vibe. I suddenly pictured a large man in a hockey mask lurking behind a hedge, ready to strike—

Something rustled in the bushes. I let out a small shriek, leaping back. Until I realized it was nothing more than a black cat, peering up at me with obvious disdain. As if to say, *And here they call* me *a scaredy cat…*

"You okay?" Lilli asked, raising an eyebrow.

I laughed uneasily. "Trash mob. What are you going to do?"

She giggled. "It does feel a little like a video game, doesn't it?" she remarked, shining her flashlight down the dark street. She switched to a movie-announcer voice. "Can our brave heroes make their way down the forbidden Oak Street? Past the dastardly mailboxes of doom?"

"Will they brave the terrible traffic lights?" I continued, joining the game. "Will they make it past the Petersons' puppies of peril?"

"And what will await them at the end…in the Epic Fun Play dungeon of doom? Will they find Wi-Fi? Or will they find *death*?"

We both broke out laughing so hard we could barely

walk. Lilli kept telling me to shush—no need to alert the neighbors to our secret quest—they might call Aunt Robin. A truly terrifying boss mob we definitely didn't want to have to face alone.

I pushed down my laughter as we continued to our destination. Still, I couldn't help feeling a little excited about the secret mission. It'd been a while since I'd done something even remotely daring. I had to admit, it felt pretty good.

It took longer than it would have if we'd had our bikes—our usual mode of transportation—but we made it to the arcade about fifteen minutes later. I let out a breath of relief as my eyes caught the familiar neon sign above, lit up like daylight. The first light we'd seen since the power had gone out. Like a literal light at the end of the tunnel.

"We made it!" I declared. "Quest complete."

But when I grabbed the door handle? It was locked.

"Or…maybe not," Lilli said with a sigh.

CHAPTER SIX

I groaned, banging my fist against the door in frustration. So much for an easy quest. I leaned against the nearby brick wall, staring out into the dark night. "If only you had real-life lock-picking abilities," I remarked to Lilli, remembering her epic skills back from our Dragon Ops days.

She snorted. "Right? Though—real-life breaking and entering might lead to a very bad game over. As in go directly to jail. Do not pass go. Do not collect two hundred dollars."

"Good point."

I turned back to the door, then looked up. Was that a faint light I saw in the upstairs window? Maybe Maddy was up there working on her art. Maybe if we knocked, she'd hear us and let us in, even though she was technically closed.

It was an emergency, after all. Or it might be, anyway. We still weren't quite sure.

My mind flashed back to Ikumi's message.

Help.

I rang the doorbell, then knocked with my fist, just in case. "Maddy?" I called out. "Are you there? It's me—Ian Rivera!"

We waited, for a moment hearing nothing. Then my ears caught a rummaging beyond the door. There was the click of a lock, and the door swung open. Maddy stood there, dressed in a big fluffy bathrobe with a weird array of cats wearing space helmets plastered all over it. She rubbed her eyes with her fists, then blinked back at us.

"Hey, Ian," she said. "What are you doing here so late?"

"It's not that late," I pointed out. "It's only eight thirty."

She glanced at her wrist as if expecting to see a watch there. Then she laughed. "Oh, right. Sorry. I'm still on Tokyo time."

"You went to Tokyo?" I asked, impressed.

"I wish. I was just on a Zoom call with my publisher over there," she explained. "They need three more chapters of artwork by the end of the month to stay on schedule, and we were going over the text to make sure I got it right."

"Cool," I exclaimed. And I meant it, too. Imagine drawing manga for a living! That was almost as good as being a video game programmer like Uncle Jack!

"Sorry," Lilli broke in. "I'm Ian's sister, Lilli. And we didn't mean to wake you. It's just…the power's gone out everywhere, and we knew you had a generator."

"And…you needed a late-night video game fix?" Maddy raised an eyebrow.

"Your Wi-Fi, actually," I explained.

The eyebrow went higher. "*You* want to use Wi-Fi?" she asked. She made a big show of looking outside from left to right. "Did the world get taken over by pod people while I was on deadline?"

I blushed. I hadn't thought about how weird that would sound, coming from me. After all, how many times had I told Maddy in the last three months that I didn't "do" the internet anymore? She'd thought it was so funny—this twelve-year-old Luddite, obsessed with old-school video games and denying all things online.

If only she knew why.

"It's kind of an emergency," Lilli piped in.

Maddy gave her a skeptical look. "Emergency-emergency? Or, like, you need to learn some new TikTok dances emergency?"

"The first," I assured her. "We have to check on someone. Make sure they're okay."

Rain started to fall again, splashing onto my shoulders. Maddy looked up and sighed. "Fine. Come in before you get soaked to the skin."

She hustled us through the front door and into the arcade. The place had been shut down for the night, and the screens to all my favorite games were dark. Until, that was, Maddy walked behind the prize counter (she gave out the *best* prizes in town) and everything came to life. The screens loaded with their blocky graphics. Their eight-bit theme songs cheerfully beeping and booping through the arcade.

Lilli let out a low whistle, turning in a circle to take it all in. "Wow," she said. "This place is like Ian heaven. No wonder you come here so much."

I breathed in the familiar stale air, feeling my body relax for the first time all evening. Lilli wasn't wrong. This was my safe space. The one place I could come and still feel like a gamer. I trailed a hand along an old *Galaga* game, having the instant urge to stick in a quarter and start playing.

But we had more important things to do now. So I plopped down at one of the tables in the corner, which Maddy used to host *Dungeons and Dragons* sessions on weekends. Reaching into my bag, I pulled out Lilli's laptop.

"Come on," I said, beckoning to Lilli. "Let's get this over with."

I could feel Maddy watching us curiously as Lilli came over and pulled up a folding chair next to me. "Everything all right?" she asked.

"We don't know," I admitted. Which was something I'd

normally never say to a grown-up. No need to get them all worried and up in our business. But Maddy was different. I was pretty sure if something really went wrong, she'd have our backs.

After connecting to the internet, I drew in a breath, then loaded up *Fields of Fantasy* again, selecting the mail icon on the load-in screen and pulling up Ikumi's message.

Help!

I bit my lower lip. What did she mean by that? Did she want me to help her? Or her dad? Both? A little more information might have been useful in this case.

"Why don't you write her back?" Lilli suggested.

I nodded, placing my hands on the keyboard again. *Hey, it's Ian and Lilli,* I typed. *Sorry it took us a while to reply. Is everything okay? What do you need?*

I glanced back at my sister. "Does that sound all right?"

"Yeah. Send it. Then we can wait—see if she replies."

"Good idea." I pressed Send on the message. Then I turned to Maddy. "Do you mind if we hang out for a little bit? We're waiting to hear back from our friend." I paused, then added, "We don't know for sure, but she might be in some trouble."

"And…she doesn't have a phone?" Maddy asked, raising an eyebrow.

"Her dad's really strict," Lilli said quickly. I shot her a grateful look.

Maddy didn't look entirely convinced. But in the end, she nodded. "Fine. But you gotta make yourselves useful if you're staying. Help me clean the machines. These games get crazy dirty during the day." She tossed me and Lilli some rags and a bottle of Windex. "I can use all the help I can get."

And so we got to work, wandering the arcade, wiping off the screens and controllers of the various game cabinets. Maddy wasn't wrong; some of them were filthy. Definitely needed to remember to wash my hands after my next visit.

"What on earth is this game?" Lilli asked a few cabinets down, squinting at a bear in a party hat being chased by killer trees. "It looks weird. And it doesn't even have a . . . What's it called? A joystick?" She rolled her rag over the little trackball that sat in its place.

"*Crystal Castles*," I said, stepping over to her side. "It's supercool. You, like, run around this maze, collecting gems."

"So like *Pac-Man*."

"Uh, yeah, except completely different!" I exclaimed, a little offended. I mean, really! *Crystal Castles* and *Pac-Man* were not even remotely the same. That was like saying Mario and Zelda were the same! *Fortnite* and *Apex Legends*!

Lilli rolled her eyes. "So sorry. My mistake."

Maddy walked over to us, placing a hand on my shoulder. "I swear this kid was born before his time," she declared. "Before *my* time, even."

Lilli giggled. I groaned.

"Whatever, haters," I said, walking over to the *Dragon's Lair* cabinet and watching the familiar animated scene of Dirk the Daring and Princess Daphne play out on-screen. "These games might not have the flashiest graphics or soundtracks sung by celebrities, but they're still awesome. The building blocks of today's most important games."

Lilli groaned. "Here we go again."

"He's not wrong," Maddy relented, leaning against a *Centipede* machine. "Some of the stuff we take for granted in games now was totally revolutionary in their time. For example, did you know Sega released a home version of virtual reality glasses back in the eighties? They're super primitive compared to what we have now. But at the time it was a huge deal. And it paved the way for the VR systems we have today. Even that mixed-reality theme park they're building out in the South Pacific." She tapped her finger to her chin. "What's it called again?"

"Dragon Ops," Lilli and I both said together.

"Yes! Right!" She laughed. "I wonder if they'll ever open that place....Seems like it's had a lot of technical difficulties."

I gave Lilli a look. Maddy had no idea! And, of course, we couldn't tell her anything. That would be going against our no-talking agreement. Not that I was anxious to relive the experience anyway.

I patted the side of a *Gauntlet* machine. "I wish I lived back then. Everything was much simpler."

"Yeah, right," Maddy scoffed. "I mean, hello? If we wanted to rent a video, we had to drive to an actual store and then return the tape the next day! No streaming. No movies on demand. Even Netflix mailed you DVDs."

"The horror!" Lilli said, fanning her hand in front of her face, laughing.

I sighed. Honestly, it all sounded pretty good to me. No Wi-Fi, no internet. No crazy AI dragons...

Maddy peered at me curiously. "Are you sure everything's okay, Ian?"

I paused, unsure what to say. I wanted to tell her; I really did. But we couldn't risk it. Cool as she was, she was still a grown-up. Which meant she would either not believe us or believe us so much that she'd want to call our parents. Or the police, even.

"Any mail message yet?" Lilli asked, walking back over to her laptop. She peered down at the screen, pressing her lips together. "Maybe you should log in all the way—see if she's online or something. A lot of people never check their in-game mail."

I wasn't sure about that. In fact, my guess was if you sent a help message through the game mail system, you probably would stick around to see if someone answered it. But then, she did send it two days ago, and we hadn't replied until now. Maybe she'd given up on us.

I set down my rag and forced myself to walk back over

to the laptop, trying to ignore the all-too-familiar feeling of anxiety creeping through me as I sat down and selected my character. Lord Wildhammer, the eighty-five-level warrior I'd modeled my Dragon Ops role after, was big and burly, with huge plates of metal armor covering all his vital parts and a horned helmet protecting his head.

In other words, basically the complete opposite of real-life me. But that was the beauty of video games. You could be anyone. Do anything. Lord Wildhammer wasn't afraid of some silly old dragon. And as long as I was playing him, well, I shouldn't be afraid, either, right?

"Wow," Maddy said, coming over. "This really brings me back. I was a huge fan of this game back in the day. I haven't played lately, though—too busy with work to get sucked back in. My poor mage Allora—I'm pretty sure I last left her hanging out in some random tavern years ago. I hope she's at least made friends with the locals."

"Ian used to be a superfan of *Fields of Fantasy*," Lilli informed her. "You couldn't get him offline if you tried." She laughed.

"I'm still a fan," I muttered, half to myself. "Just…have other things going on right now." In fact, just seeing the loading screen was making me miss gaming more than ever. But it was also sparking my anxiety big-time.

Please don't let Atreus be there. Please don't let—

The screen flashed, and Lord Wildhammer appeared. At

first I wasn't sure where I'd landed—it'd been so long since I last played. But then I started recognizing the background. The bloodstained rocks, the bone-strewn floor. The chunky crystal-studded walls.

ROAR!

The sound ripped through the laptop speakers, and I nearly leapt out of my skin. With trembling hands, I spun the game camera around, already knowing what was behind me before I even saw it.

The great dragon Atreus. And he did not look pleased.

CHAPTER SEVEN

O
n instinct, I drew my sword. The dragon growled again, his mouth creaking open, revealing a familiar cavern of razor-sharp teeth. I held up my shield over my body, a pathetic attempt to protect myself. One blast from that fiery mouth and I was a goner.

"Dude, just get out of there," Lilli scolded. "You'll never beat him by yourself. Without even a healer." She drummed her fingers on the table. "Man, I wish we brought a second laptop."

"I've got mine," Maddy broke in. "Just get out of aggro range and give me a second to port over to the Crystal Temple." She grabbed her laptop from under the prize deck and walked over to the table, flipping it open. Her eyes glittered with excitement.

And why not? My brain reminded me. After all, this

wasn't the *real* Atreus—the artificially intelligent robot that had tried to kill us in Dragon Ops. This was just the classic video game version. A simple program, designed to perform a simple function, dressed in a dragon's skin.

Still, try to tell that to my stomach, which rumbled uneasily as the massive dragon padded forward, closing the space between him and my game character. His tail swished behind him, and his wings cracked at the air like twin whips. My mind flashed back to that fateful day in Dragon Ops. In the real Crystal Cave, with the real Atreus looming in front of us. Fire dancing on his blackened tongue.

When one wrong move would be game over—forever.

You're not there, I scolded myself. *This is just a game. A dumb, harmless game.*

"I'm here!" Maddy cried. "Let's get this guy."

I forced Lord Wildhammer forward, ready to pull aggro and strike. The dragon roared, swiping at me with his claw, taking out almost half my hit points with one blow. From behind me, Maddy's mage shot a blast of ice straight at him, freezing him in place.

"Ugh. Ice," Lilli shuddered and turned away. Maybe she was thinking about the time back in Dragon Ops when we'd fought an ice dragon and she'd been frozen in much the same way. At the time, I thought she was a goner. Until Ikumi showed up and unfroze her.

"Heal up!" Maddy barked at me. "You've got ten seconds before this wears off."

I clicked on my inventory, digging through my game junk to find a potion. Wow—I'd left my bags quite a mess. Finally, I found the icon I was looking for, clicking on it to drink. My character on screen gulped it down, and my hit points ticked back up.

Just in time, too. Maddy's spell expired. Atreus unfroze. He lunged again, this time swiping at me with his paw. I held up my shield, allowing it to absorb the blow. Then I charged forward, driving him back as Maddy prepared her next spell.

"Aw, man. I really wish I was playing," Lilli said, leaning over to take in the action.

"We could have used you," I agreed as the dragon blasted me with fire and my hit points plummeted again. At least it didn't hurt in real life like it did back in Dragon Ops. Still, it wasn't looking good for us. I couldn't use another potion—there was a five-minute cooldown on those—and we had no healer in our party to get me back into fighting shape. Which meant basically one more blow and we'd be wiped.

"Come on, Maddy!" I called out. "What are you waiting for?" I turned from the screen to glance at real-life Maddy next to me. She gave me a helpless shrug.

"He gagged me!" she said. "Sorry!"

Ugh. Being gagged was basically the worst thing to

happen to a mage. It literally shut you up—meaning you couldn't cast any spells until it wore off.

In other words, we were doomed.

I considered running. Maybe I could get out of aggro range and reset the fight. But it was too late, I realized. If I turned back now, he'd just attack me from behind. Better to die head-on with glory and honor.

At least in this case, it was only a game.

I raised my sword. "Come at me, man," I declared. "Just try it!"

Atreus roared, stalking forward. I slashed at his nose, my blade singing true. Just a nick, but enough to wound him. My sister and Maddy cheered.

"That's it! Hold him off. Just twenty seconds more!" Maddy cried.

"I'll do my best!"

Okay, I had to admit. This was fun. Like, ridiculously fun. Even though we were totally getting our butts kicked. Just to be playing again. To feel the adrenaline rushing through my veins. My skin prickling with excitement.

Gaming. Man, I had really missed gaming.

Atreus roared, knocking Lord Wildhammer backward. Then he followed it up with a blast of poisoned breath. My hit points ticked down rapidly. Maddy was still gagged behind me. Atreus's eyes flashed fire as he took a triumphant step in our direction. Lifted his head and—

BOOM!

I yelped in surprise at the sudden noise blasting from my speakers. A noise that definitely had not come from Atreus. I spun the game camera, trying to figure out where it had come from. Had a new group arrived, fresh for battle?

Atreus also seemed confused. He stopped his attack, his gaze turning upward…

BOOM!

A large blast of electricity slashed through the sky. At first I thought it had come from Maddy, but she was still gagged, and anyway she was an ice mage, not electric. Atreus let out a horrible roar, convulsing violently as the lightning hit him straight on. He crashed to the ground, for a moment struggling to regain his footing. But at last he surrendered, collapsing heavily, his eyes rolling back into his head.

Dead. But how?

I turned my game camera to the sky, my heart pounding in my chest. To my shock, I found another giant dragon. This one was a shiny silver, with three heads attached to three long necks. It swam through the sky with impossible gracefulness. I watched, mesmerized, as it began to come down for a landing.

Was it a friend? Or another foe to deal with?

Maddy's cell phone rang. She made a face, then looked at the screen. "Tokyo again," she told us. "I gotta take this. Sorry." She rose to her feet. "I'll be back. And thanks for the game. I forgot how much fun it was to play." She smiled at us. "Hope everything's okay with your friend."

"Thanks, Maddy," Lilli and I said in unison.

As she headed upstairs to her apartment, I turned my attention back to the game—namely to the new dragon arrival. I had to admit, it was so beautiful. So majestic. And yet at the same time, it looked weirdly... familiar.

"Why, hello, my favorite adventurer! Fancy finding you here! And in dire peril, too. Just like old times!"

I stared at the screen. The English-accented voice was clearly coming from the silver dragon. I'd recognize it anywhere.

"Yano?" I asked through the laptop microphone. "Is that you?"

The three-headed silver dragon did a fancy barrel roll before coming in for a graceful landing. "The one and only," he declared. "How do you like my new look? Just like my namesake, Yamata-no-Orochi, the three-headed dragon of legend."

"You look amazing," Lilli cried, scooting in closer.

"Is that Lilli?" Yano asked, peering out from the computer screen. It was then that I realized he couldn't see the real-life us from inside the game. Only Lord Wildhammer. But he could hear us both just fine.

"Yes! I'm here, too!" Lilli assured him. "It's great to see you again!"

"It's great…not…to see you," Yano replied. "But I'm sure you look as lovely as you always have. I mean, not as stunning as me, of course. But still, relatively well kept, I'm sure."

I couldn't help a smile. Good old Yano. He'd been such a loyal guide during our Dragon Ops adventures. There was no way we'd have ever made it through without him.

"I thought you were guiding Ikumi now," I said, remembering how he'd appeared to me the last time I'd played *Fields of Fantasy*. When Hiro let his daughter out of the game, he also released the dragon, so she'd have a companion. Someone to keep an eye on her—keep her safe. My eyebrows furrowed with sudden concern. "Is she all right? We got this message—"

"Right. Yes. That was from me. I used her account to send it because I didn't know how else to reach you. You're never online anymore." His voice held a slightly accusing tone.

A sudden cold washed over me. "What's happened? Is something wrong with Ikumi? Is she okay? Do you know where she is?"

Yano's heads turned, no longer facing Lord Wildhammer in the game, but rather staring out directly at real-life us through the screen. "They've got her," he said slowly. "And they're not planning on letting her go."

CHAPTER EIGHT

"They? Who are *they*?" I demanded, my voice trembling. It was a good thing I was already sitting down—my legs felt like Jell-O. This was what we'd feared all along. But to hear it confirmed. Ikumi—kidnapped. A chill tripped down my spine.

"You're serious," Lilli broke in. "I mean, you're not messing with us or anything?"

"I would never joke about something so terrible," Yano assured us. "It's completely serious. Worse than the time they ran out of fresh porg meat on that new *Star Wars VR*. And that was a crushing state of affairs, let me tell you."

"So what happened?" I demanded, trying to get him back on the subject. Which was sometimes a problem with Yano. He was smart, but... easily distracted.

"I'm not entirely sure," Yano admitted. "All I know is

she disappeared about a week ago. Which wasn't a big deal at first. The girl likes to take her little trips around the digital world. And she often prefers to travel solo. I've told her time and time again how dangerous this is, of course. But does she listen to her guide? Does anyone ever listen to—"

"Then she's just gone?" I interrupted impatiently. "And you think someone took her?"

This was not good. This was so not good. Ikumi had been through so much already. If something else had happened to her...

"I wasn't sure at first," Yano replied. "I mean, it was as if she disappeared off the cloud entirely. I searched, of course, as any good guide would. But I came up empty-clawed. Until one morning I woke up to a distress signal, pinging away. I'd given her this in case of emergencies. But the sound was so faint, I had difficulty pinning it down. That's when I first realized she was in trouble."

He opened his mouth, puffing out a small cloud of smoke. We watched, fascinated, as a blurry hologram seemed to pop up in the middle of it.

A hologram of Ikumi.

She was dressed in a strange silver suit, almost like something you'd see an astronaut wear. Around her was a set of glowing green bars, like a laser prison. Behind her was a window, and out that window was a brilliant array of starlight. Was she in outer space?

Her gaze turned to us. As if she could see right through the monitor to the arcade. Her eyes clouded with tears. Her mouth wobbled, then opened. "Help me," she begged. "Ian and Lilli, I need your help."

I rose in my chair, almost knocking it backward. My heart pounded in my chest. "Ikumi!" I cried, even though on some level I knew she couldn't hear me. That this was just a recording. When had she made it? And where had she made it from?

The smoke drifted into the air and her image disappeared. Lilli pushed me out of the way and sat down in my chair. "Where is she?" she asked Yano. "Do you have any idea? You said someone took her. Who? Was it the same people who took Hiro?"

For a moment Yano's face seemed to darken. "Hiro?" he repeated. "What about Hiro?"

"He's missing, too," I explained. "They don't know where he is."

Yano gazed at us solemnly. "Then this is worse than I feared," he replied. "Your friend—and maybe her father, too—is in grave danger."

I swallowed hard. "You said *they* won't let her go. Who's they?"

The dragon tossed his three heads. "Have you ever heard of Admiral Appleby?" he asked.

"Obviously," I said, surprised. "He's a legend. And he's

from here—Austin. I think his gaming company is head-quartered just outside of town."

In fact, Admiral Appleby was almost as famous as Atsuo Takanama, Ikumi's grandfather, who created *Fields of Fantasy*. He got his start designing eight-bit games for Atari back in the day and had always been known for being a little on the eccentric side. Which was the nice way of saying he was super weird. For one thing, he wasn't really an admiral. He'd never been in the military at all, from what anyone could tell. And for another, he always dressed as if he were an officer of some sort of futuristic space squad, even on a Tuesday.

Most recently he'd been in gaming headlines for developing an updated version of Mech Ops, a futuristic horror massively multiplayer role-playing game that had originally been released in the eighties as an eight-bit side-scrolling game. The new version was meant to be state of the art. A new kind of virtual reality experience no one had seen before. Online, people were chomping at the bit to get their hands on an early copy.

But what did that have to do with Ikumi?

"I don't understand," I said to Yano.

"Of course you don't. Humans hardly ever do!" The dragon blew more smoke from his nose. "When I received the distress signal, I realized I needed to track her down. Through my extensive data mining online, I was finally able to match the background of her distress call with a short scene from the new Mech Ops game trailer that was just released," he explained. "So...putting two and two together, which is really not hard for a very advanced AI like myself..."

Lilli and I exchanged horrified looks. "Wait. Are you saying she's trapped in a video game?" Lilli asked. "Like, *another* video game?"

"But she just got out of Dragon Ops!" I cried, furious. My heart ached as I thought of poor Ikumi. Once again held against her will. It wasn't fair. "They can't do this to her!"

"They can, and they evidently have," Yano replied matter-of-factly. "And now it's up to you to break her out."

Uh, what?

"How are we supposed to do that?" I demanded, trying to ignore the fear rising inside. "I mean, it's not like Dragon Ops, where we had an in with our uncle. And Mech Ops isn't even out yet. In fact, it's not due to be released for at least a year!"

"All true," Yano agreed. "But lucky for you, the company is holding a beta test competition at their headquarters this week. If you can impress them and get them to select you as early players, you will receive a VR gaming rig and a demo of the game to take home and test." Two of his three mouths grinned. "It's the perfect gateway to getting into the game and finding our girl."

Right. I leaned against the *Frogger* machine, my mind spinning. "But even if we do get selected, how are we supposed to find Ikumi? It's not like they're going to just leave their digital prisoner in the demo," I reasoned. "If anything, they've probably got her locked away, deep in the game in a majorly encrypted section we'd never be able to reach, never mind crack."

"Of course. But you're forgetting your secret weapon," Yano pointed out. "The beta will get us through the front door. Once inside, I can hack the game code and access deeper levels, where they've most likely stashed her."

Of course. Yano, like Atreus, was also a pretty intelligent AI. And unlike Atreus, he used his powers for good.

Lilli leaned backed in her chair. "That's great and all, but we'd have to win a beta competition, right? How are we supposed to do that? We've never even seen this game before."

"No one has," Yano reminded us. "It'll be new to everyone. And I have full confidence in you. You're gamers, after all. The best of the best! No one can even come close to your greatness when it comes to navigating through virtual worlds."

I raised an eyebrow. "Wow. And here I thought you considered us noobs." Let's just say our guide, while sometimes charming, had often been...critical...of our gaming performance in the past. Evidently things change.

Yano's three heads blushed in sync. "Well, of course. But that was before you beat the almighty Atreus, right? Clearly I've reassessed your gaming brilliance."

I snorted. "Clearly."

"So what do you say?" the dragon continued. "Are you with me?"

I glanced at Lilli, who was looking back at me. I could tell what she was thinking before she opened her mouth. What choice did we have? Ikumi was trapped again in a video game. We couldn't just leave her there.

I drew in a breath. "Okay," I said. "We'll try out for the beta."

"That's the spirit!" Yano chirped. "All right. Assuming you get in, send me your log-in info the second you get home. That will allow me to meet you in the game. And then we'll take it from there. Saving the world—once more with feeling!"

He cheered loudly, then rose back to the sky. I watched him go, my heart thudding in my chest. What had we just agreed to do?

Lilli closed the laptop. "This is crazy," she said.

"What's crazy?"

We turned to see Maddy coming back downstairs. She rubbed her eyes sleepily. "Are you guys almost finished? I really should get some sleep. I've got a big art deadline tomorrow."

"Sorry." I grabbed the laptop, tucking it under my arms. "Thanks for letting us in. We really appreciate it."

"Yeah," Lilli added. "This place is supercool. I'll have to come back sometime."

Maddy smiled. "I'm glad I could help. Even if it was just for a *Fields of Fantasy* fix," she added teasingly. If only she knew.

I started for the door, then stopped. "Maddy?"

"Yeah?"

"Do you know anything about a Mech Ops beta test competition coming up?"

"Sure," she said. "I read they're holding it on Sunday afternoon out at their headquarters in Dripping Springs. Why?"

"Is it open? Like, anyone can try out?"

"I think so. But..."

"What?"

"It's just..." She shrugged. "I don't know. It's, like, sci-fi. Spaceships and robots and stuff. Doesn't really seem your jam."

"I like them," Lilli broke in, saving me. "And I saw this trailer about it? It looks amazing. I want to try it out."

Maddy walked behind her desk and rummaged around for a moment. Then she held up a flyer with a triumphant grin. "Here we go," she said. "They dropped it off a week ago and wanted me to hang it up. I forgot all about it until you mentioned it."

"Awesome," I said, grabbing the flyer. Maybe since she hadn't hung it up to publicize the event, there wouldn't be a lot of people there to compete against. "Thanks again."

"Anything for my favorite eight-bit gamer," she teased,

ruffling my head like I was some little kid. I groaned. But still, I was more than thankful she'd hooked us up.

We stepped out of the arcade and into the night. It appeared the power had come back on since we'd been inside, and I hoped that meant the Wi-Fi was back, too. I needed to do some serious research about Admiral Appleby and the Mech Ops game before we headed there Sunday to try out. Despite Yano's confidence in our gaming abilities, I knew this was going to be a serious test.

But we had no choice. Ikumi needed us to step up. Her life was once again at stake. Whatever it took, we had to get her out. Even if it meant playing online games again.

Even if it meant risking running into Atreus.

CHAPTER NINE

"**W**ow! That's a lot of people."

I stepped out of the car, my eyes scanning the massive crowd standing in front of Mech Ops HQ. In fact, the parking lot was so packed that Dad had to drop us off at the side of the road. He rolled down his window and handed us the signed waivers for the competition. Because we were under eighteen, we needed parental permission. Thankfully, he was happy to grant it. Even though he wasn't a gamer himself, he was married to Mom, so he got it.

"You sure you don't want me to go in with you?" he asked, looking at us doubtfully.

"No, we'll be good," I assured him. The last thing we needed for our secret mission was our dad tagging along. "We'll call you when we're ready to be picked up."

"Okay. I'll be right across the street at Starbucks if you

need me," he said. "But if your mom asks later? I was with you the entire time."

"Absolutely. You even tried and failed the test miserably," I assured him with a grin.

"Humiliated beyond belief," he agreed solemnly. Then he laughed. "Good luck, guys! Knock 'em dead."

With that, he pulled away, leaving Lilli and me alone. For a moment we just stood there, taking in the crowd. So many people! It was as if we were at a massive music festival or sporting event instead of a video game beta test.

Worry wormed through my chest. This was going to be harder than I thought.

I shouldn't have been surprised. After we got back from Epic Fun Play, the Wi-Fi had come back on, and I'd spent half the night reading up on anything and everything to do with the upcoming Mech Ops VR release. It was evidently hyped to be the game of the century, a massively updated version of its eighties predecessor, which had been so big back in the day it had spawned its own movie and animated series. Think Mario Bros. with zombies. It still had a cult following, too. With entire Reddit boards devoted to artwork and memes and people cosplaying the characters at comic cons. And when they had first announced they were doing a brand-new updated version—complete with an immersive VR experience? The internet had practically blown up with excitement.

From what I read, the new game would be similar to *Fields of Fantasy* in some ways. A massively multiplayer role-playing game where you could create a character, do quests either alone or with small groups, level up, and get rewards. The only difference? It was set in the future, not a fantasy kingdom. Instead of dragons, there were zombies and robots. Instead of majestic castles, there were ruined skyscrapers. It was even rumored there were spaceships you could actually fly around in.

Also, in addition to the main story line, there were supposed to be quite a few mini games available for players to earn extra rewards and gear. Player versus player—or PVP as they called it—where you competed in games like starship races, capture the orb, and huge battle royale arenas where you fought the other players, hoping to be the last man standing.

Kind of like video game sports. Not really my thing, but Lilli would probably love it.

My sister scanned the crowd, biting her lower lip. I could tell what she was thinking before she opened her mouth. Most of the crowd was made up of adults. Adults who likely had been playing video games years before we were born. How on earth were we going to stand out in a crowd like this? A trail of doubt began to worm its way through me.

But Ikumi needed us. There was no way we were going home now.

"Let's do this," I said.

As we grew closer to the compound's front gate, my eyes fell upon a twentysomething girl sitting in a wheelchair in one corner. She had dark skin, large brown eyes, and long brown hair that fell around her shoulders in ropy braids. A dragon tattoo snaked up her arm. I squinted at her for a moment, puzzled. Why did she look so familiar?

Suddenly it hit me. "Oh my gosh! That's Starr!" I realized aloud. "Whoa."

"Starr?" Lilli questioned.

I groaned. "Seriously, have you been living under a rock? Starr is, like, this total Twitch celebrity! She streams all the big games online and is completely epic at every game she tries. She's super funny, too, and has, like, ten million followers." I stared at her in awe, not able to help myself. This was like seeing a movie star—only better! "I had no idea she was in a wheelchair in real life."

I watched as Starr held her phone up to her face, chatting away. Probably streaming live to her channel this very second. I felt a thrill of excitement roll through me. I wondered if it'd be okay to go up and say hi. Get her autograph maybe? But then she probably got mobbed by fans all the time. I didn't want to annoy her.

Also...another more disturbing thought came to me. Starr was probably the most amazing gamer I'd ever watched online. And she was here. Along with so many other gamers who probably had their own Twitch channels or competed professionally.

And then there was us. How on earth did we expect to get picked?

"Don't freak out, Ian," Lilli scolded, catching my face. "All we can do is try. Besides, you're a good gamer. Don't forget that. I mean, none of these people made it through you know where," she added, lowering her voice on the last part.

I winced at the mention. I didn't want to admit it to her, but that was the other thing that was bothering me. I hadn't gone online in months to avoid Atreus. And now I was willingly going into a VR game for an extended period of time. What if he found a way in, too? What if he tried to sabotage our chances of rescuing Ikumi? It would be Dragon Ops all over again. Dragon Ops... with robots and zombies.

That would not be good.

Lilli patted me on the back, trying to be reassuring, maybe. "I'm going to go grab some waters," she said, pointing to a food truck on the other side of the parking lot. "You want anything?"

"Nah. I'm good."

I watched as she wove her way through the crowd, leaving me alone. I turned back to Starr. Wondering again if I should say hi or if that would be uncool. Before I could make the decision, a shadow crossed over me.

"Rivera! I should have known *you'd* be here today."

I whirled around. To my shock (and, let's face it, extreme annoyance), my soccer teammate Josh was standing behind me, regarding me as if I were dog poop he'd found under his shoe. His mop of curly blond hair hung in his eyes and he was wearing jeans and a T-shirt instead of his normal soccer attire. His T-shirt read IT'S OKAY IF YOU DISAGREE WITH ME. I CAN'T FORCE YOU TO BE RIGHT. Which was so on-brand for Josh it wasn't even funny.

I groaned. And this day just got better and better.

"We're here for the beta test," I told him, though I suppose that was pretty obvious. What I really wanted to ask him was why *he* was here. After all, this was about as much Josh's scene as soccer was mine.

"We?" Josh raised an eyebrow, making a big show of looking around. "What, you and your invisible friend?" He laughed at his own dumb joke. Man, this guy was the worst.

"Yes, Josh. Me and my invisible friend. Mario. He's a plumber and really good at video games."

Josh snorted. "Yeah, well, you and Mario better bring your A game." He gestured to the crowd. "It's freaking geekapalooza around here today. Nerds flying in from around the world just to compete in this thing. Professional gamers and everything. What makes you think you...and Mario...have a chance?"

"What makes *you* think you do?" I shot back, surprising myself with my quick comeback.

"Oh!" He laughed as if I'd said the funniest thing ever. "I'm not competing. I've got way better things to do than nerd my day away in some random VR apocalypse. Real life, baby! That's where it's at!" He pounded his chest with his fist. I resisted the urge to roll my eyes.

"Sure," I said instead. "But...you're here. Why are you here?" Maybe he had an older brother or sister competing? Maybe even his dad or his mom?

But Josh was no longer listening to me. He was glancing across the parking lot, a surprised look on his face. "Wait," he said. "Is that your sister over there? You drag her into this thing, too?"

"I didn't drag her," I protested, following his gaze and spotting Lilli on approach. "She actually happens to like nerding her day away in random VR apocalypses from time to time."

"But she's...um..."

"She's what?" I asked, confused. What was he trying to say?

He seemed to catch himself. "She's on the soccer team."

"What does that have to do with anything?" I squinted at him, confused. What was he trying to imply? That sporty people couldn't play video games? "How do you even know Lilli, anyway?"

Before he could answer, a man wearing an Appleby Games T-shirt walked up. He tapped Josh on the shoulder.

"There you are!" he exclaimed. "Didn't I tell you to stay inside? He wants to talk to you. Now."

I frowned. The way the guy said "he" I could tell he meant someone important. Like, really important. Could it be Admiral Appleby himself? But why on earth would a legend like Admiral Appleby want to talk to a tool like Josh?

Josh's face turned bright red. He scowled. "Yeah. Whatever. I'll be right there." He turned back to me. "Good luck, Rivera. You're going to need it."

And with that, he turned and walked away, escorted by the clipboard guy. I watched him go, feeling utterly confused. What was that about?

"And there he goes! Crown Prince of Appleby Games."

I turned, surprised at the new voice. To my amazement, I realized Starr had rolled up next to me. She watched Josh being escorted away, wrinkling her nose in distaste. "He's as obnoxious in real life as he is online, isn't he?"

"Um...You mean Josh?"

"Oh. Yeah. I guess that's his real-life name. Better known as Crash Zero, the most obnoxious kid on the internet and heir to the almighty throne."

"Throne?" I asked, super confused now. Since when did Josh have a throne? "What are you talking about?"

Starr raised an eyebrow. "You don't know? He seemed to know you. I just assumed..."

"We play soccer together. What does he have to do with this place?" I asked, feeling completely lost.

"Are you kidding? He's Admiral Appleby's grandson. And his only heir. All of this? It'll all be his someday." She waved a hand around the compound. "Of course he'll probably burn it to the ground just for spite."

I stared at her, flabbergasted. "Wow. I had no idea." And here I thought the guy was just an annoying jock. Instead, he was an annoying jock with a video game empire.

Seriously, sometimes life was so unfair. There was already crazy competition here. And now—with Josh on the inside? There was no way he was going to let me win this. Not after the whole soccer thing.

We had lost before we'd even begun playing.

"And two ice-cold waters," Lilli announced, handing a bottle to me. Then she turned to Starr and smiled. "Hi. I'm Lilli."

Starr held out her hand. "Nice to meet you, Lilli. I'm Felicia. Felicia Johnson. Though most people call me Starr."

"I know who you are," I confessed, shaking her hand after she shook Lilli's. "I mean, I've seen your channel. Actually I subscribe. I love your *Old School Saturday* streams. Like when you did that run-through of the original *Doom* on nightmare mode. That was so amazing. And—"

Lilli snorted under her breath, and I blushed hard. *Oh man, Ian. Could you sound more like a dork?*

But Starr only smiled. "Thank you," she said. "Most people don't appreciate *Old School Saturday.*"

"Ian's not like most people," my sister teased.

"So I've heard," Starr replied, giving me an overexaggerated wink.

I frowned, suddenly confused. "Wait, wh-what?" I stammered. "You've heard? What do you mean, you've heard?" How could this famous gamer have heard of me?

"Come on. Give me a little credit. You guys are practically legends. Well, in some circles, anyway. But don't worry." She grinned. "Your secret is safe with me."

My sister and I exchanged glances. "Um, I think maybe you're thinking of someone else?" Lilli suggested hesitantly. "We're not famous or anything."

"We don't even have a YouTube channel," I added, suddenly kind of wishing that we did.

"No," Starr replied. Then she leaned forward, lowering her voice. "But you did beat Dragon Ops, right?"

CHAPTER TEN

I stared at her, too stunned to speak. "Wh-what did you just say?" I stammered.

"Dragon Ops? You're the kids, right? The ones who got stuck in the game and fought their way out? Wow." She gave a low whistle. "For some reason, I thought you'd be taller."

"I'm plenty tall for my age," I protested, then realized I had just basically admitted to being the Ian she was talking about. Which I was definitely not supposed to do, legally speaking. "I mean, if I *were* that Ian. Which I'm totally not saying I am."

Starr held up her hands. "I get it. They made you sign stuff. It's cool. I don't want you to get in trouble."

"How did you even hear about this?" Lilli asked. "It's never been talked about online."

"Maybe not on the *public* internet," Starr agreed. "But on the Dark Carnival, you guys are practically heroes. The two kids who outwitted the *Camelot's Honor* sabotage. Who fought Atreus and won."

I felt a shudder cross over me at Atreus's name, but I shook it away. Tried instead to concentrate on the whole "hero" thing. *Take that, Josh!*

"The Dark Carnival? What's that?" Lilli asked curiously.

"It's this message board I belong to," Starr explained. "A lot of hackers and gaming people use it. It's ... well, you can't google it. It's hidden. But it's the best place to find out cool stuff going on in the tech and gaming world."

"Have they ... been talking at all about Hiro Takanama?" Lilli asked hesitantly.

Starr frowned. "The Dragon Ops game maker? I don't think so. I mean, I haven't been on in a while. I've been in a deep dive researching for this beta competition. Why? Is something up with him? Has there been another delay in opening the Dragon Ops park? More sabotage?"

I shot Lilli a warning look. We could not be talking about this. Starr seemed cool and all, but we had no idea if we could trust her. She had a Twitch channel, for goodness' sake! She could spread anything we told her to the world—instantly.

Lilli seemed to catch my look. "Oh. I have no idea. I was just wondering—"

Thankfully, at that moment a loud horn blew, interrupting

the conversation. We all turned to the compound's entrance, where a small stage had been set up. A young woman dressed in a futuristic metallic camouflage jumpsuit stepped up onto the podium and adjusted the microphone.

"Thank you all for coming out today," she said into the mic after the chatter died down. "It's always wonderful to see how much love and support Appleby Games has garnered in the gaming community. From way back in the 1980s, when we launched our very first game, to the moment last year when we announced our thirtieth title—the Mech Ops remake—your love and support has been a true honor. And today we're inviting all of you to level up—literally." She chuckled at her own joke. "To test-drive the future. Or should I say ... fly."

Everyone in the crowd cheered.

"Now for the bad news," the woman continued. "As you can see, there are a lot of you here. So for most of you, this is your one-day free pass to try out this new VR experience. Have fun with it, enjoy your time inside our little world, and remember it will be on sale sometime in the first quarter of next year. Consider this your sneak peek."

A few boos from the crowd. The woman smiled knowingly. "Don't worry," she assured them. "We won't make you go home empty-handed. We have some lovely parting gifts for all of today's participants. Including a ten-dollar-off coupon for the game when it comes out and ..." She paused for dramatic effect. "A limited-edition ruby power-up. Exclusive to those who preorder the game today."

The crowd erupted in excited chatter. Evidently ruby power-ups were a big deal. I wondered if they were some kind of real-life collectible or something you used in-game, like a cool weapon.

The woman was still talking. "But for those who really stand out from the crowd today, we have something much greater to give you. An exclusive chance to become part of our team. To sign on as an official Mech Ops beta tester. You will receive a full gaming rig—headset, sensor gloves, console . . . the works—to take home and try out for the next three months. You will record your gaming experiences, help us find bugs in the system, and basically make sure Mech Ops fulfills its promise to be the best VR game ever made."

Now the crowd went super wild, cheering and whooping. Clearly everyone here wanted to be one of the lucky chosen ones. I wondered again how Lilli and I would ever be able to stand out from the pack. At least one of us had to go home with a VR rig!

The woman waited patiently for the crowd to calm down. Then she grabbed a clipboard from the podium and held it up in the air. "I need each of you to grab one of these from our volunteers," she said. "Sign the waiver, which will serve as your NDA."

NDA stood for "nondisclosure agreement." Our parents

had to sign one of those for us when we first went to Dragon Ops—and another after, when we received our settlement. It was basically a promise that you wouldn't talk about the game to anyone—whether in person or especially online. Otherwise the game company could sue you for a lot of money.

The volunteers wandered the crowds, handing out clipboards. Each of them was dressed like the woman onstage—in a metallic camo jumpsuit. I wondered if this was something from the game itself. Maybe what players wore to show off their various factions?

Lilli scored three clipboards—one for each of us and one for Starr. We started filling them out. Simple things at first: name, address, all that good stuff. The second page, however, was a little more detailed. It wasn't part of the NDA, but rather a questionnaire about our gaming experience. What were our favorite games, how many hours a week did we game, did we game online or off? Did we prefer to play with friends or strangers? Had we ever played a fully immersive VR game before?

Hm. How to answer that one?

Lilli poked me. "What's wrong?" she asked. "You look worried."

"It's just…" I dropped my voice so our new friend couldn't overhear. "You know what Starr said—about us being famous on the Dark Carnival?"

"Yeah, so?"

I glanced up at the high, imposing walls of the Appleby Games compound. The ones we were about to enter. "What if *they* know about us, too?"

"Oh." Lilli pursed her lips. "I hadn't thought about that."

"If they know who we are, they're going to be super suspicious about why we want to join the beta test. Like, they'll think we're spies or something, working for Hiro."

"Um, we nearly got murdered in Hiro's game. I doubt they're going to assume we're superfans."

I hadn't thought of it that way. "But still..."

"Look, if they don't want us, they won't pick us. We'll go home with a ruby power-up—whatever that is. End of story."

"*If* they let us go home..." My mind flashed back to Uncle Jack discussing Hiro's disappearance. As far as we knew, the game maker was still missing. What if he, too, had tried to go into Mech Ops to find his daughter? What if he, like Ikumi, was now trapped in the game?

What if we were about to be next?

Lilli looked at me with concern. "What do you want to do?" she asked in a whisper. "Do you want to call it?"

I thought about it for a moment, then I shook my head. "No," I said. "We can't wimp out now. Ikumi needs us. We can't just abandon her in the game. No matter what the risks."

"Agreed. Besides, it's not like we didn't know this was going to be dangerous. We just need to be extra careful is all."

"Careful of what?" Starr rolled back over to us, her paperwork all filled out. She peered at us curiously.

"Oh, nothing!" Lilli said quickly. "Just VR sickness. Ian gets it super easy. I told him that he needed to go in slow the first time."

"Actually he doesn't," Starr said. "The new tech they've got on this game? You supposedly don't feel sick. That's its major selling point. Most people can't take normal VR for more than, like, twenty minutes 'cause it messes with their equilibrium. This game? You could play for days and not get the least bit dizzy."

"Days?" I repeated. "What, do you wear a diaper? How do you eat?"

Starr laughed. "Not real days. The game has time compression built in. You must have experienced that in Dragon Ops, right?"

We had in fact. The game had felt as if it were days long, but in the end, we'd only been in it for hours. It was the weirdest feeling, and I wasn't exactly thrilled to experience it again. I hated that disconnected-from-real-life sensation. But I supposed every VR game would start using that now. You couldn't very well live in another world if you had to pee in real life all the time.

"*If* we played Dragon Ops," I reminded her.

She snorted. "Right. If."

The woman at the front clapped her hands. "All right, everyone," she called out. "Are you ready to go inside?"

Everyone cheered and rushed the gates. I thought for a moment Starr might get left behind in her wheelchair, but then I realized she was already ahead of us. I grinned at Lilli, and we joined the mob, a thrill of excitement mixed with fear rushing through me.

This was it. We were in.

But what we were walking into? We had no idea.

CHAPTER ELEVEN

"Whoa."

My jaw dropped as we passed through the gates, entering the Mech Ops compound. "No way!" I cried. "Lilli are you seeing this?"

You gotta understand. I'd expected this part to be boring. A corporate courtyard leading to various nondescript office buildings. Instead, it was as if we'd stepped into another world entirely. A futuristic city packed with life-size models of robots and spaceships. Some looked really cool and new—like something out of a video game. While others had this sort of dorky retro look. As if they had come from an imagined future that never came to pass a long time ago.

But that wasn't the coolest part. Not by far. Instead it was the giant robot standing in the center of the courtyard that had me gaping. He had to be at least forty feet tall and was dressed in huge plates of purple and silver armor, so brilliant it was almost blinding to look at it.

"Rocky the Robot," I whispered, recognizing him from my earlier research. The mascot for the Mech Ops game. I had to admit, he was supercool-looking. Like, tough and futuristic, but almost medieval at the same time. I wondered if there was a way to play him in the game. Or fight with him. Or maybe he was the bad guy? Blazing across the robot's body was the Mech Ops logo, complete with its catchphrase: *Gear up, Mech Heads! And welcome to tomorrow.* I felt a chill of excitement flow through me. Wow.

I reached instinctively for my cell phone, wanting to take a picture, before remembering they had taken our phones at the front gate when we walked in. Which wasn't surprising. Appleby HQ was notorious for keeping its corporate secrets, from what I'd read online. Even Admiral Appleby himself was known to be a bit of a recluse, hardly ever appearing out in public. In fact, this was the first time in years that they'd let anyone who wasn't an employee through the front gates. No wonder so many people had shown up.

Everyone crowded the spaceships and robots, their excited voices rising into the air. It took me a moment to realize what was getting them so worked up. Turned out each spaceship had a ladder or staircase. So you could actually go into them and check them out. Even Rocky the Robot had a door in his chest, leading into his cybernetic body. How cool was that?

Excited, I started over to the robot, wanting to get in line. But Lilli ran after me, grabbing my arm and pulling me back. "What are you doing?" she demanded.

"Uh, checking out the awesome?" I said, as if that wasn't obvious. "Look. Everyone's doing it."

"*Everyone* is not here to save Ikumi," Lilli scolded. "Maybe a little focus, please?"

"Right." I reluctantly walked away from the line, not able to help feeling a little disappointed. I mean, when was I ever going to get another chance like this? Still, I knew she was right. We were here on a very serious mission, and we couldn't allow ourselves to be distracted. This wasn't Disney World. This was the vile compound of an evil mastermind who may or may not have kidnapped my friend and her father.

In other words, no robots for me.

We crossed the courtyard, weaving through the throngs of excited gamers. At the end, we found Starr waiting by herself outside a locked set of double doors where a sign read BETA TEST ENTRANCE. She was writing in a small notebook on her lap.

"No spaceships for you, either?" I joked as we approached.

She looked up. "Not exactly wheelchair accessible, are they?" she said with a smirk as she pointed to the ladders.

Ugh. I hadn't thought of that. I glanced back at the ships. Sure enough, not one of them had a ramp or an elevator or anything.

"That's so uncool," Lilli declared. "And probably illegal, right?"

Starr waved her off. "Whatever," she said. "These spaceships don't interest me, anyway. I only care about the real ones in the game."

It was an odd thing to say, but it made sense in a way. While these spaceships and robots were technically real—as in, they had real walls and doors and paint—at the end of the day, they were still only models. Metal shells that couldn't fly or do anything interesting beyond looking cool.

In the game, however, it would be a different story.

"Anyway, I wanted to be first in line," Starr added. "There's a lot of people here. I do not want to miss my chance to try out."

"Yeah, us too," I said, giving Lilli an appreciative glance. Good thinking, skipping the touristy stuff. Now we were second and third in line after Starr.

Starr slipped her notebook into a pocket hanging off the side of her wheelchair. "So," she said, looking up at us, "why are you two really here?"

"What do you mean?" I asked, something uncomfortable churning in my gut. "We're here like everyone else. To try the demo. Become beta testers."

"Sure." Starr pursed her lips. "But you guys are *Fields of Fantasy* players. Most people who play *Fields of Fantasy* like fantasy games, not sci-fi games."

"People can like both!" I protested.

"Yes," she said, giving me a pointed look. "But do you?"

A nervous feeling spun down my spine. She was suspicious. And if she was suspicious, wouldn't the Mech Ops people be suspicious, too?

"Actually, *I* do," Lilli broke in, saving me from answering. "Ian's just here as my backup. I'm the sci-fi superfan."

Starr raised an eyebrow. "Are you?" she asked. "*Star Wars* or *Star Trek*?"

Lilli's face turned red. Uh-oh. While my sister had a lot of fine qualities, let's just say sci-fi fandom was not one of them. "Um, *Wars*? That's the one with the lightsabers, right?"

"Favorite captain?"

Lilli's blush deepened. "Captain...Crunch?"

"Favorite Doctor?"

"My pediatrician, Doctor Lillian, is pretty nice..."

D'oh.

"Look," I blurted. "No offense, but we didn't come here to prove our geek cred. We came to get on this beta. And that's what we're going to do." I placed my hands on my hips for emphasis, hoping it made me look tough.

Starr smiled as if amused. "Fair," she said. "And I'm going to help you do it."

I dropped my hands, surprised. "You are?"

"Sure," she said. "As long as you agree to be on my channel someday."

"You want us on your channel?"

"We can't talk about Dragon Ops stuff," Lilli broke in. "I mean, even if we were the ones who played Dragon Ops. Which I'm not saying we are," she added quickly, shooting me a glance.

Starr held up her hands. "It's okay. You don't have to talk about anything you don't want to," she assured us. "I just want to prove I know you." She looked at us pointedly. "So do we have a deal?"

"Absolutely," I said. Why not? We needed all the help we could get. And going on my favorite online celebrity's channel? That was just icing on the cake.

"Great." She grabbed her notebook and flipped a few pages. "I have some inside info. This may turn out to be nothing, but I figure it's worth a shot. Anything to get an edge, right?"

"Totally," I declared, excitement rising inside of me. "What is it?"

"Well, according to one of my *Old School Saturday* fans who is a huge Mech Ops geek from way back when, in the original eight-bit scroller version of the game, they placed a chest at the very beginning in a secret room at the back of the starting area. To get to it, you had to start the game by pushing the joystick backward, which, of course, no one would ever think to do in a scroller game. You'd just move forward, like you're supposed to. And you'd miss the chest altogether."

"Cool," I said. I always loved Easter eggs placed in really old video games. They were much rarer than they were today. And also, because there was no internet back then, they stayed secret longer.

"But this isn't side-scrolling," Lilli reminded her. "Do you think they still added the chest?"

She shrugged. "I honestly don't know. But it would make sense, right? At least for a beta test like this one. A chance to prove you're a real fan. Someone truly worthy to play their game."

"Right," I said. "That makes total sense."

"It could end up being nothing," Starr added. "But if it's there, it'll give you a huge weapons cache right off the bat. Which would give you a big advantage over the other team. Maybe even enough to eke out a win. In any case, it's worth the few seconds it'll take you to look for it."

My heart pumped with excitement. This was exactly the kind of thing we needed to set ourselves apart from the other, more experienced players.

"Thank you," I said to Starr. "We really appreciate this."

"No problem!" Starr declared. "Anything for the Dragon Slayerz!"

I exchanged a guilty smile with my sister. Wow. She even knew our guild name. Which made me wonder, what else did the Dark Carnival know about us?

Or...Atreus, for that matter. Maybe Starr knew what was going on with Atreus?

I opened my mouth to ask, but at that moment the door in front of us began to creak open. The woman from the podium stepped out. She scanned the crowd, then her eyes dropped to us. She smiled approvingly, and I felt weirdly as if we'd passed some kind of test by skipping the tourist attractions and heading straight to the game.

"Are you ready?" she asked.

We looked at one another. Lilli grinned. Starr gave two thumbs-up. Excitement welled inside of me.

"Absolutely," I said. "Game on!"

CHAPTER TWELVE

"**O**kay, space cadets! Are you locked and loaded? We're just waiting on one more recruit and then we're clear for launch!"

A mustached man in a silver jumpsuit—our mission commander—walked over to each of us, checking our game rigs in turn. Each setup contained a large headset that could have doubled as a space helmet, a backpack with the battery pack and game console inserted inside, and two gloves, one for each hand, that would work as game controllers.

It was a totally different setup than we'd had in Dragon Ops, where we put on goggles and walked around the park in real life. Since this was only virtual reality, all we had to do was sit in a chair and turn on the game. Which meant even couch potatoes like me could rock it.

At least I hoped so.

Since we'd already been waiting at the gates when the woman first came out, we'd ended up first in line for our test. And bonus, Starr had gotten to join our team, too—Team Red. We'd been ushered into a small room with computer monitors at first, where we designed our characters and picked our starting armor. Unlike Dragon Ops, you didn't pick a character class—like warrior or mage. It was the armor that gave you your abilities. Some of it was really cool, too. Like an amazing lion's head helmet that I spent half my allotted starting cash on. I'd be broke but awesome-looking.

Next we'd been fitted for our gear and brought in here, which looked like the inside of a spaceship with tons of blinking lights and monitors spitting out numbers. Lilli sat on one side of me, Starr on the other. I glanced over at Starr. She gave me an enthusiastic thumbs-up, looking excited.

Meanwhile, I was just short of petrified, wondering what I had gotten myself into. Three months of being offline, and now I was jumping back in with both feet. Fully immersing myself in VR. What would it be like to be back in a game?

And what if Atreus found me there? He couldn't hurt me in real life. But in the game...

Don't think about it, I scolded myself. *Think of Ikumi. She needs you. You have to be brave for her.*

The door opened with a loud groan. My jaw dropped as the last person I expected to see stepped into the room. Josh's eyes locked on me, then Lilli, his mouth curled into a smirk.

Oh no. No, no, no!

"Fashionably late again, are we, Josh?" the mission commander tsked, giving him a disapproving look. But Josh only grinned.

"Fashionable, definitely. Late? Actually, it looks like I'm right on time." He crossed the room and sat down in the empty chair beside my sister. "Hey, Speedy," he said, poking her in the arm. "What's up?"

Lilli raised her eyebrows in surprise. "Wow! Josh!" she greeted him. "I did not expect to see you here!"

"Yeah. I thought you weren't competing," I broke in. "I thought you said this was only for nerds."

Josh grabbed his helmet. "It is, and I'm not," he replied easily. "But when Grandpa says jump, we all must ask ourselves how high." He smirked. "Evidently he saw you in line and thought it would be nice for me to play with some kids my own age."

"But not your own maturity level?" I muttered under my breath. I could feel Lilli give me a sharp look before turning back to Josh.

"Grandpa?" she asked curiously.

Josh's cheeks colored a little. "Oh yeah. He owns this place. And my parents are off saving the rain forest somewhere in South America. So I'm stuck here for the month."

"Awesome!" Lilli declared, flashing him a big smile. "I mean, not that you're stuck. But lucky for us. We can use all the help we can get. You ever play this game?"

"Unfortunately." Josh made a face. Then he grinned at my sister. "Don't worry, Speedy. I'll get you up to *speed*."

Lilli giggled. I rolled my eyes, willing myself to stay silent so Josh didn't decide to get us kicked off the competition. Still, I couldn't believe it. Of all the rotten luck. This was going to be hard enough without having to deal with Josh on top of it all.

"Don't let him shake you," Starr whispered, leaning close so only I could hear. "We got this—with or without His Royal Jerkness. Just ignore him; let him do his thing. He'll only manage to get himself killed. Meanwhile, we've got a secret weapon, remember? A whole stash of them if we're lucky."

I nodded, feeling a little better. Thank goodness we met Starr and she ended up on our team. I could already tell she was worth more than ten Joshes put together.

"Okay," the mission commander barked. "The rules of this game are simple. Capture the other team's orb and bring it back to your base. Meanwhile make sure to protect your own orb. The first team to capture the other team's orb twice will be declared the winner." He looked over at us. "Sound good?"

"Stellar," Josh replied with over-the-top fake enthusiasm.

The mission commander sighed. From his look I was guessing this wasn't the first time he'd gotten stuck with Josh. "All right," he said. "Hang on to your helmets, space cadets. You are now clear for launch."

He reached out and pressed a red button affixed to the wall, cutting the lights. A moment later the room around me vanished, and I was plunged into pitch-darkness without even a pinprick of illumination. I looked around, my heart beating fast in my chest, trying to see something—anything. But the blackness was unending. It was eerily quiet, too. Like that old *Alien* movie my dad always quoted. *In space, no one can hear you scream.*

Honestly, I really wanted to scream. What was going on? Were we in the game? No one had mentioned it would be dark. Was there a way to turn on the lights? I fumbled for menu settings but came up blank. There was nothing.

Nothing.

Nothing.

And then…a prick of light. Tiny at first, like the head of a pin. Then it grew a little larger. And larger. Like a light at the end of a long tunnel. Growing wider and wider and—

Liftoff! a voice whispered in my ear.

This time I did scream as my body suddenly rocketed toward the light, like a space shuttle hurtling into open space. It was so fast and so real that my stomach dropped out from under me and I was positive I was going to vomit all over myself back in the real world. I thought this game wasn't supposed to make you sick!

I waved my arms, trying to slow myself down. But I found I had no control as I shot through the air toward a now huge, glowing white hole. Until—

WHOOSH. I was sucked into the ball of light. And everything went blank once more.

CHAPTER THIRTEEN

When I opened my eyes again, I was no longer spiraling uncontrollably through space. Instead, I had been dropped into a decrepit old warehouse that looked as if it had been hit by a bomb. The crumbling walls were scorched with black soot and covered in old graffiti, and the cracked cement ground was piled high with trash and twisted pieces of metal.

Whoa. I turned around slowly, taking it all in. It looked so real. Just like Dragon Ops had. But unlike Dragon Ops, I was walking around in a body that wasn't my own. It felt so weird. Not like any other VR I'd tried before, where you were still aware of your regular body and could still move your arms and legs and feel them when you did. Here it felt as if we'd entered another plane of existence entirely. Become another person. It was disorienting and strange but also, I had to admit, kind of cool.

I spotted our orb at the back of the warehouse, shining bright and spinning in midair. It was golden, about the size of a soccer ball, and really beautiful. I had to resist the urge to pick it up and turn it over in my hands. Did it feel warm or cold? Hard or soft as silk? I couldn't tell by looking at it.

"Amazing!"

I turned to see Lilli had appeared beside me. She was dressed in a golden jumpsuit with zippered pockets all over it and a pink belt buckled around her waist. Her normally short brown hair was now bright pink and piled high in a ponytail on the top of her head. Her skin was shiny—almost metallic looking.

"This is so cool," she breathed. "I feel like I'm really here."

"Me too," I agreed. "I've never seen anything like it."

Starr appeared next, blinking into the room. She was dressed similarly to Lilli, but she was no longer in a wheelchair. Instead, she was hovering two inches off the ground, held up by what appeared to be a shiny pair of metal wings. I'd seen them when we were picking our armor, but hadn't chosen them—as I'd already spent all my starting game cash on my cool helmet. Which now I totally regretted. I'd thought the wings were just decorative—I had no idea they actually worked!

Starr fluttered her wings, her eyes shining. "Sweet!" she said. "I like this game already!"

Josh appeared next, unfortunately. I'd hoped he'd changed his mind and bailed at the last second. But there he was, decked out in some sort of super fancy purple space armor I hadn't seen on sale in the shop, complete with a shiny metallic breastplate and matching elbow and knee-pads. On his head, he wore a silver helmet shaped like Rocky the Robot's. I had to admit, he looked supercool. Not that I'd ever admit that to him.

"Wow," Lilli said, looking impressed. "I didn't see that armor in the store. I totally would have picked it myself."

Josh pushed up his helmet's visor and winked at her. His character was ten times bulkier than his normally skinny real-life self. "It's custom," he explained. "I had some of the artists design it for me a few months ago. I figure if I'm going to be stuck playing this game, I at least ought to look good."

Of course. The kid who didn't even care about the game was the best dressed—and best equipped, I bet—of our whole group. Totally not fair. But whatever. As long as his playing was as good as his look.

"Enemy approaching. Hatch will open in T minus three minutes," Rocky the Robot's voice announced over the airwaves.

"Oh no! Not the enemy!" Josh joked sarcastically, leaning

against a trash pile and giving an exaggerated yawn. "I'm *so* frightened."

I squeezed my hands into fists, anger welling inside of me all over again. I just knew Josh was going to mess this up for us. And why not? He didn't need to win this! He didn't even want to be here. He was just stuck here because his grandfather had ordered it. Why would he even bother to do his best?

Argh.

I grabbed Lilli by the arm and dragged her a short distance away. She looked at me and frowned. "What's wrong?" she asked.

"Josh, of course!" I snapped. "He's going to make us lose!"

"Why would he do that?" She looked honestly perplexed.

I ran a frustrated hand along my helmet. "Isn't it obvious? He's not taking it seriously. He doesn't care. And if we lose our chance to rescue Ikumi because of—"

"Relax, Ian," Lilli interrupted. "We're going to be fine. Josh is just being Josh. But trust me—he's way too competitive to let anyone else win—even in a video game. Besides, we should be happy to have him. He's the only one who's ever played this before. He probably knows all sorts of tricks and strategies."

I scowled. I knew she was probably right. Not that it made me feel much better. Especially the idea that Josh would be good at this. Video games were supposed to be my thing. Josh made fun of me for playing them. And yet he was probably going to end up the better player. Yet another thing he could rub in my face.

Also, how did my sister become such an expert on Josh? I didn't even realize before today that they knew each other. I thought back to the room in Mech Ops HQ. Josh had even called her by a nickname. That didn't exactly scream casual acquaintances...

I opened my mouth to ask her, but at that moment, Starr flew into my line of sight.

"Um, are you guys going to just stand around or help me look?" she asked.

Oh. Right. The weapons cache. I'd almost forgotten. I forced myself to push Josh out of my head. I could deal with him later. Right now we had to focus on our mission.

"Where is it?" I asked. "Do you know?"

Starr tapped a finger to her chin. "Not exactly. But it'll probably be in a small secret room in the back if it's here. Let's split up and look for it. If you find it, yell."

Lilli and I nodded, and we broke apart, heading toward the back of the warehouse to start our search. Which wasn't going to be easy, I realized as I looked around in dismay. There was trash and debris everywhere. Old spaceship parts, rusty tools, discarded robots that looked as if they'd fought in a war and lost. It was a lot to look through in less than three minutes.

"Hey!" Josh called after us. "Where are you guys going? Don't tell me you're retreating already!"

Ugh. We didn't have time to explain this to him. "We're looking for weapons," I said, starting toward the back of the warehouse.

Josh leapt in my path. "Weapons? There's no weapons here, dummy. They're in the center of the game board. Once the gate opens, we rush to get them." His tone was patronizing, as if speaking to a child.

"I know that," I ground out. "But there might be some here, too. It's a long story. But just, we're going to look real quick."

"Enemy approaching. Hatch will open in T minus two minutes," Rocky announced.

Josh groaned. "I thought you wanted to win this thing."

"I do!"

"Then get to the starting gate! You have to be there when it opens to get to the weapons pile first. That's the only way to win this." He was starting to sound anxious. Maybe Lilli was right about his competitiveness...

"You go, then. We'll meet you there," I said, kicking over a pile of rusty parts. Nothing. Nothing. *Where was it?*

"Don't tell me you're scared," Josh continued, evidently not willing to take a hint. He stepped into my path again. "Don't tell me you're going choke like you did on the soccer—"

"I said we'll meet you there!" I cried, instinctively reaching out and shoving him hard. To my surprise, he went flying across the room, slamming into a huge pile of precariously stacked garbage. The pile collapsed, burying Josh in debris.

Uh-oh.

"T minus one minute…"

Okay. I have to admit, I considered just leaving him there. I mean, seriously, he more than deserved it, right? But in the end, I ran over, grabbing handfuls of garbage.

"Hang on!" I cried. "I'll get you out."

The garbage smell assaulted my nose as I dug, stinking to high heaven. That was one nice thing about Dragon Ops— no smells! Here, on the other hand, they'd clearly perfected the technology.

"T minus thirty seconds!"

"Hurry!" cried Josh. I could see him thrashing around inside the pile. "We don't have much time!"

"Help me!" I cried to Starr and Lilli. I hated to make them stop looking for the weapons, but maybe it was a lost cause, anyway. Maybe it was only something in the eight-bit game.

I heaved a large piece of metal to the side and Josh came tumbling out. He shook himself, garbage flying from his fancy armor, which was now stained and dented. I waited for him to yell at me. Maybe even shove me in the other direction. Instead, something sparked in his eyes. He slapped me on the shoulder.

"That was borderline impressive, man," he said. "I didn't know you had it in—"

"Look! There it is!" Lilli suddenly burst out. I turned to see what she was pointing at. Sure enough, behind the garbage pile I'd just dug Josh out of, there was a small opening.

"Is that it? Is that the room?"

Josh frowned. "What room? What are you talking about?"

But Starr was already diving through the tunnel, and I was right behind her, Lilli at my heels. For a moment Josh just stood there, glancing at the game clock, still ticking down. Then he sighed and followed us in.

The tunnel was long and tight. It reminded me a little of that tunnel we'd crawled through in the water cave back in Dragon Ops that almost crushed us when it started collapsing. But I pushed the thought from my brain, concentrating on the light at the end.

Eventually we came out on the other side. And there, in the center of the room, shining brightly, was the biggest golden chest I'd ever seen.

Score!

"Whoa! What is that?" Josh asked, staring at it in fascination.

"Oh, just our secret weapons," Starr said, yanking off the lid and revealing its contents. "Literally."

I stared into the chest, my eyes bulging from my head.

Starr hadn't been kidding. This was a huge treasure trove of weapons, many looking far from beginner level. From swords to crossbows to metal staves that crackled with electricity. It was a total score.

Maybe we had a chance to win this after all...

"No way!" Josh cried, reaching into the chest and rummaging around. His eyes were about as big as mine probably were. "How did you know this was in here? I've never heard anything about this before."

Starr smiled smugly. "A dork's gotta dork."

Josh grabbed what looked like a laser crossbow and arrow, yanking it free from the pile. "Sweet!" he cried, switching it on. It glowed with a purple light that matched his armor.

Starr reached down and grabbed what looked like a throwing star, flashing with inner fire. And Lilli grabbed a staff that was crackling with pink electricity. Of course. Once a mage, always a mage.

As for me? I was still a warrior. I grabbed the last weapon—a laser sword that looked a lot like a lightsaber. I swung it around, testing it a few times. It made the coolest whooshing sound as it sliced through the air. I loved it already.

"T minus five seconds."

"Let's do this!" I cried, diving back through the tunnel and into the main room, my teammates scrambling behind me. By the time I reached the hatch, I was out of breath, my lungs feeling as if they were burning in my chest. Which was odd, considering I was literally sitting on my butt back at Mech Ops HQ in real life. This game was super realistic, to say the least.

"Gates opening," Rocky announced cheerfully. "Gear up, Mech Heads. And welcome to tomorrow!"

I turned to Lilli and Starr, flashing them a grin. They smiled back at me, brandishing their weapons, looking eager to start. Even Josh seemed kind of excited—he kept checking out his crossbow when he thought we weren't looking.

The gates creaked open, revealing a massive ruined cityscape beyond.

Game on.

CHAPTER FOURTEEN

"All right," Starr said. "They're gonna go straight to the middle of the map. That's where the weapons cache is. Let's cut them off at the pass. Get a go at them before they're armed. We'll take them out and storm their base while they're waiting to revive in the graveyard."

I nodded, accessing my game menu and opening my map. It was a simple layout—a bombed-out city street with buildings flanking each side. There were a bunch of cars, many still on fire, that we could use as cover. At the very other end of the street was the Team Blue base. Where we'd find their orb.

"Someone should stay behind," I suggested. "To guard our orb."

"Yeah, have fun with that," Josh replied. "I'm a center,

not a goalie." He raised his crossbow and started running down the street.

"Wait for us!" I cried, annoyed. But he was already halfway to the weapons cache. So much for being a team player. But I should have guessed that from his soccer style.

"I'll stay and guard," Starr said. "Yell if you run into trouble." She fluttered her wings, taking flight, then laughed. "This is so cool."

Lilli's eyes sparkled as she turned to me. "Let's do this!"

She dashed down the street in the direction Josh had gone, her steps literally leaving trails of fire in their wake. She must have chosen speed boots at the store, I realized in dismay as I tried to keep up with her, only to be left in her dust. (Or fiery inferno, as the case might be.) I tried to remember what awesome abilities my new outfit had but came up blank. To be honest: I'd picked it 'cause it looked cool—and I had no idea what it did.

Rookie move, Ian.

I kept running anyway—too late now. When I finally did reach the center of the map, I found Josh perched on a huge pile of crushed cars, picking off the other team with his crossbow as they attempted to retrieve the weapons from the cache. One by one, they fell to the ground wounded and screaming and completely confused as to how the other team had managed to roll up fully armed.

Okay, I felt a little like a cheater. But, hey—all's fair in game and war, right? Especially when Ikumi's life was at stake.

"Yeah, baby!" Josh cried, stopping to reload his cross-bow. "Cry to your mama!"

The other team tried to stand up. But we were ready for them. Lilli and I attacked, staff and sword slashing down at them where they stood. Unarmed, they had no prayer of getting near us, and we were blocking their access to the pile of weapons. In a few seconds, all three had blinked off the game board, presumably teleported back to the graveyard behind their base. There, they'd have to wait a full minute to revive before they could play again.

In the meantime, their orb lay unprotected.

"Let's go!" Lilli cried, dashing forward with her boots of lightning speed. Josh slid down the hood of one of the cars, launching after her. I was last again. Seriously—would it have killed me to check the stats of my gear before selecting it?

Just then I caught a flash of movement out of the corner of my eye. Something white—behind a burned-out car. I stopped in my tracks, then switched directions, heading back to the weapons cache. Josh and Lilli could deal with the orb. I needed to take out this guy, who was clearly a little craftier than his teammates.

But not too crafty for me.

I drew my sword, watching and waiting for him to make a move. He poked his head out for a moment and caught my eye before ducking back out of sight. I circled the car, my laser sword swinging, ready to strike.

Unfortunately, in doing so, I'd managed to leave the weapons cache unguarded. The enemy launched into the air, throwing himself on the pile. I chased after him, but as I swung, his fingers locked onto a sword and he met my blow, our blades clashing together, sparks flying, before sliding apart again. The guy smirked at me, something wicked gleaming in his silver eyes as he backed up, keeping his sword raised and ready. As if to say, *How will you do in a fair fight?*

He was good—I could tell. Probably a pro gamer. Someone who did this kind of thing for a living. Traveled the world. Played in tournaments.

My heart pounded in my chest. How was I going to defeat him?

You beat Atreus, man, something inside me whispered. *One of the most advanced AIs ever built. Surely you can beat some sorry gamer.*

Inspired, I charged at my enemy, slashing with my laser blade. He dodged easily, rolling himself across the hood of a nearby car. I didn't pause, leaping onto the hood to go after him—a move I could have never done in real life. Maybe that was my gear's superpower? Leaping? Just for fun, I tried again, jumping as high as I could.

I shot into the air like a rocket. Going at least twenty feet off the ground.

Sweet!

Of course what went up had to come down. A second later I found myself hurtling back to the earth. I crashed into the car, hitting it just off center and losing my balance, careening to the hard cement below. It didn't hurt, of course, but my vision blurred on impact, and I couldn't see anything for, like, three seconds. When it cleared again, the guy was right on top of me, his sword raised and ready to strike.

Crap. I rolled to the side, scooting under the car, out of his reach. His sword slashed down, sparks flying as it hit the ground. He let out a curse, realizing I'd slipped away, then dropped to his knees to find me. I lay on my back under the car, panting, not sure what to do. I could try to slip out the other side, but he could easily circle around and take me out before I could stand.

Meaning I was trapped.

Argh. This was not good. Should I just give up and let him send me to the graveyard? Then I could start my sixty-second reset. Otherwise I was just wasting time. But still! Josh would have a field day if I ended up being the first man down.

Annoyed, I punched the car's metal undercarriage above me. To my surprise, it shot up easily under my fingers, and I found I was suddenly holding up an entire car with just one hand.

Holy super strength! Was that another one of my armor's powers?

I had no time to think about it. Instead, I just shoved the entire car upward and to the side. The Blue team player screamed in surprise as the car came crashing down on top of him.

A moment later, he blinked off the game board. Back to the graveyard.

"Sweet!" I cried, raising a fist in a cheer. My first knockout. And by car, too! How cool was that? Forget super speed. I was like Superman in here!

"If you're done congratulating yourself?" Lilli broke in, panting as she raced past me. (Speaking of super speed.) "I could use a little backup?" She held up the glowing orb in her hands triumphantly, then motioned to the Blue team behind her, now revived and in hot pursuit. Where had Josh gone off to?

I turned to the new arrivals, ready to take them on. At first I figured I'd simply throw the car at them again, like I'd done to their friend. But when I tried to lift the vehicle a second time, it was unbearably heavy. It was then that I noticed a strength meter blinking at the corner of my vision. A limited power, maybe—and I'd already burned it out.

Guess I was fighting the old-fashioned way.

I raised my sword. "Come and get me!" I cried, stepping into their path. The three of them stopped, looking uncertain. They were still unarmed, so even without my super strength, I had an advantage. The big burly one yelled something to his friend. Then they took off running in the other direction, toward the weapons cache instead of me and Lilli. They must have figured they'd basically lost this round anyway. Time to prepare for round two.

I considered running after them, trying to stop them, but they were too close to the weapons now, and there was no way I could take on all three by myself once they were armed. Instead, I ran back to the base, wanting to help Starr and Lilli in case the fourth guy showed up again.

I barely made it before the buzzer sounded.

"The orb has been captured by Team Red!" Rocky the Robot announced. "The score is one to zero."

"Woo-hoo!" Starr cried, flying in circles around the orb. As she passed me, she held out her hand in a high five. I had to leap to reach it. Lilli was also there, jumping up and down with excitement.

"Nice going!" she cried. "They never even got near our base."

Starr floated to the ground. "I know, right?" she crowed. Then she sobered. "But we're not done yet. We need another point to win. And now they'll have their weapons. Our advantage is over."

"Right," I said. "We need a plan." We had thirty seconds while the orbs reset. Then it'd be game on again.

"There's a power-up in the east quadrant," Josh announced, popping back into the base.

"Where have you been?" Lilli scolded. "You totally disappeared on me out there!"

He waved a hand. "Please. You didn't need my help. They were unarmed. Even Ian here could have scored."

"Um, I took out a dude with a car," I informed him, annoyed. "I mean, just saying."

"Twenty seconds…" Rocky the Robot droned.

"Whatever," Josh said. "We need to get that power-up."

"No way," Starr argued. "We don't need it. We have the lead. We just need to play quick and smart. Go straight for the orb. Bring it back. Nothing fancy. That's how we'll win."

"It's not going to be that easy!" Josh shot back. "They have weapons now. You can't just roll over them. We need an advantage if we're going to keep our lead."

"Ten seconds," Rocky announced happily.

"We're wasting time arguing," Lilli cried. "We have to work together if we want to win."

"Which means we need to go after the orb," Starr said stubbornly.

"The power-up," Josh corrected.

"Five seconds…"

"Whatever," Josh muttered. Which I wasn't sure was agreement or not.

But there was no time to question. The gates began to lift. Round two had begun.

CHAPTER FIFTEEN

"Go, go, go!" Starr cried, flying out of our base and onto the city streets. We followed her out, me in last place again. (Not that I cared anymore—I could throw cars! Leap from buildings!)

Suddenly I stopped short, digging my heels into the pavement. Something was different this time. The landscape had changed. Sure, it was still a city straight out of a zombie apocalypse film. But unlike before, when it was just burned-out cars and crumbling buildings, now it was alive and teeming with large robotic sentries on patrol. Giant metal creatures perched on long spindly legs, crawling up and down the city streets, their laser eyes darting to every corner, seeking out intruders and zapping them into oblivion. I watched as one of them locked onto a large rat that had crawled out from an old gas station. A laser beam shot out, obliterating the rat and leaving only an oily black stain on the sidewalk where it had stood. Whoa.

The sentry turned, scanning in our direction.

"Take cover!" Starr called, dropping behind a car. We joined her, hearts pounding.

"Okay, who upped the difficulty level?" I joked, though it didn't come out as funny as I wanted it to. The sentry took a few steps forward, still scanning. If it found us, we were toast. Burnt toast.

Josh rolled his eyes. "So...anyone for a power-up?"

I sighed. I didn't want him to be right. But I was starting to agree with him. There was no way we could just barrel our way through those robots to get to the orb. Not without help.

"Look," Starr said. "If you're so hot for the power-up, just go get it, okay? Meanwhile we'll try to sneak through the buildings. It looks as if they're connected on the second floor. Maybe we can get through that way without attracting the robots' attention."

"Yeah, good luck with that!" Josh muttered. He turned to me and Lilli. "What about you guys?"

"I'll join you," Lilli said, surprising me. When I raised an eyebrow, she shrugged. "Why not? It could help, you know."

"Why not, indeed," Josh agreed, grinning at me as if he'd won something. Then he turned to Lilli. "All right, Speedy. Let's burn some space rubber." And with that, they started running back toward the base in the direction of the power-up, Lilli's boot trail still flaming in her wake.

Leaving Starr and me alone.

"Forget them," she advised, beckoning me into what looked like an old pharmacy. We ducked inside, and I looked around, taking in the scene. The place was as trashed as the rest of the city. Shelves knocked over. Broken bottles everywhere. A dim light above fizzled on and off and on again, buzzing loudly while rats scurried across the floor. Charming.

My mind flashed back to the beautiful Dragon Ops world, with its majestic mountains and lush forests. Maybe it had gone bad, but it had always been beautiful. This, on the other hand, was the stuff of nightmares. I would never understand the appeal of these kinds of games.

I followed Starr up a broken staircase and down a dark hallway lined with ripped wallpaper and teeming with black mold. She was skimming the ground with her toes, her wings keeping her above most of the debris. I, on the other hand, had to look each time I leapt and nearly ate it a few times, tripping over random boxes and loose floorboards in my path.

"Slow down!" I called out to her. "Wait for us mere mortals!"

Starr laughed but slowed her pace, and I caught up with her at the end of the hall. As she had predicted, there was a bridge-like walkway stretching between the two buildings. What she hadn't predicted, however, was that its bottom had fallen out, making it totally impassible—at least for those of us without wings.

"Really?" Starr asked. "Are you kidding me right now?" She stared at the broken walkway in dismay.

"Now what?" I asked. "Do we go back down?"

She scratched her head for a moment. Then her eyes lighted on an old clothesline stretching out between the two buildings. A thoughtful look came over her face.

"Oh no," I said, reading her mind. "No way. I don't do heights."

"You better learn quick," she shot back. "It's the only way we'll have a chance." She gave me a reassuring glance. "Look, it's really no big deal—just think of it as a zip line."

"I don't do zip lines, either." I glanced nervously at the ground below. Which, for the record, was really, really far down. "Remember, you have wings. I'm going to splat."

"If you do, you'll revive in the graveyard," Starr reminded me. "But if you don't—well, we have a chance to win this thing right now. Isn't that worth the risk of a little virtual splat?"

I nodded grimly, realizing she was right. We needed to win this. And if zip-lining to my death was what it took to win? I needed to suck it up. Besides, it wasn't like real-life dying. It wasn't even like Dragon Ops, where it would real-life hurt. If I fell, I'd reset. No big deal.

But it still felt like kind of a big deal.

Starr handed me a thick piece of wire she'd pulled from her wings. She instructed me to wrap it around the clothesline and then use it to slide down. I did as I was told, my hands shaking the entire time as I gingerly stepped out onto the broken walkway, trying not to look down.

"I am seriously a crazy person," I muttered, then jumped.

WHOOSH. The air rushed at my face and past my ears as I flew down the clothesline at breakneck speed. My stomach dropped, possibly to ground level, and I fought not to puke all over myself. (Could you virtually puke? I wasn't sure.) The window of the next building rushed closer and closer and—

"Ian! Jump! Now!"

I kicked my feet out, using my jumping power to leap through the window. I ducked my head as I crashed through the glass and somersaulted three times before slamming into a wall and stopping short. The impact knocked the air from my lungs, and for a moment I just lay there, gasping for breath. Then I recovered, scrambled to my feet, and ran to the window.

I waved up at Starr, grinning, rather proud of myself.

"Your turn!" I cried.

She gave me a small salute, then jumped out the window with ease, using her wings to keep from dropping to the ground. For a moment she looked like an angel floating across the sky. The first beautiful thing I'd seen in this game. And then—

BOOM! A blast rocked the building, knocking me backward. One of the robot sentries below had taken out a member of Team Blue on the ground. Which, of course, was a good thing. Until I realized his partner had survived, dashing into the alleyway to avoid the blast. When she looked up, her eyes locked on Starr—in midair, unprotected.

She raised her crossbow.

"Watch out!" I cried, frantic.

But the warning came too late. The arrow arced through the air, hitting its mark. Embedding itself into the middle of Starr's left wing. She flailed, knocked off balance, her wing smoking and sparking behind her. The other wing working overtime to keep her afloat.

But in the end, it wasn't enough. She began plummeting to the earth.

"No!" I cried.

Her eyes flew to me at the window. "Keep going!" she cried. "Get the orb!"

And with that, she hit the ground, blinking out of view. Straight to the graveyard.

Leaving me alone.

I abandoned the window, my mind racing. What to do? What to do? I could go for the orb alone, like Starr had suggested, but once I grabbed it, my hands would be full and

I couldn't use my sword. Which meant I wouldn't be able to defend myself on the way back. I needed backup. Where were Lilli and Josh? Had they gotten the stupid power-up yet? Were they on their way?

I couldn't wait around to find out. The girl from Team Blue had to have heard me shouting. She'd be heading inside any second now to finish me off. I had to move, and fast.

I raced through the building, an old movie theater, I realized as I ran through a projection booth, tripping over film reels and machinery. Pushing the far door open, I took the stairs two at a time, landing in the theater lobby, wanting to make a break for it while I still could.

But just as I was about to exit, I heard voices. Team Blue was there, right behind the door. I dove behind a popcorn machine, trying to find a hiding spot. Unfortunately, I managed to knock over a stack of soda cups in the process. They fell to the ground with a loud crash. (Which was seriously louder in-game than it had any right to be. They were just paper cups, after all!)

"There he is!" cried the girl who had taken out Starr. "I told you he was still in there!"

"Let's go get him," her partner exclaimed, sounding way too eager for my liking.

Crap. I glanced around, desperate for a better hiding spot. My gaze landed on an open door leading into the theater itself. Drawing in a breath, I made my move, praying it wouldn't prove to be a dead end.

Inside the theater was dark. Only dim floor lighting gave off any sort of illumination. I ducked down behind a row of moldy red velvet seats and began crawling toward the other side. Thankfully, there did seem to be an exit at the front by the ripped screen, its light faintly glowing in the darkness. If I could get to it, I would be able to escape.

But the other team had entered the theater now. One on each side, walking down the rows, peering into each one. I had four—no three—rows before they spotted me. And then I'd be a sitting duck.

What to do...? What to do...?

It was then that I remembered my superpower. I could leap. Maybe I could leap as far as the door. They'd be startled—not expecting the move. Maybe I could make it outside before they knew what was going on.

It was worth a try.

"Hey, cheater. We know you're here," one of them called. "Just give up already. We've got you surrounded."

I clenched my body tight, preparing for the jump. If this worked, I'd never complain about a lack of super speed again.

Three...two...

I shot into the air, throwing myself at the exit.

"What the—"

"He's getting away! Stop him!"

They dashed down the aisles, the girl raising her crossbow as she ran, trying to get off a shot. But I was already there, shoving open the exit. Accidentally activating my super strength and knocking the whole door off its hinges. I burst out into open air...

...straight into a robot sentry.

BOOM!

Everything went black.

CHAPTER SIXTEEN

When I came to, I was lying in the graveyard behind our base. I felt a little achy, but nothing near the level of pain you'd feel when getting hit by a real-life laser beam, thank goodness. Just sort of tingly and winded. Rising to my feet, I watched the counter in my field of vision slowly tick down from sixty to zero—the time I had left before I could revive and play again.

I couldn't help feeling a little discouraged. I mean, that whole run had been awesome. I dashed, I zip-lined, I outwitted my enemy and leapt to freedom. All to get blasted by a stupid tank. All to end up back in the graveyard without the orb.

It was almost as bad as my last soccer game.

Finally the clock ticked down to zero and the revive

chime rang in my ears. I was free! But as I ran back into the base, ready to make another attempt, the buzzer sounded, indicating a score.

Not ours this time.

I sank to my knees, frustrated. Well, that was that. So much for our awesome plan. So much for our lead. We were now tied one to one. The next score won the game.

And we had no advantage left.

"Okay, that isn't great," Starr muttered, checking her wings. They seemed to be working again, at least.

"Your top-secret plan didn't work?" Josh asked innocently.

"Maybe it would have if we'd had some backup," Starr shot back. "Instead of half the team running off on a waste-of-time side mission."

"Waste of time? I don't think so." Josh nudged Lilli. "Show them, Speedy."

Lilli grinned, holding up two glowing white balls the size of baseballs. "Anyone for a power-up?" She tossed one, then the other, to Josh. He caught them easily.

"Nice!" I cried, proud of my sister, even if Josh was still the most annoying guy on earth. "What does it do?"

"It disrupts electrical impulses," Josh explained. "Which means if we throw one of them out onto the street, everything electric stops in its tracks."

"Like the sentries, for example," Lilli added, her eyes shining with excitement. "We can take them out entirely."

"Okay, I got to admit, that's handy," Starr said grudgingly. "Those things are no joke."

"Yeah, but does it help us win?" I asked. "I mean, taking out the mechs helps us, but it also helps the other team the same way."

"Not if they're already dead," Lilli said proudly.

"What?"

"We're going to play defense."

"I don't understand."

"It's easy," my sister said. "We don't throw out the power-up right away. We wait here at the base, guarding the orb. The other team will have to fight their way here. Hopefully, the sentries will take most of them out on the way. Then we take care of any stragglers who happen to make it."

"And while they all peace out to the graveyard," Josh continued, "we throw the power-up, knock out the sentries, and make our run."

Starr wrinkled her nose. "I don't know..."

"Come on!" Lilli pleaded. "It's a brilliant plan, and you know it."

"Okay, fine," Starr said. "We'll give it a try. What do we have to lose, right?"

We had a lot to lose. Everything, really. But I did agree with my sister; it was a good plan. Josh might be a pain in the butt, but he clearly knew the ins and outs of his grandfather's game. It was an advantage we couldn't afford to refuse.

"T minus ten seconds," chimed Rocky the Robot.

"Okay, positions," I barked out. If we were going to do this, we needed to be prepared. "Josh—you've got the cross-bow. So you go high. Try to pick them off before they enter the base." I turned to my sister. "Lilli, you hide near the left entrance. If anyone comes that way, take them out. And, Starr, you can guard the orb. With your wings, you can fly around it, covering the most ground."

"What about you?" Lilli asked.

"I'm the bait. I'll bring them right to you." I bounced in the air, practicing one of my leaps. "Just be ready."

"Doors opening," Rocky the Robot announced. "Gear up, Mech Heads! Welcome to tomorrow!"

Everyone scrambled to take their positions while I headed directly out the front gate, stepping into the ruined city. The robot sentries were still there—but they looked as if they'd been upgraded since the last round. More laser can-nons. More electric eyes searching for a target. I shuddered as I thought back to the one that had taken me out behind the movie theater. While it hadn't exactly hurt, it still felt really uncomfortable. Let's just say I wasn't eager to repeat the experience.

I dropped down behind a large chunk of cement, then slipped quietly to the next, watching and waiting for Team Blue to appear. It took them a while; they had to deal with upgraded sentries, too. But at last I spotted three of them sneaking behind the pharmacy, just out of the sentries' range.

That would have been a good strategy last round, I realized. But ours was going to be better.

"Hey!" I burst out into the open air, waving my sword. "Over here! Come and get me!"

To my delight, they took the bait, charging in my direction. I waited for them to get close, then power leapt back toward our base. They followed, as I knew they would, walking right into our trap. Josh let loose a barrage of arrows. One of which hit its mark dead-on. I watched as the girl who had taken out Starr screamed and dropped to the ground, popping out of sight. I let out a silent cheer.

One down. Three to go.

The others stopped in their tracks, now wary. They dove behind cars to get out of Josh's line of fire. I ran back into the base—heading to the left entrance, where Lilli was waiting, hoping at least one of them would follow me.

"How's it going?" Lilli whispered as I reached her.

"Josh got one of them. They didn't even see it coming."

"Nice!" My sister gave me a high five, and I beamed.

But our celebration didn't last long. Suddenly Lilli yelped

in shock and surprise. When I turned around to see what was wrong, she poofed in a bright flash and disappeared.

What on earth?

Confused, I spun around. Who had gotten her? There was no one here! Except...

My eyes caught a shimmer in the corner of the room. As I squinted at it, I could just make out the outline of a person sneaking up the stairs. My jaw dropped. Did their armor give them invisibility?

I charged after him, slashing down with my sword. The player yelped in surprise; clearly he hadn't realized his power had worn off enough for me to see him. He fell to the ground, then blinked out of view.

Two down. But now we were down one player, too.

I ran back into the base to let Starr know. When I got there, she was already in battle mode. One member of Team Blue— the bulky guy—had gone straight through the front door, not knowing Starr was lying in wait for him at the orb. She spun in the air, winding up, then throwing her star at the intruder. It spun madly, then hit the guy square in the forehead.

"Hasta la vista, baby!" Starr crowed.

"Nice!" I cried as she dipped back down to the ground. "I took one out in the hall."

"And I got the girl outside," Josh added, coming back down the stairs.

"So there's one left," I said. "Did you see him?"

Josh shook his head. "No. He must have gone back to the base."

I wrinkled my nose. Annoying. I would have liked to have taken them all out before using the power-up. But we couldn't waste any more time. We needed to go now—while the other three were in the graveyard.

Three of us against one of them. We had the odds at least.

"Okay! Use the power-up!" I told Josh.

He raised his hands. They began to glow. A ball of white light crackled at his fingertips. I had to admit, it looked supercool. I watched as he wound up his arm and vaulted the ball out into the city.

Everything immediately ground to a halt.

"Yes!" I cried, so excited I could barely stand it. No more robot sentries. Our path to victory was wide open.

"Go, go, go!" Starr shouted. "I'll stay here, in case that last guy shows up."

Josh didn't need a second invitation. He dove down the street like he was on fire, his purple armor blazing in the sunlight. I followed, using my leap ability to keep up with him.

We raced past the dead sentries, now standing like useless metal hulks, thanks to Josh's power-up. I wondered how long it lasted—would we have to face them again on the way back? Whatever. That was Future Ian's problem. Right now we had to get the orb.

Finally I reached the Team Blue base. Josh was already

there, going for the orb. But before he could put his fingers on it, a figure leapt from the shadows. The last member of Team Blue! He grabbed Josh from behind, stabbing him in the back with his sword.

Josh screamed in fury, but it did no good. A moment later, he popped off the map.

And the enemy turned to me.

CHAPTER SEVENTEEN

I held my breath as the player stalked toward me. He'd already used his super leap, but I didn't know what other powers he might have up his sleeve. Maybe super strength like me? Or invisibility? Super speed?

Whatever it was, it couldn't be good.

I drew my sword and we circled each other, eyes not leaving the other's face. He was bigger than I was. Taller, bulkier. But hey—the bigger they were, the harder they fell, right? And there was no time to hesitate—in a few moments his teammates would revive from the graveyard nearby. And the sentries would wake back up.

It was now or never.

With a mighty yell, I abandoned my sword, grabbed a huge hunk of machinery that was lying on the ground, and heaved it in his direction. It crashed down on top of him, not knocking him out, unfortunately, but pinning him to the ground—at least for a moment. As he struggled to free himself, I made a leap toward the orb, pulling it into my hands. It felt warm and tingly as I hugged it against my chest like a football.

I glanced over at the enemy. He was almost free. Time to make my exit.

I dashed out of the compound. I could hear the angry shouts from the other players—they had just revived and were running back into the base and realizing the orb was gone. They dashed out after me, and I tried my best to pick up the pace. It was going to be close, but I was pretty sure I had enough leeway to make it.

ROAR!

The sudden sound ripped through my ears. I dug in my heels, stopping short. Because suddenly, standing where nothing had been a moment before, was a dragon. A big, huge, red-scaled dragon. Mouth creaking open. Sparks dancing on his blackened tongue.

"No," I whispered. "Oh please no!"

My hands shook. My legs gave out from under me. I fell to the ground, barely able to breathe.

Please not now. Not now—when we're so close.

"You're not real," I whispered, struggling back to my feet. "You're not *real*."

But then, maybe this time he *was*. After all, this wasn't

like seeing him on a soccer field in the real world, a place he couldn't possibly be. We were in a game. Which meant he could have found his way in, too. Finally tracking me down after all these months to get his revenge.

Do you want to play again?

Do you want to play again?

Do you want to—

"Ian! What are you doing? Run!" I could vaguely hear Josh's voice. But it sounded a million miles away.

Suddenly I felt the orb being ripped from my grasp. I turned to find a member of the Blue team laughing at me as he cradled the sphere under his arm, taking off in the other direction. "Nice choke, loser!" he yelled as he dashed full speed back to his base.

"What did you do?" Josh cried, reaching me out of breath. "Why did you stop in the middle of the field? We totally had them!" His face shone with annoyance and disappointment, just as it had on the soccer field.

I turned, heart in my throat, searching for the dragon again. But the street was empty. If he had been there, he was now long gone.

I felt like I was going to puke. What had I done? Had I just cost us the game?

Josh gave me another disgusted look, then dashed down the street toward the enemy base, shooting arrows from his crossbow without pause. The guy with the orb put his hand up in a rude gesture, easily dodging each blow. Josh was fast, but the guy had a big head start.

And the sentries were moving again.

Oh no. No, no, no!

They started to turn, their laser eyes locking onto Josh. I could hear them warming up. Readying their strikes.

"No!" I cried. "Josh, watch out!"

On instinct, I jumped into the sentries' path. Their sensors caught the sudden movement and whirled around, locking onto me instead. I tensed my body, waiting for the blow.

BOOM!

Back at the graveyard once again. Awesome.

I thrummed my fingers against my armor, chomping at the bit for the timer to tick down. Hopefully my sacrifice hadn't been in vain and Josh got the orb and was now running it back to the base. I wanted to scream as I thought of how I'd frozen out there, just like I had in the soccer game.

Had Atreus even been there at all? Or had it all been in my head? The other players hadn't seen him—they would have at least reacted if they had, right? But was it possible he only appeared to me? In real life that would be impossible. But in a game…

The timer dinged and the bars came down. I bolted from our base just in time to see Josh sprinting through the gate. He was panting heavily, and the other team was right behind him, ready to pounce. Starr and Lilli ran to intercept, but they were too far away. Josh wasn't going to make it.

Unless…

"Kick it!" I yelled as loud as I could. "Kick it to me, Josh!"

Josh looked up in surprise. For a moment, doubt crossed his face—probably remembering our fateful soccer game. Or, you know, me choking just a few moments before. But in the end, he dropped the orb to the ground, wound up, and kicked it hard in my direction milliseconds before the other team took him out and he disappeared into the graveyard.

I watched, breathless, as the orb arced through the air, then dropped inches from my feet. I scooped it up and ran to the pedestal, triumphantly placing it on the platform.

The game world blinked. The sky outside exploded with fireworks. The other team vanished from the map. The word *Winner* flashed across my field of vision.

And then everything went black.

CHAPTER EIGHTEEN

I felt hands at the sides of my head. A moment later, my headset was pulled away. I blinked, my vision still super blurry as my eyes attempted to readjust to real-life mode again. Thankfully, I didn't feel like I was going to puke like I did when I left Dragon Ops.

Once I could see again, I looked around. We were back in the launch room, sitting in our chairs. Lilli was pulling off her own helmet. Josh was rubbing his eyes. Starr was shaking her head in amazement, a big grin spread across her face.

"So," our mission commander said with a smile. "What did you think?"

"It was amazing," I blurted out before I could remind myself to play it cool. "I've never played anything like it."

"It felt so real," Lilli added, still looking a little dazed. "Not like regular VR. I felt as if I was really inside the game."

The mission commander smiled. "Very good," he said. "That's exactly how it's supposed to feel. As if you're entering an extended dream. As far as your brain is concerned, it's real."

"Except you don't really croak," Josh pointed out. "So, not *really* real."

"Of course not!" The mission commander barked out a laugh. "Who would play a game where you could die?"

Lilli and I exchanged glances, remembering Dragon Ops. Who indeed?

"You did well, my friends," proclaimed a new voice.

We looked up as the door opened and a strange little old man hobbled through. He was dressed much like the mission commander, in a space uniform, but his was bright purple, matching Josh's armor in the game.

"Whoa," Starr whispered. "Admiral Appleby!"

My heart practically stopped. It was all I could do to not let my jaw fall to the floor. Admiral Appleby. *The* Admiral Appleby? Standing here, in our game room?

I glanced over at Lilli, my heart racing. Was this the evil man who had stolen away our friend? Trapped her in a video game for some nefarious purpose yet to be discovered? Did he know why we were here? Did he suspect we knew about Ikumi?

But no. That was impossible. Right?

"I see my reputation proceeds me," Admiral Appleby

said, turning to Starr. His watery blue eyes seemed to shine with an inner fire. "Yes. I am your admiral. I have just warped in from the Zeta Quadrant to congratulate you on your recent victory in the city of Empire. You fought bravely against a mighty foe."

I blinked in surprise. Whoa. He role-played? The evil game designer role-played?

Josh groaned. "Seriously, Grandpa?" he demanded. "You're really going to do this now? In front of my friends?"

The admiral turned to his grandson, giving him a solemn look. "Ah, yes, young Crash Zero," he said. "I am happy to see you have returned in one piece. I fear every time you so valiantly go forth and face our enemies that one day you will not return."

"I should be so lucky," Josh muttered.

Admiral Appleby's mouth twitched, and I could tell he was trying not to laugh. Which I grudgingly had to admit was pretty funny. Josh getting trolled by his grandfather—nice!

"It was indeed a rough battle," Starr declared, picking up on the role-play. "But working as a team, we were able to finish victoriously."

The admiral turned to her, giving her a sharp look. "I applaud your victory," he replied in a solemn voice. "But I do wonder at your methods. Was it indeed teamwork? Or was it...something else that gave you your winning edge?"

I stared at him, confused for a moment. What was he talking about? The power-up, maybe?

Then it hit me. The weapons cache. It'd been so long at this point since we'd found it, I'd almost forgotten.

But Admiral Appleby clearly hadn't.

"The Mech Ops Academy operates under a strict code of honor," the admiral went on, a frown etching into his already well-lined face. "Virtue. Honesty. Fairness." His eyes narrowed. "We don't abide cheaters here."

My heart sank. I stole a glance at Lilli. I should have known a move like that wouldn't go unnoticed. And now? What if it cost us the beta? Because they thought we cheated? And if we didn't get the beta...

No. I wasn't going to accept that. I couldn't accept that.

"You dare call us cheaters, sir?" I cried, going into full role-play mode. Couldn't hurt, right? "Forsworn, an accusation like this should not be made lightly. We are honorable space knights, toiling in your endless war. Should we not fully embrace all that has been given us? Should we not fully discover every advantage at our disposal to take down thine enemy? Call it not cheating. Call it resourcefulness. Ingenuity. Something I did not see from Team Blue."

"And...Ian's gone full-nerd," Josh muttered. "It was only a matter of time, I guess."

Admiral Appleby's blue eyes locked on me. For a moment he looked so fierce, I thought he was going to kick me out of the building altogether. Do not pass go. Do not collect a VR rig.

Then, to my surprise, he burst out laughing.

Josh groaned. "Seriously?"

Admiral Appleby kept laughing. Peals of laughter so hard he had to lean against a nearby wall to hold himself upright. We looked at one another, not sure what to do. What to say. What was so funny?

"Um, is everything all right?" I tried to ask. "Look, I'm really sorry if—"

Appleby cleared his throat, the laughter fading from his face. "I have to admit, I had my doubts," he declared, no longer in role-playing mode. "You're the youngest players here today. I didn't think you'd be able to compete against the more accomplished of our ranks. Especially not with Mr. Grumpy Pants on the team," he added, throwing a look at Josh. "But in the end? You were smart. You were creative. You worked as a team. And it paid off."

I let out a breath. Phew.

"So...you're not mad about the weapons cache thing?" Lilli asked.

"On the contrary, my dear, I'm extremely impressed! How did you know it was there?"

"We have our sources," Starr said, a little smugly.

"Well, whatever you did, I admire it. I've always been a firm believer that the best games go beyond the screen and bleed into real life. So even when you're not actively playing, the game is still part of your reality. That's the way a true gamer sets him- or herself apart from the rest." He smiled broadly. "You, my friends, are true gamers."

Wow. A wave of pride rolled over me at his words. True gamers! That was high praise coming from someone so legendary in the industry...

Who might also be super evil, I scolded myself. *Let's not get drawn in to his game. He might act nice now, but what would he do if he knew what we're truly after?*

"We did our best," I assured him, trying to play it cool. Evil or not, I needed him to think we were on his side if we were to have any chance of winning the demo. "It's an amazing game."

"And you have only touched the tip of the iceberg," the game maker declared. "A mere microcosm of a vast universe. The capture the orb game was just a gateway to something so much bigger. A massively multiplayer role-playing game the likes of which no one has ever seen before. An entire universe, just waiting to be explored. I daresay you could spend years wandering my game and never see the same place twice."

I gulped. Normally a virtual world that vast would be the ultimate in coolness. But we had to find Ikumi. The bigger the world, the harder that was going to be.

"How much of the game will the beta have open?" Starr asked. "Will we get to see everything if we get chosen?"

"Unfortunately not. Thanks to legal. You know how they can be!" He shook his head, as if gravely disappointed by whoever this "legal" was. "I can only open up one planet for the beta. But don't worry—there are plenty of story lines, quests, in-games to play. Even a whole player-versus-player realm. Trust me, you won't be bored."

I looked up. "Does this mean we're in?" I asked, holding my breath.

Admiral Appleby smiled warmly at me. "You're in, kid. You too," he added to Starr and Lilli. "Just go to the main desk to sign out your new VR rigs." He gave us a firm salute. "Gear up, Mech Heads! And welcome to tomorrow."

Josh groaned. Admiral Appleby looked at his grandson and sighed deeply.

"Now, if you'll excuse me," he said. "I've got other potentials to observe. I will see you soon." And with that, he and the mission commander exited the room, leaving us alone.

"I can't believe we're in!" Starr cried, her eyes bright with excitement.

"I know, right?" I agreed. "We did it! We really did it!"

"Congrats, team," Josh said, rising from his seat. "Now, if you'll excuse me, I have a real life to get back to." He gave us a mock salute, then started toward the exit.

"Wait!" Lilli said suddenly.

He stopped, turning and raising an eyebrow at my sister. "Yes, Speedy?"

"Thank you," my sister said sincerely. "We couldn't have done this without your help." Then she shot me a meaningful look. I sighed.

"Yeah," I agreed. "Thanks and stuff."

"You may not like this kind of thing? But you're pretty good," Starr added grudgingly.

Josh shrugged. "Yeah, well...not like it's hard," he said. But I caught a small smile at the corner of his mouth. "Anyway, it's been...well, *not* real." He snorted at his own joke and headed out of the room.

Once he was gone, Starr turned to us, her brown eyes sparkling. "So," she said. "Who's ready to gear up?"

CHAPTER NINETEEN

"**S**o what was it like?" Mom asked as she hustled to get dinner on the table. She'd gotten out of work late and had picked up pizza since she hadn't had time to cook. Not that anyone was complaining. "To be inside the legendary Appleby headquarters?"

"Pretty awesome," I told her. "They had all these full-size spaceship and robot models. There was even a giant Rocky the Robot you could go into."

"So. Jealous." Mom sighed. "My kids are living the dream. Meanwhile I'm stuck at work." She grabbed a slice of pizza. "You'd better let me try out that demo at some point. I'm dying to see what they've done with the game. I used to play the original version, you know."

"Cool," I said. I hadn't realized she was a fan. "Yeah, you can definitely check it out."

Dad entered the room, scooped a slice of pizza out of the box, and shoved half of it into his mouth in one bite. A splotch of cheese dripped from his lips, and he grinned as he slurped it up. Mom snorted.

"What did *you* think of the place?" she asked him.

He froze. "Um, it was...awesome?" he tried. "Right, kids? Super awesome. Robots. And video games. And..."

Mom gave him a suspicious look. Dad smiled innocently at her, then turned to Lilli. "Hey, Lills, you want to go out and work on the zip line after you finish eating?"

He and my sister had been constructing this crazy zip line in the backyard that started from the balcony off the game room on the second floor of our house and went all the way to our old treehouse at the very back of the yard. Mom thought it was ridiculous and dangerous, and worried what the neighbors would think. But Dad only laughed this off. It was going to be the fastest zip line in Texas when he and Lilli were through, he'd declared. As if that addressed even one of Mom's concerns.

"Maybe later, Dad," Lilli apologized, pushing back her plate. She'd barely eaten any of her pizza. Not that I'd done much better with mine. The adrenaline was still raging inside me from today's adventure at Mech Ops and had messed with my stomach big-time. "I, uh, promised Ian I'd try out the new game with him."

Uh-huh. As if she wasn't as eager to break out the new VR as I was.

Dad sighed. "Haven't you played enough video games today? Don't you want a little fresh air and exercise?"

"I do!" Lilli assured him. "Just…maybe tomorrow?"

"Fine. I'll go work on it myself for bit," Dad said resignedly. He knew he never won video game arguments in our house. Not with Mom being as big of a player as we were. "Come on out if you change your mind and want to help." He addressed this to Lilli, of course. He had no illusions about me pitching in on this particular project.

"Okay, Dad," Lilli said. "I will!"

He headed outside. We pushed back from our chairs, bringing our plates to the sink before making a mad dash for Lilli's bedroom, where we'd stored the VR rigs under her bed. Her bed was way bigger than mine, which was good thing, since the equipment they'd sent us home with was totally bulky. Back at Dragon Ops, it was all about these tiny little goggles—not much bigger than a pair of sunglasses—and a sleek SensSuit that fit your body like a glove. These setups, on the other hand, were massive—with large space-helmet-like things you put over your entire head with a bulky battery pack attached, the size of a fully stuffed school backpack. I had to say, it was a good thing this was virtual reality and not augmented reality like Dragon Ops. I couldn't imagine walking around in real life with all this gear strapped to my back.

But with VR? That was no problem. We didn't have to move. We just sat down, jacked in, and entered a whole other world.

Ready or not, here we come.

"I still can't believe they just gave us these," Lilli remarked as she pulled the helmet over her head and fumbled for the On switch. The helmet whirred to life, lighting up electric blue and emitting a loud fan noise, presumably to keep the thing cool while it was on her head. "I mean, out of all those people, I never thought they'd pick us."

"Well, we can thank Starr for that," I said, fumbling with my own helmet. "I mean, if she hadn't known about the chest, there's no way we could have won."

"And Josh," Lilli added. "You gotta admit, that power-up thing turned out to be pretty useful."

"I guess." Something tugged in my stomach. "You never told me you knew Josh," I added, my voice sounding perhaps a bit more accusatory than I meant it to.

Lilli shrugged. "I didn't?" she asked. "I guess it never came up. I mean, I don't know him well. Sometimes the teams get together, you know. I guess we met that way."

"Yeah," I said. "Sure." That made perfect sense. So why was I still bothered by this? Who cared about Josh? We were on our own now. We didn't have to deal with him anymore.

"You know what's weird?" Lilli said suddenly, sitting up in bed. "It's been bugging me all day."

"What?"

"Admiral Appleby. He didn't seem like a bad guy. I mean, certainly not the type of bad guy you'd find in a movie. If anything, he seemed nice. Like a regular old grandpa. A little weird, maybe—but certainly not the type who would kidnap someone and hold them in his game."

"Yeah, well, it's not like this is a Marvel movie or something," I reasoned. "I mean, no one just goes and acts like a supervillain in real life. Otherwise you'd never get away with your evil plan, right?"

"I suppose," Lilli said, though she didn't sound totally convinced. "Anyway," she added. "It was fun to play today. It's been way too long since we played anything."

I nodded. "Yeah," I agreed. "It was fun..."

Suddenly my mind flashed to a particular moment on the street that hadn't been so fun. Atreus looming in front of me. Teeth bared. Stomach warming with fire. Had he really been there, in the game? Or was it just my freaked-out imagination again? I honestly couldn't tell. Which made it even more terrifying.

I thought about mentioning it to Lilli, then decided against it. If it *was* all in my head, which, let's face it, it probably was, it'd be way too embarrassing. I mean, the two of us had gone through the exact same experience in Dragon Ops, and she came out completely fine.

While I was still seeing dragons everywhere I went.

I let out a small moan. *Stop thinking about it, Ian!* I scolded myself. But that was easier said than done. What if Atreus had truly tracked me down in Mech Ops? What if he was there, even now, waiting for me to log back in? After months of avoiding him, was I about to willingly step into his line of fire?

Do you want to play again?

But in the end, I knew I had no choice. Ikumi was in there, trapped. And we were her only hope of getting free. And that meant I had to go forward. I had to play this game. And if Atreus did find us inside? Well, I'd have to deal with him, too. We'd fought him once and won. We could do it again.

Maybe...

At least we weren't totally alone. Yano was going to meet us in-game. When I'd first gotten back from Mech Ops, I'd sent the account information we'd been given directly to Ikumi's message account on *Fields of Fantasy*, as the dragon guide had instructed. This would allow him to log in and meet up with us in-game. So we'd have one dragon on our side, at the very least.

Though could Yano take Atreus in a fight?

Hopefully we wouldn't have to find out.

"You ready?" Lilli asked, peering at me expectantly.

I sighed. "As I'll ever be," I replied.

I pressed the On button on my helmet. It whirred to life, locked and loaded. I squeezed my eyes shut and pressed the Sync button.

And entered another world.

CHAPTER TWENTY

"**G**reetings, Mech Heads. And welcome to the end of the world."

I opened my eyes. Lilli's bedroom was gone. So were the headset and all the equipment. The real world altogether. Instead, I found myself standing in the middle of an abandoned warehouse that looked similar to—but definitely not the same as—the capture the orb event one.

It was a large, open two-story building, sunlight streaming through its half-collapsed roof. On the far wall were a number of windows, most of them smashed. And the cement ground was stained with crusty browns and suspicious-looking reds. Plopped down in the center of the room was a huge shipping crate about the size of a train car with rusted edges, surrounded by a trash heap of rotted-out cardboard boxes, muddy piles of cloth, and rusty parts that could have come from a car or a tractor—maybe a man-eating robot? Let's just say it was a depressing scene.

But, hey! There was no killer AI dragon in sight, so that was a bonus.

There was, however, a robot. Rocky the Robot, to be precise. He was trotting toward Lilli and me, a big grin on his goofy mechanical face.

"Welcome, beta testers!" he greeted us enthusiastically. "We are so happy to have you join our little team! We've taken every detail into consideration to make this game the best you've ever played. So if there's anything I can do to make your experience more fun—please don't hesitate to ask."

"Maybe some maid service to start?" Lilli suggested breezily, nodding to the piles of trash. "I mean, just saying."

"Ha ha ha!" Rocky laughed loudly. His laugh was hollow and forceful and, well, a little unsettling, to be honest. "That's a joke!" he exclaimed. "I love jokes! Especially apocalyptic jokes. I make apocalyptic jokes like there's *no tomorrow!*" He paused, looking at us expectantly. "Get it? Apocalypse? No tomorrow? 'Cause it's the end of the world, and there's—"

"No tomorrow," I finished for him. "Good one. Hilarious."

Wow. If I really was beta testing this game, I'd have to make a note on this guy. Not funny at all.

"Anyway." Rocky cleared his throat and straightened his shoulders. "Before I let you out into the game, I just want to update you on a few simple rules. Are you ready to hear them?"

"Go for it, dude."

"Very well. Rule number one: Mech Ops is a fully immersive VR experience. Which means you will feel as if you're really here—in the flesh, in your real body. Everything you do will seem real. And all five senses will be engaged. If you eat an irradiated rat, it will taste bad. If you breathe in toxic fumes, you will pass out. If you impale yourself on a sharp spike, you will bleed. If you are blasted by a laser-wielding robot, you will die. But through it all, your body—your real-life body—will remain safe and sound back wherever you left it. Assuming you left it somewhere safe and sound and not in the middle of the road, on train tracks, or outside on a beach during a hurricane." He gave us a pointed look. "Do you understand?"

"Yeah," I said. "We get it."

But Rocky the Robot wasn't finished. "In the end, you will leave the game just as you entered it. And bonus! The bodies you have here are a hundred percent regenerable. Meaning if you die in the game, you'll respawn in a nearby graveyard. Good as new!"

Well, that was good at least. I still remembered the anxiety I'd felt at Dragon Ops when the game malfunctioned. We had no idea there what would happen if we died. Thankfully, none of us had to find out.

"Number two," Rocky continued cheerfully. "This game contains the latest in time compression technology. Meaning you can spend days in the game world—while spending no more than mere hours in real life. But beware! Some players have been shown to become too immersed in the game, forgetting real life altogether. We recommend you set an alarm for yourselves. To remind you to log off now and then. Go back to the real world. Eat, drink, rest, repeat." He grinned madly. "And...use the facilities, please. Waking up in a pool of urine is never awesome."

Okay, I couldn't argue with him there.

"Great!" I tried. "We got it! So, can we go now?" After all, this was wasting time. We needed to get out there, get started. The last thing we needed was to get stuck in some hour-long tutorial like so many games forced you to go through before letting you actually play.

Rocky's smile dipped, as if I'd hurt his feelings. "Don't you want your first quest?"

Oh, right. I forgot. We were supposed to be actually playing through the beta. Rocky had no idea of our real mission. "Um, yeah. Sure. Lay it on us," I told him with as much enthusiasm as I could muster.

"Great! This warehouse is full of cyber-rats. We need you to catch ten of these cyber-rats and—"

I groaned, tuning him out. Of course. A rat-collecting quest. What a shock.

"We'll get on the rat thing ASAP," Lilli broke in. "But in the meantime, can you open the gates for us?"

"Absolutely!" Rocky beamed. "And remember, if you need me, simply press the Help command in your game menu. I can't solve quests or attack monsters, but I can offer helpful hints or provide assistance if you get stuck somewhere. Most of this level is finished, but there are a few places where you might possibly glitch out and fall through this world into an unfinished level. If that happens, call me immediately."

I raised an eyebrow. "What would happen if we tried to play in an unfinished level?" I asked.

Rocky frowned. "I do not understand the question. Why would you play an unfinished level?"

"I don't know. I mean, just say we did. What would happen?"

"I am not programmed to answer that question. Would you like me to put in a help ticket to HQ?"

"No!" Lilli and I shouted at once. We glanced at each other. Yeah, no need to call HQ, that was for sure.

"Very well," Rocky replied, still looking suspicious, if a virtual robot *could* look suspicious. "I can tell you're eager to get started. I wish you the best of luck and the most pleasant gaming experience." He pressed a button on his chest plate, and the warehouse door began to slowly creak open.

"Gear up, Mech Heads," he chimed, the grin back on his face. "And welcome to tomorrow."

And with that, he blinked off the game grid. As if he'd never been standing there at all.

"Finally," Lilli declared. "I thought he'd never leave."

"I know, right?" I agreed. I turned to look at her, noticing her outfit for the first time. She was dressed in what could only be described as a silver space dress, short and swingy and, well, not exactly the best outfit to fight deadly robots and zombies in. On her feet, she wore matching silver boots that came up to her knees. "Nice outfit," I teased, wondering if she'd noticed it yet.

She looked down, wrinkling her nose in distaste. Evidently she hadn't.

"Seriously?" she moaned. "This is worse than the mage robes from Dragon Ops! I'm supposed to be saving the world from the apocalypse! Who saves the world in a cute party dress and heels?"

I couldn't help a small laugh. Poor Lilli. As I did, I looked down at my own outfit. It wasn't the best, either. No cool lion helmet like I'd had for the test. Just a ripped leather vest and a pair of raggedy pants. Guess this was the kind of game where you started from nothing and worked your way up, gearwise.

"At least you got a crossbow," I said, pointing out the

weapon attached to her back. "That's pretty cool." I glanced down at myself to note I had a sword attached to my belt. Guess I'd be playing melee again. I realized my sister was still talking. "I should report this," she was saying. "They want our opinions, right? I am so giving my opinion on the female starter wear. It is not cool at all!"

"Also not cool?" I added. "I don't see Yano anywhere."

Lilli frowned. "Did he say where he would meet us?"

"No. I sent him the log-in info. I was hoping he'd be able to find us from that."

"I can and I already did," interrupted a voice. "Now, hurry up and let me out of here! My wings are cramping!"

I whirled around. To my surprise, the big metal shipping crate in the center of the room appeared to be shaking, as if there was something very large inside. I ran over, heart leaping in my chest as I swung open the door and found Yano standing there, a cocky grin on his face.

At least I was pretty sure it was Yano. The dragon had changed his look again. He was still three-headed and huge, but instead of the shimmery silver scales of a living, breathing dragon, he'd upgraded to some kind of dragon cyborg instead. His eyes were made of brilliant green LED lights, and his wings were scaled in shiny silver metal with hints of blue. Even cooler? Under his wings were two large rocket launchers. Sweet!

"Whoa!" Lilli cried. "Yano got an upgrade!"

"Nice of you to notice," he said, preening a little as he waddled out of the shipping container. "I thought it would be appropriate for our mission." He raised an eyebrow as he took in Lilli's dress. "Unlike that ensemble, for example..."

"Don't start," Lilli groaned.

"Were you in there the whole time?" I asked, unbelievingly.

"Yes. I spawned in a few minutes before you, using the log-in information you gave me. Then I hid in the crate when I saw the giant robot guy coming. I didn't know if he'd... appreciate...my presence."

"Smart," I said.

"Of course it was. I am a superior artificially intelligent creature, after all. Which means pretty much everything I do is smart. Like the fact that I chose this new look for the adventure. No one's going to bat an eye at some random, yet incredibly handsome, cyborg robot dragon flying around the place."

I wasn't positive that was true. In my research I hadn't read anything about dragons—cyborg or otherwise—being part of the game. But we'd have to take our chances. He was the only one who could guide us to Ikumi.

"So where do we go?" Lilli asked. "You said you pinpointed Ikumi's location. How do we get there from here?"

"First, you must invite me to your party," Yano directed. He flapped his wings, sending two matching shimmers of silver down his side. "Then I can share my map with you."

Right. I blinked my eyes to bring up my game menu. I found Yano in my proximity and invited him and my sister into a new group.

"The Dragon Slayerz?" Yano asked as he read the name of the group I'd picked. "Should I be concerned? Being one of dragonkind, that is?"

"Of course not!" I said with a laugh. "That was our name back in Dragon Ops, remember?"

"We'd never slay you, Yano," Lilli added with a grin. "You're far too handsome."

Yano grinned proudly. "Goes without saying, I suppose. Though please don't let that stop you from saying it." He flipped his third head. "Now, about our girl. From my research I believe she's being held in the Alpha Trinity sector of this game."

Lilli frowned. "Which is...where, exactly?"

"About as far from here as possible," Yano admitted. "Far beyond the part of the game that's open for the demo."

Right. "So how do we get there?" I asked.

"From what I can tell, this game is set up in layers. Think of it like a cake. So instead of a world that sprawls out like Dragon Ops, this one is more vertical. Once you make your way through one level, you are sent down to the next. Right now, we're near the top. Ikumi is near the bottom."

"So how do we get down levels?" Lilli asked. "Especially if this is the only one that's open."

"That," Yano replied, "is what we need to figure out. If we could play through the game, we might be able to find a locked door. I could hack that door and—"

"There's no time for that," I argued. "That would take forever. Ikumi can't wait."

Yano cocked his three heads. "You have a better idea?"

I thought for a moment. We needed to go down. We needed to...

"I got it!" I cried. "We need to fall through the world."

"What?" Lilli asked.

"You know. Like Rocky the Robot was warning us *not* to do. We search this world for an unfinished spot in the game—where the ground hasn't been fully rendered yet. We'll jump through and land in the level below."

"You really think that's going to work? What if there is no level below? What if the level below is super hard and we die instantly from mobs we aren't at a high enough level to fight?"

"Then we resurrect in the graveyards."

"What if there are no graveyards yet? We could be stuck as ghosts."

"Then we'll rescue Ikumi as ghosts," Yano broke in, sounding impatient. "Look, we can argue all day, but we're just wasting time. We don't know how long it will take for the Mech Ops people to realize what we're after. And when they do, they'll kick us out of the game—permanently. So if you want to find our friend, we're going to have to act fast and fearless."

"Besides, it's not like we're in any *real* danger," I added. "It's not like Dragon Ops. It's just a game."

But even as I said the words, doubt began to worm through me. Dragon Ops had been "just a game," too—until it wasn't. And while our bodies were safe and sound at home this time, what made me think this game couldn't mess with our heads just as easily as Dragon Ops? As we'd learned there, if your brain truly believed you were dead, it could literally stop your real-life heart from beating. And we had no idea what was down there in the unfinished levels waiting for us.

And then there was the Atreus thing. Not that I wanted to bring that up.

"Okay, fine," Lilli said, putting on a brave face. "Let's do this."

"Finally!" Yano gave out a loud cheer. "Ladies and gentlemen, we are clear for launch!"

CHAPTER TWENTY-ONE

The good news? After reviewing the game maps, Yano found a location he believed to be nonrendered and fall-downable. The bad news? It was on the top of a super-high mountain at the very other end of the level. Not exactly easy access.

I stared at the map in dismay. "Wow. This place is huge." At least there was time compression in the game. But still! I thought back to wandering through Dragon Ops with all its quests and trash mobs and bosses in the way. Would this game be the same? Would it take hours—even days—to reach the mountain at the very other end of the map? Just to get to our true starting point? "This is going to take forever."

"For you, maybe," Yano agreed. "But not for winged superior magical beings like me. For me—it's just a merry jaunt. A mere hop, skip, and a flight."

Lilli raised an eyebrow. "Um, yay you?"

"Yay me, indeed." Yano flapped his massive wings. "And yay you as well! Since I plan to take pity on your sad human state and allow you to get on my back and experience a tremendous travel experience. Now, come on. All aboard."

I watched as he lowered his metal wing, unfurling it so that the scales became like steps up onto his back. Which was really cool, I had to admit, until I got a better look at his back. No saddle, no handholds, no seat belts. No possible way to ensure you wouldn't just slide off his back midair and crash helplessly to your death below.

So...yeah. Did I mention my paralyzing fear of heights?

Daredevil Lilli, of course, had none of these concerns. She was already scrambling up Yano's wings like he was a new ride at Six Flags. I watched as she swung her leg over the dragon's back as if mounting a giant horse. Then she beckoned for me.

"Come on!" she scolded, clearly catching my look of pure dread. "It's just virtual. If you fall, you'll die. We'll pick you up in the nearest graveyard. No biggie."

Easy for her to say.

"Or we can meet you there," Yano suggested. "And you can fight your way solo through the streets of New Angeles on your way to the Radiated Forest. Of course, then you'll have to start dealing with zombies.... The Radiated Forest is *filled* with zombies. Hope you can up your sneak skills before you get there. Oh, and then there's the Pool of Piranha. That's a great zone if you like water levels."

I did not like water levels. Which he well knew.

Or zombies, for that matter.

Ugh. Fine. I forced my feet to propel me forward, then climbed gingerly onto Yano's back, settling in behind my sister and reluctantly wrapping my arms around her waist. Maybe a little too tightly, but who could blame me?

"You got something to hold on to up there?" I asked.

"I'm fine. As long as you stop cutting off my circulation," she replied with a laugh. I grudgingly loosened my hold. Just a tad.

"You ready?" Yano called out. Without waiting for an answer, he flapped his metal wings. They slapped against the ground with a loud bang that made me nearly jump out of my skin. I tried to remind myself that none of this was real. It was just a game. I was not really on a cyborg dragon about to launch into the air. I was at home, curled up in my sister's bed, safe and sound and cozy. My game body might be ready to die tragically, but my real one would be just fine.

"What are you waiting for?" I called to Yano, hoping I sounded super brave and not at all freaked out. "Let's do this already!"

I felt the dragon lower to the ground like a lion ready to leap. I held my breath, my heart pounding in my chest. *Three, two, one...*

Liftoff! Yano shot into the air like a rocket, leaving my stomach somewhere back on the ground. I screamed, instinctively tightening my grip on my sister.

"Dude! You're going to break my game ribs!" she complained.

"Sorry!" I squeaked, but I couldn't loosen my hold as we climbed higher and higher into the sky. My stomach lurched in a mixture of nausea and terror as wind blasted our faces, causing tears to stream from my eyes. At one point, I made the grave mistake of looking down, and the ground wove and spun beneath us, looking literally a million miles away.

This was so freaky. So scary. So—

"Amazing!" Lilli cheered in front of me. "Can you do a barrel roll?"

"Don't you dare!" I threatened before Yano could reply. Of course Lilli thought this was cool. Like the world's biggest, baddest roller coaster. Meanwhile I was just trying to pull my stomach back up from my knees. Even if it wasn't my real stomach. Or my real knees, for that matter.

We soared through the sky across the game world. After a while, I got up the courage to look down again. I had to admit, it actually looked pretty cool down there. We'd left New Angeles behind and were now flying over some apocalyptic countryside, with a lone road cut into the forest and winding through the trees. The Radiated Forest, I guessed. Everything was overgrown, grass and weeds sticking up through cracks in the pavement. Colorful vines climbing telephone poles and wires. Abandoned cars sat motionless in the middle of the road, as if they'd just frozen up one day and stopped running where they were. There were even a few NPCs hanging out, with silver dots over their heads, indicating quests to be given out, just like in Dragon Ops.

I had to admit, a small part of me wished we were down there. Questing, fighting, doing all the normal things we were supposed to be doing in a game like this. But we had a higher calling. We couldn't afford to become distracted. Still, it reminded me how much I'd missed gaming over the last months. And to be this close, it was quite the tease.

Finally, we reached the mountain in question. If you could really call it a mountain. Up close, I could see it was more like a giant trash heap. A towering pile of rusted metal, garbage, and other unidentifiable refuse rising high into the sky. Stuff precariously piled on stuff, teetering dangerously at some points.

"This is it?" Lilli asked, shouting to be heard over the wind.

"Lovely, isn't it?" Yano replied. "And just breathe in that sweet eau de garbage scent!"

"Ew." I buried my nose in Lilli's back as the wave of stink hit. "So gross."

"Hold on," Yano shouted. "I'm going to try to land at the top."

I swallowed hard, gripping Lilli even tighter as he swooped in, finding a large, flat plane on the very summit of the mountain. He dove down, overshooting the landing and hitting the ground too hard, causing Lilli to lose her balance. Since I was holding on to her, I fell too, tumbling off Yano's wing and crashing down onto the trash heap below. As I landed, my head smacked against a hunk of rusted metal sticking out from the ground, and for a moment I saw stars.

"Ow!" I cried, holding my head. It didn't really hurt, but it felt super disorienting. And my vision was all blurry. That must have been the game's way of replacing actual pain. It still felt awful, and I would have been totally debilitated if I had been in the middle of a fight.

"Are you okay, Ian?" Lilli asked, rubbing her own head.

"Yeah. I'm fine." Thankfully, my vision was already starting to clear. At least the effects weren't long-lasting.

Lilli stood and brushed herself off. "So is this it?" she asked, looking around. "Is this where we jump through the world?"

"I believe so," Yano replied. "There's no way to get up here unless you fly—and there's no reason to even do that. There's no quests, no treasure chests up here. It's just supposed to look cool when you see it in the background as you play the rest of the level. Which means there's a good chance the game developers didn't pay too much attention to the details. That there are potential weak spots that weren't rendered completely, since they would assume no one would be coming up here. We just have to search the area until we find one."

The dragon started stomping his heavy metal feet against the trash pile, causing the whole mountain to shake. I watched uneasily as a car hanging precariously from a hook broke free and crashed down the mountain, causing a mini garbage avalanche in its wake.

"Walk lighter!" I warned. "Or the whole place is going to collapse!"

Yano huffed, looking offended. "I am as graceful as a gazelle, I'll have you know. As light on my feet as a—"

A loud engine roar cut him off midboast. I looked up, trying to place the sudden sound. To my horror, my eyes caught a large airship hovering over us. It had a searchlight and was slowly combing the mountain as if looking for something...or someone.

"Quick! Duck!" I cried to my sister and Yano as I dove behind a nearby trash pile. Lilli joined me a moment later, panting for breath. But there was, I realized with dread, no place for Yano to hide. He was too big. Too obvious.

"Maybe they'll think he's just more trash," Lilli suggested.

"Yeah," I agreed. "Yano! Stay still. Pretend you're trash!"

The dragon turned to us, looking offended. "Pretend I'm trash? No one's going to believe a beautiful, majestic creature like myself is—"

The spotlight stopped on him, the light flashing off his scales, so brightly that for a moment I was blinded. When I could see again, the airship's hatch had slid open and giant metal spiders with parachutes attached to their backs were floating to the ground.

"I think it's fair to say they've spotted us," Lilli said with a groan.

I nodded grimly, pulling my sword from its sheath. "Gear up, Mech Heads," I muttered. "It's time to fight."

CHAPTER TWENTY-TWO

I watched, frozen, as the spiders began to land. Their parachutes detached, floating away as their eight mechanical legs hit solid ground. They were big—as big as tanks—their eyes emitting glowing red laser beams that swept the ground in front of them as they crawled forward on spindly legs. The scratching of metal skittering across metal made my skin crawl. Like nails on a chalkboard, my mom would say.

Lilli pulled her crossbow from its holster on her back, nocking an arrow. Her face was tense, her mouth pressed tight as her eyes stayed focused on the encroaching spiders. I bit my lower lip, mind racing. What should we do? Stay here, play defense? Or charge them in a surprise attack?

"We need to help Yano," Lilli whispered, nodding her head in the direction of the dragon, who was still standing out in the open. The spiders, clicking and clacking against the garbage-strewn ground, had surrounded him.

"He's a giant robot dragon! You don't think he can take care of himself?"

"I don't know. He's just standing there!"

I frowned. She was right. For some reason, our guide looked completely paralyzed. He wasn't moving, wasn't fighting, wasn't even talking—which was very un-Yano-like.

As I watched, worried, he started to flicker. Like a candle just before it goes out.

"Yano?" I whispered as loudly as I dared. "Are you okay?"

But he didn't answer. Instead, he disappeared completely. One moment he was there, the next he was gone. Blinked out of the game altogether.

Oh no. No, no, no!

"Yano!" I cried. But he was already gone.

"His system must've crashed," Lilli said, frowning.

"Or the powers that be booted him from the game," I added, worried. "After all, he's not supposed to be here. They might have thought he was a virus or something."

"That's not good. Especially if they realize we've been with him this whole time."

"No kidding. We need to find that hole in the world—fast."

Lilli peeked around the trash pile. The spiders were getting closer. "How are we supposed to do that with them right there?"

"We can't. We'll need to get rid of them first."

Lilli cringed. "How did I know you were going to say that?" She made a face. Let's just say spiders were to her like heights were to me. Ever since that day in third grade when Derek had dumped a jar of them in her desk at school just to watch her scream when she opened it. He'd gotten detention. Lilli had gotten a lifelong phobia of eight-legged creatures.

"Come on, Lills," I said with a small smile. "They're just virtual. If they kill you, you'll die. I'll pick you up in the nearest graveyard. No biggie."

She made a face as she realized I was repeating her own words back to her. "Yeah, yeah," she muttered before she began to climb up on the trash pile, her crossbow raised and ready. I watched from below, a little nervous. Joking and phobias aside, this was going to be quite a battle. There were only two of us. And at least five of them. Not great odds. Especially since we'd basically flown over the entire beginner section where a normal player would have spent time leveling up and scoring better gear. Trapping cyber-rats and all that fun stuff.

Instead, we had relied on Yano. And now Yano was gone.

Lilli fired her crossbow. "Die, you giant insect!" she cried. I was going to mention that technically spiders were arachnids, not insects, but decided it didn't matter when her arrow hit its mark, piercing the spider's armor. Black oil exploded from the wound, and the spider crashed to the ground, squealing and smoking.

"Sweet!" I cried. "Nice shot!"

She grinned. Then her gaze snapped back to the field. "Watch out," she warned. "One's coming around the side. I can't get a good shot. You'll have to take him."

I nodded grimly, crouching low, my whole body vibrating with electricity as I waited for the creature to appear. I could hear him before I could see him—his feet clacking against the ground. I raised my sword, ready to take that first strike.

Wait for it. Wait for it . . .

Suddenly we were face-to-face. The creature was even scarier up close and personal. Laser red eyes, metal fangs dripping with oil. Sharp spikes on the ends of its legs. My heart pounded in my chest. How was I supposed to kill something like this?

The spider lunged, fangs bared. I met it with my sword, slashing down and slicing off one of its legs with my laser blade. It teetered for a moment, thrown off balance. Then it recovered, charging again. I swung a second time, somehow managing to lop off another leg. Which was great, until you considered it had six more to go and seemed perfectly capable of getting around with two missing limbs.

It drew closer, snapping its jaws. I staggered backward until I hit a wall of trash, stopping me in my tracks. I slashed at the spider, trying to ward him off until I could come up with a plan. One that didn't land me in the closest graveyard, which, given our position on top of the trash mountain, wouldn't likely be very close at all. And without Yano's flying powers, we would never get back up here. Never find our hole in the world.

"Ahhhh!"

With a great cry, Lilli leapt down onto the spider's back. She had dropped her crossbow and picked up a giant hunk of metal from the pile and was slamming it against the spider's head with all her might.

Bang! Bang! BANG!

"Squash already, you mutant metal monster!" she screamed.

Sadly, the spider didn't obey. However, she had effectively distracted it, and its attention was on her now, not me. Which gave me another chance to act. I dropped down, scurrying underneath its body, using the gaps in the missing legs to squeeze through. Once in place, I thrust my sword up, straight into his belly.

"Take that, you annoying arachnid!" (See, Lilli wasn't the only one who could call out cool catchphrases.)

The spider roared in rage, sparking and smoking and gushing oil. I dove out from under it to avoid getting squashed as its legs buckled. It took one last staggering step, then dropped like a stone, Lilli still straddled on its back.

She gave a cheer, leaping onto the ground. "Nice one!" she declared, holding up her hand for a high five. I started to return it, then stopped midslap as I saw a new spider rise up behind my sister. It was bigger than the others. A boss, maybe? And covered with glittering purple scales.

"Lilli!" I cried. "Watch out!"

Lilli whirled around, but it was too late. The spider grabbed her, tangling her in its legs, dragging her closer to its vile fanged mouth. She screamed, trying to fight her way free, but it was no use. The creature was too strong. And I couldn't get a clean swipe at it. Not without risking slicing my sister in the process. I watched, helpless, as the creature opened its mouth wide.

Zoom!

Suddenly, out of nowhere, a silver star flew through the air, straight at the spider's head. It connected with a loud crunch, embedding itself into the metal scales. The spider's head popped open, gears and circuits flying everywhere as it smoked and buzzed and spouted oil. Its legs retracted, dropping Lilli in the process. My sister crashed to the ground.

"Argh!" she cried, clutching her knee. "Stupid spider!"

"Don't worry, he's not going to be bothering you anymore," came a new voice behind us.

I whirled around, stunned to see none other than Starr herself standing there smiling at us. She was dressed in the same silver armor with wings combo she'd had during the

MARI MANCUSI

beta test, the Rocky the Robot insignia emblazoned on her chest.

"Starr!" I cried, overjoyed to see her. "What are you doing here?"

"Saving your lives, evidently," she replied. "You're welcome, by the way."

"Thank you!" Lilli and I cried in unison.

"I thought I was bug breakfast," Lilli added.

"You were about to be," Starr agreed. "But it's all good. I took out the two others as well. Where did your dragon go?" She peered around the trash pile. "He ditch you already?"

Wow. She'd seen Yano? I wasn't quite sure what to think about that. "Um, I'm not sure?" I said. "He sort of just took off." No need to mention he possibly got booted because he didn't belong in-game. Didn't want Starr to get suspicious of us. "I'm sure he'll be back."

Starr put a hand to her forehead, shielding her vision as she looked out over the horizon. "Where did you get him?" she asked. "I don't remember reading anything about a dragon in the beta files."

"Maybe he was meant to be a surprise?" Lilli suggested. "After all, they can't give away all the coolness in the brochure."

"Sure," Starr said, though she looked as if she didn't believe us. "What are you guys doing up here, anyway? You flew by all the quest givers. Not to mention the armory,"

175

she added, giving Lilli's dress a skeptical look. My sister blushed.

"Whoops?" she tried.

Starr rolled her eyes. "Cute. But don't play dumb with me. I know you're up to something. After all, you guys aren't just random beta testers. You're the Dragon Slayerz. No way do I buy you accidentally flew up to a random trash mountain on some mysterious cyborg dragon that isn't even supposed to be in the beta. Clearly you're on some kind of secret mission. And I want to know what it is."

I sighed, glancing at Lilli. Of course Starr wasn't going to believe we flew up here to this random place by accident. But what could we say? Could we explain our real mission? Could we trust her to keep it quiet? What if she was secretly working for Mech Ops? Or maybe she hoped to score a job or something with them, and selling us out would be her ticket in. She could run right back to Admiral Appleby and tell him everything.

"We're just here to play," I tried. But Starr shook her head.

"If you were just here to play, you'd be down there playing. Capturing cyber-rats, sneaking through the zombie forest, collecting power-ups. You even blew past the first boss—and he's incredible! This metallic yellow robot bumblebee-type thing that shoots poison darts." She put her hands on her hips. "So spill. What are you doing up here? For real?"

"Our uncle sent us," Lilli declared suddenly, surprising me. "Our Uncle Jack. He's a game designer. He's worked on Dragon Ops and some other stuff. But he's always wanted to work on Mech Ops. So he thought if he could send us in for an insider's look into the game, we could share what we found with him. So he can seem super smart when he goes in for an interview."

"Exactly!" I agreed. Wow, my sister was kind of a genius. "Like, we can find some of the game issues, the weak spots. Then he can walk in with a plan to fix them."

Starr looked a little disappointed. I could tell she'd been hoping for some way-cooler secret mission from the kids who survived Dragon Ops. But she did seem to be buying the idea, so that was good.

"And that's why you're up here?" she asked, looking around. "You're looking for glitches?"

"For holes," I said, figuring the more honest we were, the better. "We're trying to find a way to jump through the world. A secret passage into some of the unfinished levels."

Starr's eyes shone brightly at this idea. "Cool," she declared. "I'm in."

CHAPTER TWENTY-THREE

I stared at Starr for a moment, not sure I'd heard her right. "Y-you're what?" I stammered.

"I'm in." Her grin widened. "Let's jump through the world together."

"Are you sure?" Lilli asked, stepping forward. "Remember, this violates all sorts of terms and conditions. If they find out what we're doing, they may delete our accounts. Take our VR rigs away."

Starr waved a hand. "Don't worry about me," she said. "I can take care of myself. Also?" She pointed to the dead spider. "You may need my help, no offense. After all, I did all the early quests and boss fights. I'm already level twenty. How about you?"

"You did them already?" I stared at her in shock. "We only got our rigs this afternoon."

"Oh." Starr shrugged, looking embarrassed. "I logged on the second I got home. And, uh, I read a few online guides ahead of time to get the lay of the land."

I glanced over at my sister. That was some dedication!

Then a more troubling thought hit me. How did she find us up here, anyway? And why was she looking for us to begin with? We were just kids; she was basically a grown-up. It was one thing to be partnered up in the beta when we had no choice. But surely she had someone else she'd rather play with now. Someone who, like she mentioned, was actually playing the game the right way. It was odd, to be sure. And I wondered if we could trust her. She knew a lot about us— but we knew very little about her, besides what she did on her channel.

At the same time, we needed all the help we could get. Especially from someone who was higher level and had researched the game extensively like Starr claimed she had. We were fighting blind and had no idea what was in store for us deeper in the game. Someone like Starr could help. Especially now that Yano had crashed out. Who knew when he'd be able to get back inside.

"Fine," I said, making a decision. "You can come."

Starr's face broke out into a grin. "I was hoping you'd say that."

We split up, searching the trash mountain for weak spots. At first it felt thrilling—like a secret mission. I kept looking over my shoulder for some game sentry to bust us. But after a while, I began to get discouraged. Everything felt so real. So solid. Was Yano wrong about this? Maybe the game designers had finished this section after all, even though it was remote. Maybe some quest took you up here.

I was just about to give up when I heard Starr's cry from somewhere nearby. "Um, we've got a small problem," she said. "And when I say small, I mean... well, pretty gigantic."

Before I could answer, I heard a rumbling above. I looked up, my jaw dropping in dismay as I watched three large airships approach. The same kinds of airships that dropped off the robot spiders earlier were now returning for a respawn. I dropped the soggy piece of cardboard I'd been looking under and ran back to join Starr and my sister.

"What do we do?" Lilli asked, eyes wide.

"We could try to fight them," Starr suggested.

"I don't know. We barely took out five last time. And that was from a single ship. There's probably at least fifteen now," I reasoned.

"So what, then? Should we hide?"

"Maybe..." I scanned the area, searching for hiding spots. There were plenty of nooks and crannies to slip behind, but I wasn't confident any of them would offer much protection against giant robot spiders.

A shadow crossed the sky as the ships grew closer. I watched as their hatches began to creak open. One by one, the spiders parachuted down from the sky, floating to the mountaintop. I had guessed there would be fifteen, but now it looked to be at least twenty. Maybe more.

"Spiders," Lilli moaned. "Why does it have to be spiders?"

One by one the spiders landed, shedding their parachutes and beginning to slowly crawl across the mountain. Their laser eyes scanned the territory, leaving no stone unturned as they began their hunt.

And we were sitting ducks.

"Come on!" Starr urged. "Let's get out of here."

We started running in the opposite direction. I wondered for a moment if we should try to climb down the mountain and retreat to live another day. But it looked too steep to descend, and every time I got near an edge, a piece of trash would break off from the pile, tumbling down to the earth. There was no way we'd avoid the same fate if we tried it ourselves.

But what else could we do? The spiders were closing in. We didn't have a dragon to fly us to safety. We were running out of mountain. Once we reached the far side, we'd be completely trapped.

"You should go," I urged Starr. "You have wings. You can fly away."

"And leave you two here?" She shook her head. "I joined your team, remember? Teammates don't bail on one another."

"Can we all fly?" Lilli asked. "Or maybe you could take one of us down at a time?"

"Maybe..." Starr motioned for me to come closer. She grabbed me in a hug, squashing me against her. "Let me try." She flapped her wings.

For a moment I thought it would work. We floated a good two feet off the ground. But before I could celebrate, we crashed back down, tumbling into a pile of trash.

"Sorry," Starr groaned. "The wings aren't strong enough to support two of us."

I nodded grimly, staring down, my vision swaying and blurring at the sheer height of the drop. On this side of the mountain, I couldn't even see the ground below. It was just a vast expanse of nothingness. As if we were standing on the edge of the world...

My eyes widened. "This is it!"

"What?" Lilli grabbed me, pulling me to my feet. "What are you talking about?"

"Don't you see?" I waved a hand over the abyss. "This is the end of the world. This level, anyway. If there's a hole, it has to be here."

I looked down into the nothingness, my stomach churning. I knew I had to be right. But at the same time, I kind of wished I wasn't. My fear of heights was worse than Lilli's fear of spiders.

Starr joined me on the edge of the cliff. "You could be

right," she said. "But there's no way to know for sure. Also, it's kind of a risk, jumping into oblivion. It's not like a regular hole. You don't know if there's anything underneath."

"What do you mean?" Lilli asked, looking worried.

"Have you ever jumped off the edge of the world in a regular video game? Sometimes you just fall. You fall and fall and fall, and there's nothing down there to catch you. You don't crash-land. You don't die. You don't end up anywhere else. You just fall. Forever." She shuddered. "Well, I mean at least until you reset the game. But here..."

"What if we killed each other in the air?" I asked. "That might reset us."

"Not if there's no graveyard down below," Lilli pointed out.

I frowned, my stomach churning as another worrisome thought came to me. If we glitched out and got locked in a free fall, would we even be able to access our menu screen to exit the game? Get back to real life? It wasn't like a regular game where you could simply push a physical button to reset the computer if the game glitched out and you couldn't log out the regular way. In this case, we'd need someone to help us unplug on the other side—in the real world. Someone to pull the helmet from our heads, eject us from the game.

Would Mom or Dad come to check on us? But then Dad was out working on the zip line. And Mom was working in her office. And while it felt like we'd been here for hours, it might be only minutes with the time compression thing. Who knew how long it would be before they came in to yell at us about too much screen time? Would we be stuck in free fall for days? My stomach twisted at the idea.

"Maybe we should find another way," I declared, backing away from the edge. "There's got to be—"

GRUNT. CLICK.

I whirled around, heart in my throat. The spiders had found us. At least ten of them surrounded us, eighty metal legs clicking and clattering on the ground as their laser eyes locked on us, ready to strike.

They started forward. "Jump!" Starr cried. "Now!"

She dropped into the abyss, her body soon disappearing into the mist. At first I could hear her screaming, but then her screams faded away, as if they were too far down to hear. I glanced at my sister, horrified.

"I can't…" I tried.

"You have to!" she scolded. "They'll kill you if you don't!"

The spiders kept coming. I stared down into the nothingness. "What if there's no bottom like Starr said? What if we fall forever?" I knew I sounded like a baby, but I couldn't help it.

Lilli grabbed me by the shoulders, shaking me hard. "You can do this. Remember the hang gliders at Dragon Ops? You didn't think you could do those, either. But you did. In fact, you helped Ikumi and me get ours under control. You're braver than you think."

"I don't know about that," I floundered.

"Look, I'm going," Lilli said. "You can decide for yourself what's worse. Falling forever or being eaten alive by cyborg spiders. Your choice, dude." And with that, she dove off the cliff, leaving me alone.

Awesome. I turned back to the cliff. Sucked in a breath. Tried to remember the hang gliders. Tried to remind myself that in real life I was safe in bed. That this was just a virtual thing. No big deal. *Come on, wimp. Do this!*

Suddenly I heard another noise. A roar that sounded distinctly unspiderlike. I looked up to the sky, my eyes lighting on a soaring shadow high above.

A dragon-shaped shadow.

Relief flooded through me. "Yano!" I cried, waving my hands in the dragon's direction. "Yano! I'm here! Down here! I need your help! I need—"

I broke off midsentence as the dragon swooped down below the clouds, giving me a better look at him. And what I saw? Well, it almost made me fall off the cliff right then and there.

"No..." I whispered, fear sliding down my spine. "It can't be."

But it was. The dragon circling above me was not our friendly guide.

It was Atreus.

There you are, tiny human, his voice whispered in my ear. *I've been waiting for you.*

Oh no.

His mouth creaked open. A stream of fire shot out, scorching the ground below. The cyborg spiders screeched in surprise and horror, scattering quickly to avoid getting burnt. The dragon dipped his snout as if ready to dive-bomb the earth.

And I dove, headfirst, into the abyss.

CHAPTER TWENTY-FOUR

"**A**hhh!" I screamed as I dropped like a stone, the trash mountain flying past me until it was no more. The wind rushed at my face, cold and fierce. My stomach plunged to my knees. My arms waved wildly and uselessly at my sides as I continued to fall, down, down, into the void. Going faster and faster until everything was a blur. At one point, I dared look up to see if I could still spot the shadowy dragon swimming through the air. But there was nothing. Only endless sky and space and falling.

Which was good. But also... not good. Was I glitching out? Would I fall forever?

Suddenly my eyes caught a flash of brown below, coming up fast. It took me a moment to register what it was. Ground. The pit wasn't bottomless, after all. Which meant I was about to crash.

But weirdly, I didn't crash. Instead, I met the ground and went right through. As if plunging into a pool of water that looks solid on top, but isn't. But unlike water, there was nothing beneath this thin surface. Just more open space. And now I was no longer falling. I was simply floating. Like Alice going down the rabbit hole.

Wow. Just... wow.

Once I caught my breath, I looked around. I spotted my sister and Starr floating, too, not that far below me, their eyes wide with awe. And who could blame them? It was as if we'd entered another world. The sky above looked as if it was made of *Minecraft* blocks. Nearby a purple tree floated in midair. To my right I saw what looked like a zombie swimming through the sky. It growled at me and gnashed its teeth before floating on by.

Okay, this was really getting freaky.

Finally, we landed. Floating down to a new level of solid ground. I collapsed in relief, still breathing heavily. Wow. That was intense.

I looked around, trying to get my bearings. Which wasn't easy, considering everything looked very odd. There were some finished parts. Patches of grass here and there. A small path winding into the distance. But much of it was unfinished. Just a purple grid stretching out in all directions. In the far back, you could see weird squiggly lines rising up. As if placeholders for future mountains or cities.

"Wow," I said, rising to my feet. "This is crazy."

"And completely freaky," Lilli added, looking a little nervous as she tried to lean against a nearby tree. Instead of supporting her, the trunk gave way and she fell right through it, landing hard on the ground. Evidently the object hadn't been fully rendered yet.

She scrambled to her feet, looking embarrassed. "Are you all right?" she asked. "I'm sorry I left you up there. I just...didn't know what else to do."

"It's okay," I said, scrubbing my face with my hands. "You did the right thing."

My mind flashed back to the mountaintop. Atreus soaring through the sky. A feeling of dread rose inside of me, and my heart pounded in my chest. Now I knew, beyond a shadow of a doubt, that he was really here. Actually here, in the game, and not simply a figment of my tormented imagination. His fire had scorched the ground. The spiders had scattered in terror. If he had been a hallucination, that wouldn't have happened.

Do you want to play again?

Do you want to play again?

"Lilli," I started to say. "There's something I need to tell you—"

But a loud noise suddenly interrupted my words. Looking out, I was shocked to see that the squiggly lines in the distance were beginning to straighten. A moment later, they burst into color, morphing into green mountains with gray craggy peaks, sprouting as if they were giant, fast-growing flowers.

"Whoa," Lilli whispered. "Are you seeing this?"

But I had already turned to my right, where large gray squares were springing up in the ground everywhere. They started out flat, then began to stretch before my eyes, taller and taller until they became buildings. Skyscrapers. Windows poking through their facades. Doors rising. Balconies popping into place. At first they looked like cartoon sketches. But they quickly filled in with intricate detailing. Bricks, ledges, storm drains. By the time they were finished, they looked as real as buildings in the real world.

"It's like they're building the level. Right now," Starr marveled.

I nodded, unable to look away. I'd never seen anything like this. Structures rising, then blinking out of existence, as if the game designers had changed their minds. Cars, trees, street signs. In mere moments, it had transformed from an almost blank canvas into a total futuristic cityscape.

A *ruined* futuristic cityscape, I realized as the details continued to fill in. Buildings that had just grown out of nothing a moment before started to buckle and wear before my eyes—going from brand-new to centuries old in a flash. Overgrown ivy climbed up their sides, graffiti slashed across their walls. Spiderlike cracks crawled down windows while others were smashed to smithereens. Apocalypse rising in all directions.

"Hm," Starr said. "Maybe we need to—"

But she never got a chance to finish her sentence. For at that moment, the ground shifted under our feet. I staggered, trying to keep my balance, my heart in my throat. Was it an earthquake? Or something worse?

Lilli's eyes were wide with fear. "We need to move," she declared. "Right now."

She started to dash away, but before she could get very far, the ground began to rumble again. And suddenly we found ourselves thrust straight up, high into the sky, as if we were on an elevator gone mad. It took me a moment to realize what was happening. But when I did, my heart sank.

"We just got built under," I exclaimed.

I stepped closer to what was now an edge, looking down—way down—back to the scene below. Sure enough, they'd literally built a skyscraper under our feet. And we were now on the roof of that skyscraper. Far, far away from the ground.

"Oh no!" Lilli exclaimed. "What are we supposed to do now?"

Starr paced the building. "I could fly down. But I don't want to leave you guys here." She tapped her chin with her finger. "Maybe we could jump? We might die, but we'd be resurrected, right?"

"Where?" Lilli asked, looking around. "No graveyards, remember?"

I shuddered. "I, for one, have jumped enough today," I declared.

I looked up, scanning the horizon, suddenly worried that maybe Atreus had followed us here. But thankfully the sky remained empty. Which reminded me, where was Yano? Was the dragon having difficulty getting back in the game? Or did he simply not know where we'd gone? Maybe we were untraceable in the unfinished levels.

"Mech Heads! I'm so glad you're here! I am in need of your help!"

We whirled around at the sound of the new voice. A little girl stood behind us—a girl I was positive hadn't been there a moment before. She appeared to be Japanese and about six years old. Her hands and face were streaked with mud; her clothes were tattered. Very apocalypse-chic. Above her head was a silver dot. A quest giver, I realized. They must be adding quests now!

"Where'd you come from?" Lilli asked, looking concerned. "Are you lost?"

"She's an NPC," I whispered, not knowing why I was whispering. Was I afraid of hurting her feelings?

"Zombies have taken over the building," the little girl told Lilli. I wasn't sure if she was answering her question or just repeating her programmed lines. "I got separated from my parents and ended up here. Will you help me? I need to get back to my mommy and daddy. They will reward you if you get me to them safely."

"Sorry, we don't have time for quests," I interjected. "Also, if you haven't noticed, we're kind of trapped up here, too."

The girl pointed down. To my surprise, a trapdoor appeared in the floor.

"Sweet!" Starr exclaimed. She reached down to pull open the door, revealing a darkened hallway below. I squatted to get a better look. Dim yellow lights flickered on and off, giving the building a super horror movie vibe. And what was that sound? I strained to listen. A weird creaking. And was that a groan?

Oh, right. The zombies. Awesome.

"You sure this is a good idea?" Starr asked, raising an eyebrow.

"Not at all," I admitted. "But I don't have a better one." I started to drop down into the building.

"Wait!" the little girl cried. "Where are you going? Aren't you going to help me?"

"Like I said, no time for quests," I muttered. But Lilli grabbed my arm.

"We can't just leave her here!" she protested.

"Why not? She's not a real person, Lilli. She's just a computer program."

Lilli frowned. "I know. But... I mean, look at her!"

I glanced over. The girl was crying now, hugging a ragged teddy bear I was sure someone had just rendered for her. Ugh.

"She'll slow us down," I argued.

"Or she might show us the way," Starr broke in. "Maybe it's a follow quest. Like, we follow her through the building, killing zombies to keep her alive, and she leads us out. And bonus, you'll rack up some experience points. Which, no offense, but you really need. Especially in these harder levels."

I sighed. She was right. "Okay, fine," I said. "Lilli, go accept the quest."

My sister looked relieved. She ran over and tapped the girl twice, as we did to accept quests back in Dragon Ops.

The girl frowned. "Why are you poking me?" she asked.

Oops. Maybe that wasn't how it worked here.

"Sorry," Lilli said, looking embarrassed. "I was just trying to accept the—um, let you know we're going to help you."

The little girl's face brightened. "Thank you!" she cried. "Oh, thank you so much! Allow me to introduce myself. My name is Ikumi."

CHAPTER TWENTY-FIVE

I stared at the little girl, shocked beyond belief. Ikumi? Could it really be her?

"Ikumi?" I whispered, my heart thudding in my chest. "You're Ikumi?"

The girl nodded eagerly. "Yes. My name is Ikumi. I live in this city. I got separated from my parents and ended up here. Will you help me? I need to get back to my mommy and daddy. They will reward you if you get me to them safely."

I groaned, realizing she was repeating her lines. It wasn't her. It was just an NPC with the same name.

"Wow, you guys are really bad at this, aren't you?" Starr groaned. "Come on, little game character. We got your back." She dropped down into the building.

I glanced at Lilli. "That's weird, right?" I asked in a low voice so Ikumi couldn't hear. "That she has the same name?"

"Yeah." My sister frowned. "Maybe just a coincidence. But I don't know. Do you think Admiral Appleby named a character after our Ikumi?"

"Well, not *our* Ikumi. 'Cause, remember, her real name is Mirai. The real Ikumi was Hiro's wife, remember? Our Ikumi's mom."

Lilli's eyes widened. "That's right. I wonder if Admiral Appleby knew her somehow."

"I don't know. I guess it doesn't matter. But it is definitely weird."

"Definitely. This whole thing is bizarre beyond belief."

"Also..." I started, biting my lower lip. "There's something else I need to tell you. Before I jumped off the trash mountain? I saw—"

"Hey!" Starr suddenly interrupted from below. "Y'all gonna sit up there all day, or you want to escape this tower?"

Oh, right. "We're coming!" I assured her. I'd have to tell Lilli about Atreus later. Right now, we had more pressing priorities.

I slipped down through the trapdoor into the hallway below. It was narrow and dark, with faded, ripped wallpaper and stained carpet. It smelled rank, too. It was hard to believe this had just been rendered a few moments before. It appeared to have been decaying for decades.

Lilli called down to me. "I'm going to lower Ikumi. Go ahead and grab her when you see her."

I looked up to see little NPC Ikumi's legs dangling from the trapdoor above. I grabbed her and helped her to the floor. Once she was settled, Lilli dropped down behind her.

"Are you okay?" she asked the little girl.

Ikumi nodded. She looked around the hall. "We need to be careful," she warned. "They could be anywhere."

A shiver tripped down my spine. *They.* As in zombies.

"Do you know which way to go?" Starr asked. "Which way leads down?"

But NPC Ikumi only shook her head. "I thought *you* would!" she proclaimed, looking even more nervous.

I groaned. "So much for it being a follow quest," I muttered. I knew we should have just left her up on the roof. She was going to be more of a hinderance than a help. And we didn't need to be taking on random quests to distract us from our mission.

Lilli shot me an annoyed look. She put a protective hand on Ikumi's shoulder. "Come on," she said to the little girl. "We'll figure it out together."

We headed down the corridor, trying to ignore the way the floor vibrated under our feet, as if it were ready to collapse at any moment. Thankfully, we located a staircase at the far end of the hall and ran down it. Unfortunately, it ended one floor down, dropping us into another long, bleak hallway.

"Who designed this place, anyway?" Starr muttered as we started down the new hallway. What else could we do?

But we didn't get far before we heard another low moan. This one sounding much closer.

"Um..." I said, stopping in my tracks. Two shadowy figures lumbered out from behind an old rotted-out door. My heart sank.

Zombies. Guess there was no avoiding them.

The two creatures shambled toward us, moaning and groaning. They were dressed in rags. Their feet bare and filthy. Their fingernails ragged and torn. But it was their eyes that were the worst. Or rather the blackened, empty sockets where eyes had once been.

"Brains!" one moaned. "BRAINS!"

At least they were slow zombies. Not like those ones who ran and could climb walls in the newer horror movies. I raised my sword.

"Actually, I'd rather keep my brain, thank you very much," I replied. "You, on the other hand..."

I dashed toward the zombies. When I reached them, I slashed out with my laser sword, somehow managing to cut both of them in half with one blow. Their tops slid from their bottoms as they fell, bloodless, to the floor. Lilli let out a cheer. Ikumi clapped her little hands in delight.

"Great job!" she cried. And I felt a tinge of pride at her words. Even if she was just a computer program.

I headed back to the group, a grin on my face. "Too easy," I declared. "Piece of—"

"BRAINS!"

I stopped dead in my tracks. "There are more of them, aren't there?" I asked, my heart sinking. Starr, Lilli, and Ikumi nodded their heads in unison, looking horrified. Reluctantly, I turned back around to see more zombies lumbering down the hall.

A lot more zombies.

"Run!" Starr cried.

CHAPTER TWENTY-SIX

We raced back through the hall. Back toward the staircase we'd come down. But when we finally reached the place it had been, it was no longer there. Instead the hallway continued on, seemingly endless.

"Um," Lilli said. "That's weird."

"They must still be changing stuff," I said. "Come on!"

We continued down the hall, searching for another staircase. The place was like a maze, room connecting to room, then dead-ending for no reason. A kitchen became an office became a workout room—sometimes when we were still inside it. As if the designer was changing things in real time.

"Make up your mind!" Lilli shouted into the void. "And put in some darn stairs!"

Her words sent a chill down my spine. Up until that moment, I'd assumed there were stairs—and we just hadn't found them yet. But it was very possible that no stairs existed. That they hadn't been built yet. Like when I used to mess with Lilli's Sims game, taking away the ladder from the pool, leaving the poor Sims with no way out. I used to think it was funny to watch them drown. If I ever got out of this alive, I would never laugh at them again.

"Hang on a second. Let me check down here," Starr said, disappearing into an adjoining hallway. With her wings, she was faster than we were. Lilli and I leaned over, taking advantage of the break to catch our breath. Ikumi's eyes darted in every direction.

"This is not good," she whispered in her tiny voice. "This is really not good."

Lilli knelt down and put her hands on the little NPC's shoulders. "It's going to be okay," she said. "I promise it's going to be—"

ROAR!

Ikumi screamed as a zombie leapt out from a doorway, teeth bared and arms raised. She wrenched out of Lilli's grasp and started running down the hall.

"Stop!" Lilli cried. "Ikumi!"

The zombie caught the movement and charged after her, cutting her off from us. We could see Ikumi trying desperately to run, but the hallway had changed again, and she hit a dead end. She was crying and screaming at the top of her lungs as the zombie reached her, grabbing her by the arm and yanking her to it, hugging her little body against its rotten, decomposing chest. Its sharp blackened teeth chomped greedily; its lips dripped with slimy yellow goo.

Lilli's eyes bulged from her head. "We have to help her!" she cried.

"No we don't!" I argued. "She's not real! She'll die and just respawn! We can't risk our lives to—"

But my sister wasn't listening. She raised her crossbow, charging toward the zombie, a look of rage on her face. The zombie whirled around, its teeth gnashing as it caught sight of bigger prey. It dropped Ikumi like a hot potato and stomped toward my sister.

"No!" I cried. "Lilli, get out of there!"

Lilli ignored me, trying to get a shot off her crossbow. But the zombie was too quick, knocking the weapon from her grasp. She screamed in frustration and tried to dive after it, only to have the zombie dodge at the last minute, causing her to go crashing into the next room. I could hear her slam against something large and scream with frustration. The zombie huffed, then returned to its original prey: Ikumi, who was still on the ground, crying.

"Help!" she cried. "Help me, please!"

It was up to me now. I drew in a breath, raising my sword. "Come and get me, ugly!" I called out to the zombie, trying to distract it. But the creature only had eyes for Ikumi now—probably part of the quest. If she died, we'd fail. Which I didn't really care about. But at the same time, seeing the little girl—who looked so real—begging me for help with pleading eyes was tough to ignore.

I braced myself, ready to charge. It was only one zombie. I could do this. I started forward—

Suddenly, the zombie stopped. It turned away from Ikumi to look at me, its lips curling in a ghastly grin. As I watched in horror, the creature's face seemed to swim in and out of focus, then morph before my eyes.

No longer a zombie's face.

But Atreus's face.

Somehow the zombie now had Atreus's face!

Well, well, tiny human. You ready to face me again?

I dropped my sword. It went clattering to the ground.

"No!" Ikumi cried. "Please don't let him eat me!"

Her voice sounded a million miles away, muddled with mud. I tried to will myself to grab my sword, but my hands refused to work. I couldn't move. I couldn't breathe. I could only stand there, literally paralyzed with fear, watching the Atreus zombie lean over Ikumi once again…

WHOOSH!

Starr's throwing star zoomed past me, driving straight into the zombie's skull. It screamed in pain and staggered back to its feet. Lilli, seeing her chance, burst out of the other room, diving for her crossbow and pointing it straight at the dragon zombie's head. She let loose her bolt, and the head exploded, the smell of burnt flesh permeating my nose.

"Awesome," Starr declared. "Now come on. I found a place where we can hole up and regroup."

"Not until we help Ikumi!" Lilli protested, dropping to her knees and scooping the little girl up in her arms. I realized Ikumi was no longer moving. And her face was extremely pale.

Like, zombie pale...

"Lilli!" I cried. "Put her down! Now!"

"What are you talking about? We can't just leave her here!" Lilli's voice took on a frantic tone.

"Look at her, Lilli. Look at her face."

My sister obeyed, thankfully, glancing down at Ikumi. The little girl's eyes began to open.

They were bright red.

Lilli screamed in horror, dropping her to the ground. She landed in a crumpled heap, then started to rise again with jerky motions.

"Come on!" Starr cried. "We need to go. Now!"

Lilli let out a wrenching sob. She started toward us, and we turned to run, following Starr down the hall till we reached a small room. We ran inside, and Starr slammed the door shut behind us, wedging a chair under the doorknob to secure it. My sister collapsed on the ground, burying her face in her hands.

"Oh my gosh," she whispered. "Oh my gosh."

"Are you okay?" I managed to choke out.

Her eyes shot up to me. "What were you doing?" she demanded, her voice rich with rage. "You just stood there! You could have saved her!"

"You don't understand," I tried. "It was..."

I trailed off. How did I explain? She didn't know Atreus was in the game. If I tried to tell her he'd taken over the body of a zombie...

She'd never believe me. She'd think I was crazy.

"You shouldn't have gone after the zombie in the first place!" I shot back, trying to deflect my rising guilt. "We don't need to be risking our lives on stupid quests."

"What was I supposed to do? Just let a little girl die?"

"She wasn't a little girl!" I protested. "She was just a computer program."

Lilli's eyes locked on mine. He voice turned to ice. "So is the real Ikumi. You want to let her die, too?"

I staggered backward, as if I'd been shot. "That's not the same, and you know it!"

"What are you guys talking about? Who's the real Ikumi?" Starr broke in.

I clamped my mouth shut, realizing we'd said too much in the heat of our argument. Of course Starr had no idea who the real Ikumi was. Or why we were down here in the first place. And we still didn't know if we could entirely trust her with the truth.

"Long story," Lilli said quickly. "And it doesn't matter now. We failed the quest. But we still have to get out of here. I'm going to go out there and see if I can find an exit. If not stairs, maybe a hole in the floor. There's got to be something we jump through or climb down."

"We'll go with you," I said.

Lilli shook her head. "No offense, but you're terrible at sneaking. I'll be able to move better on my own."

I sighed. She had a point. Though I was pretty sure that wasn't the only reason she wanted to fly solo. My guess was she wanted to check on NPC Ikumi. Maybe put her out of her zombie misery. And she didn't want me there, telling her she was being ridiculous.

Which I wouldn't have done, for the record. But try telling her that at this point.

"Fine," I said, slumping into a nearby chair. "But be careful."

"And don't go too far," Starr added. "You need to make sure you can find your way back."

"I'll be fine," Lilli said, sounding a little impatient. She moved toward the door, opening it and slipping back into the hallway. Starr flew over to shut it behind her. Then she turned back to me.

"You okay, kid?" she asked.

I hung my head. "She's mad at me."

"I noticed that. What'd you do? Besides fail a quest, that is. Which happens to the best of us."

"It's not just the quest." I sighed unhappily. "It's that I froze. Right when Lilli needed me. Let's just say it's not the first time it's happened. Whenever things get crazy, I start...well, I start seeing things. And I can't always tell if they're real or just in my head." I squeezed my eyes shut, remembering Atreus's face on the zombie's body. That one had to be in my imagination, right? But the one on the trash mountain—that was real. I think...

I groaned. "That sounds really stupid, doesn't it?"

"Actually, it sounds about right, considering what you went through in Dragon Ops."

I opened my eyes. "What?"

"Sorry." Starr held up her hands. "If you are *that* Ian, of course."

I groaned. "I think you know I am that Ian by now." There was no use denying it at this point, right?

"Yeah," Starr said with a nod. "I know." She was silent for a moment. "I also know it's okay to still feel a little traumatized after what you guys went through. In fact, it'd be weird if you didn't."

"What do you mean?"

"Look, I don't pretend to know exactly what happened when you were in the game. But from what I read, it sounded pretty awful. You were trapped, you were being hunted by a rogue AI dragon, you thought you were going to die. All that kind of stuff—all that trauma? It can change a person. Trust me, I know from experience."

"What, were *you* trapped in a video game, too?" I shot back bitterly before I could stop myself. I didn't know why I was lashing out at Starr. She was only trying to help. But still, I just felt so pathetic. And it was easier to take it out on someone else.

"No. I wasn't," she replied. "But let's just say I've gone through some tough times, too. It can take years to recover. And it doesn't just happen on its own. You have to do the work."

"Not if you're Lilli," I muttered. "She's totally fine."

"Is she, though? Girl puts on a good act, sure. But I'm not convinced she's not hiding some pretty serious issues deep down. Otherwise, why would she react the way she did about the little NPC girl? Like you said, it's just a computer program. It shouldn't have been that big of a deal. But she really took it to heart for some reason. I think that shows you there's more going on inside than she's willing to let you see."

I pursed my lips. Was Starr right? Was my sister still suffering like I was, but was just better at hiding it?

"Have you ever talked about any of it with her?" Starr pressed. "Have you ever told her what you're dealing with? Or asked her how she's been doing?"

I scowled, the anger returning. "We're not allowed to talk about it. With anyone. Even each other. In fact, if they knew I was talking to you about it, I'd be in serious trouble."

"Well, I won't tell if you don't," Starr said with a small smile. "And if you ever need someone to talk to, I'm here. I'll listen. And I promise not to put it on my channel unless it's really good stuff." She laughed, holding up her hands. "Kidding! I'm a vault, kid. What you say to me stays in that vault."

I nodded stiffly, feeling an unwanted tug of appreciation for her offer. Part of me wanted to tell her I didn't need to talk. That I was fine, no big deal. That she was making way more of this than she needed to.

But at the same time? Man, I did want to talk about it. To her—or anyone. It had been building up inside of me for so long. Like a water balloon ready to burst.

"Thank you," I said at last, not sure what else I could say. "I'll...keep that in mind."

She smiled. "You do that," she said. "I'm here when you're ready."

At that moment, the door opened. Lilli stood on the other side. "Coast is clear," she announced. "And bonus—I found a hole in the floor we can jump through."

"Nice!" I cried, stepping toward the door. But then I saw something behind my sister's back that made me stop in my tracks. Make that some*one*. "Are you kidding me right now?" I demanded.

"What is it?" asked Starr behind me. "More zombies?"

"Worse," I said with a sigh. "It's freaking Josh."

CHAPTER TWENTY-SEVEN

"**H**ey, Rivera." Josh greeted me cheerfully, waving a purple-armored hand as he stepped into the room. "Miss me?"

"Like a *Minecraft* Creeper," I muttered. "What are you doing here?"

He shrugged. "Just bored. I'm stuck at my grandpa's all week, and there's nothing to do. It's pouring rain, so even soccer's out. I figured I'd see what you guys were up to."

"How did you find us?" Starr asked.

"Oh, that was easy. Grandpa keeps a copy of the master game controls locked up in his virtual Fortress of Solitude. I simply accessed your profiles and tracked you down."

I raised an eyebrow. "Virtual Fortress of Solitude?"

"It's a Superman joke, evidently," Josh clarified. "The place is like his own private level on the server that no one can access unless they know the password. This way he can control the game from the inside if he wants to. Find any player, warp anywhere. It's pretty awesome. What he doesn't know is I figured out the password a long time ago." He grinned. "It's my birthday backward. You'd think a mastermind game creator would be more crafty with his passwords, but Grandpa has always been sentimental. Which gives me the keys to the kingdom."

"Um, congratulations?"

"Thanks." Josh looked around the room. "So where are we, anyway? This doesn't look like the beta." Then his eyes widened. "Ooh! Are we off-grid?"

"Um..." I didn't know what to say. I could try lying, but he would easily figure it out. Maybe playing dumb was best. "I don't know. We just jumped off this cliff and ended up here."

"Nice," Josh exclaimed. "I've been wanting a chance to spy on the new levels. Grandpa told me they're off-limits until they can be proven safe for users. Evidently there's some nasty glitches down here that can delete your character files completely. Make you start over from the beginning and lose all your experience, level gains, and items. Which would totally stink, if you cared about those kinds of things. Which I don't."

"Of course you don't," I muttered. We, on the other hand, definitely did. We'd already spent so much time just getting here. Imagine having to start over from the beginning!

"Well, we're glad to have you," Lilli assured him. "We're still pretty low level for this place, and we actually just failed a big quest." She still looked a little troubled by this. "Which means we could use all the help we can get in trying to escape this building… and the zombie horde."

"Cool." Josh grinned at her. "Escaping zombie hordes is practically my superpower."

I rolled my eyes. Sure it was. Also, what was my sister thinking? That last thing we needed was to have Josh tag along. What if he figured out what we were really up to? It was bad enough to be lying to Starr. Now we had to lie to Admiral Appleby's actual grandson, too? What would Josh do if he found out we were trying to spring his grandfather's prisoner? Would he report us? Get us kicked out of the game?

But then again, what choice did we have? He already knew we'd gone off-grid. If we made him mad now, he could report back to the powers that be that we'd violated the game's terms of service and get us kicked off the server for good. Better to keep on his good side for the time being, at least; let him think we were on the same team.

"Lilli, you said that you found a way down to a lower floor?" I asked.

"Oh, right. Yes! Hopefully it's still there." She beckoned for us to follow.

We headed out of the room and down the dimly lit hall, tiptoeing as we went to avoid any more zombie encounters.

Thankfully, NPC Ikumi was nowhere to be seen. Maybe Lilli had disposed of her body when she was out by herself. Or maybe the quest had reset by now.

When we reached the end of the hall, Lilli beckoned for us to enter the room to the left. Inside, we found what looked like a large classroom. Guess the office building had now turned into a school? Or what used to be a school, anyway. Desks were overturned, windows were broken. On the far wall there was a dirty, stained whiteboard with a cartoon drawing of Rocky the Robot. Underneath, someone had written *Gear up, Mech Heads* in what looked suspiciously like blood. Ew.

"So where's this hole?" Starr asked, scanning the ground.

My sister walked behind the teacher's desk. "It was right here," she said, frowning. "I swear. It was huge. But now it's gone."

My heart sank. The designer must have fixed it before we got here. "We'll keep looking," I said. "There's got to be something—"

"BRAINS!" came a moaning voice from outside.

"Crap. They're back!" Starr cried, running to the door and slamming it shut. "Help me!" she commanded, and I ran and grabbed a chair, propping it under the door handle to help keep it closed. The zombie smooshed its rotting face against the window, slime oozing from its skin and onto the glass.

"BRAINS," it moaned again.

Josh made a dash for the door, tapping on the window. "Sorry, ugly! No brains for you!"

The zombie moaned, thrashing at the door. Josh laughed, dancing goofily in front of the glass. "Mmm. Delicious brains," he added, pointing to his head. "Come and get 'em while they're hot!"

"Don't tease the trash mobs," Lilli scolded, dragging him away from the window.

Josh grinned. "Sorry, Speedy. I just didn't like the way that one was looking at me."

"Can we please focus here?" I broke in, exasperated. I knew we had no choice but to keep Josh around, but did he really have to be so annoying? "How are we supposed to get out of here?"

Lilli abandoned Josh and headed over to the windows. "Well, there's definitely no way to jump," she mused. "We're too high up."

"And the new floor is solid concrete," Starr added, tapping it with her foot. "I don't see any cracks or holes, either."

I slumped my shoulders, glancing out the door's window again. More zombies had shown up and were shambling around outside. We could try to fight them, but there was no guarantee we'd survive. And I didn't relish the idea of having my brain munched on, virtual or not. Plus, what Josh had said was still bugging me. What if when we died we glitched out and were sent back to the beginning and had to start all over? That would not be good.

"What about that?" Josh suggested, pointing up. My gaze rose, following his finger until I saw a small air duct near the ceiling. "People *always* escape through air ducts in the movies," he announced. As if he were some major expert expounding on a little-known fact that everyone here didn't already know.

Still, he did have a point. Unfortunately.

"It's kind of small," Starr said, walking over to the duct and peering up at it worriedly.

"Yeah. But I think we'll fit," I said, joining her. "I mean, it's worth a try. There's really no other way out."

"I don't know..." I realized her face had turned kind of ashen. "I'm not really big on closed-in spaces."

I wasn't, either, but it beat my fear of heights. And, well, my fear of zombies.

"Look," I said. "How about you stay here and keep the zombies' attention at the door? We'll go through the air duct and climb down into the next room. Then we'll circle back and take out the zombies from behind and clear the door for you."

She looked relieved. "That's a great idea," she said. "I can do that."

"Cool. Help me get this desk under the vent."

Together the four of us dragged a few desks over until

we'd made a ledge under the vent. Then we climbed up onto the desks, and Josh yanked the grate free, tossing it to ground. He peered inside for a moment, then nodded.

"Let's give this bad boy a try," he said, boosting himself up into the vent.

"Can you fit?" Lilli called after him.

"Totally," he called back, his voice echoing. "No problem at all. Come on, Speedy. Get up here and see for yourself."

My sister boosted herself up into the air vent, also disappearing from view. I glanced at Starr, who, now that they were gone, still looked a little nervous. Make that a *lot* nervous.

"You gonna be okay?" I asked her.

She shot me a half smile. "I'm sure it'll be fine. It's just a game, right?"

"So they keep telling me." It was funny; in a weird way it made me feel a little better to know that someone else was nervous about things. Lilli was always so overconfident. And Josh—well, I didn't even want to talk about him.

But Starr's face told me I wasn't alone. I wasn't crazy to be freaked out.

I climbed up onto the desk, trying to exude confidence. She'd made me feel better a few minutes before. Now it was my turn. "We'll be back for you in minute. Just hang tight."

She nodded, then walked back to the door. Knocked on the window with her fist. "Hey, uglies!" she called. "How about you pick on someone your own state of decay!"

Feeling confident she was going to be all right, I boosted myself up into the vent, wriggling my body into the passageway. Josh was right. It was tight, but I could crawl just fine. As long as I didn't think too much about it as I was doing it.

Speaking of Josh. Where was he? I peered down the vent. Or Lilli, for that matter.

"Josh?" I called out. "Lilli?"

No answer. Ugh. Seriously, would it have killed them to wait five seconds for me?

Annoyed, I started crawling through the vent. What else could I do? The air up here was dusty, and I had to stop and sneeze several times, not to mention brush thick cobwebs from my hair. As I pushed forward, I looked for more grates—entrances to other rooms—but came up empty. Which was weird, right? Something else the game designers hadn't added yet, perhaps?

Finally I got to a fork in the road. Two vents—one going left and the other right. I peered down each passageway in turn, trying to figure out which one my sister and Josh had chosen. But both looked empty. Where were they?

They must have found a grate and climbed down, I told myself, even as my heart started to pick up its pace. They were probably already down in another classroom. Maybe they were halfway to rescuing Starr, even.

But why didn't they wait for me?

Irritation rose inside of me. Was my sister still mad at

me about the whole NPC Ikumi thing? Was that why she was so eager to pal around with Josh? If so, she was fooling herself; Josh wouldn't have cared about some computer program any more than I had. Probably less, since he had no respect for the game.

Though at least he wouldn't have frozen like I had.

Exasperated, I looked down each pathway one more time, then forced myself to choose. I turned left, crawling farther down the vent, hoping for some kind of exit. But there was nothing. It just went on and on. *Maybe I should turn around*, I thought. Retreat back to the room I'd come from. Maybe Josh and Lilli had done the same.

I started to try to turn. But in doing so, I realized I couldn't. The vent wasn't big enough. I was stuck. And I couldn't even use my sword to try to cut my way through as the passageway wasn't wide enough to pull it out from its sheath.

My heart started pounding loudly in my chest. Panic gripped my lungs, making it difficult to breathe. What if there was no exit? What if I was trapped in here? My fingers began to shake so hard it was difficult to keep from collapsing.

In the end, I decided to try to crawl backward. Retreat to the safety of the classroom with Starr. Josh and Lilli would have to take on the zombies themselves and rescue both of us. It wasn't ideal, but it was better than being stuck.

And so, slowly, I started to inch my way back. It wasn't

easy by any stretch. And I hated not being able to see where I was going. The walls felt as if they were closing in, tighter and tighter the farther I crawled. At first, I figured it was my imagination. But then I realized it might not be. What if the designers were shrinking the tunnel right then and there? What if it got too small when I was still inside? My stomach swam. I felt like I was going to throw up. Or scream.

"Help!" I cried, my voice shaky and barely audible. "HELP!"

Suddenly, I heard a noise. Which could have been good—help on the way, and all that. Except it didn't sound like help. It sounded more like…scratching. Scraping. Like a giant—

RAT!

"ARGH!" I cried as the hugest rat I'd ever seen started running in my direction, its brown furry body almost as big as my own. As it got closer, I realized in horror that it wasn't just a rat, either. It was a zombie rat. With glowing red eyes. Sharp fangs.

And it was coming straight at me.

I tried to back up. I banged my head on the ceiling. My wrist turned the wrong way, and my arm buckled out from under me. The rat gnashed its teeth, growing closer.

I opened my mouth in a scream.

And everything went black.

CHAPTER TWENTY-EIGHT

"**I**an!"

I yelped as something grabbed my arm. For a moment, I thought it was the rat chomping down on my skin. Then my headset was yanked from my head and I could see again.

Namely, I could see Mom standing over me, in real-life mode, arms crossed over her chest. More terrifying than any zombie rat.

"You're still playing? Did you even go to bed?" she demanded.

"Um…" I blinked, desperately trying to re-register with reality. Everything around me looked blurry, as if I were underwater or something. Though I didn't feel sick to my stomach, I noticed, like I had when exiting Dragon Ops. That was something, at least. Still, I didn't remember feeling quite so disoriented then. As if I'd been living another life outside of my real body and had just been dumped back in without warning.

Beside me, Lilli was also trying to get her bearings, blinking furiously and looking a little ill. How many hours had we been in the game? It was then that I noticed Lilli's window. Or, more precisely, the yellowish glow coming from her window. The sun! Had we really been playing all night long? So much for the whole time-compression thing. Maybe it didn't work on the unfinished levels.

Mom grabbed the headset off the bed, turning it over in her hands. A small smile crept to her lips, telling us she knew she was supposed to be angry at all the screen time but kind of understood. "So the game's that good, huh?"

"It's pretty incredible," I admitted. "I mean, I'll never like apocalypse games more than fantasy games, but the world is intense. Super realistic."

Mom nodded, her eyes taking on a dreamy look. "Man, I used to love this game when I was a kid. Of course it was a lot different back then. I remember there was this secret chest at the beginning. Like a weapons cache..."

I glanced at Lilli. She was looking at Mom, impressed. Wow. Guess we should have hit up Mom before diving in. She might have known more secrets than Starr.

Mom started to slide the helmet over her own head.

"What are you doing?" I cried, alarmed.

"You promised I could try it!" she protested. "Just for a minute!"

I watched, helpless, as she sat down on the bed. She turned her head from left to right. Then back again. Her arm waved in the air. Was she fighting the giant rat? Should we grab the helmet off her head?

But it turned out we didn't have to. A moment later, she removed the helmet herself. "Pretty cool," she said. "Though you didn't get very far. I thought you'd played all night."

I cocked my head in confusion. "What do you mean?"

"You're at the starting area. In the warehouse. I remember it from the eight-bit game." She smiled, handing the helmet back to me. "It looks so much different now, though. It was like I was really there."

"Wait, we were in the starting zone?" I asked, my heart sinking. Oh no. Had we glitched out like Josh had said? Maybe we died and there was nowhere to send us but back to the beginning. Or Mom shut off the game before it auto-saved. If it did even autosave on an unfinished level...I shot a look at Lilli, who mimicked a face-palm.

"I think so." Mom rose to her feet. "Anyway, I gotta get to work. I'm already running late. And don't forget, you two have camp today."

"Camp?"

"Uh, yeah. Basketball camp? Remember you begged me

to sign you up at the beginning of the summer? And, Lilli, you're at soccer camp again this week."

Ugh. I'd totally forgotten about that. Back when I was trying desperately to stay away from video games, I'd had this crazy idea to sign up for every sports camp under the sun. To help keep me in real-life mode all summer long.

But now...

I put my hand to my forehead. "I'm actually feeling kind of sick. I might need to skip today."

"Same," Lilli agreed, lying back on the bed and sighing dramatically.

"Real sick or sick from staying up all night playing computer games?" Mom asked, giving us a suspicious look.

Yeah. I should have known she wouldn't buy that one. Guess it was better to just come clean. "Look, I'm sorry," I said. "I really didn't realize we had been playing for so long."

Mom gave a long sigh. But I knew, of all people, she understood. "Look, I'll let you stay home today. But that's it. And I don't want you playing any more of this thing, at least until I get back. It's not healthy to be in a virtual world for that long."

"I know. We won't. I promise," I said, crossing my fingers behind my back.

"We'll sleep all day," Lilli added. She offered up a huge yawn, covering her mouth with her hand.

Mom smirked. "You two look totally trustworthy," she deadpanned. "Now, go get yourselves some breakfast. Even gamers have to eat."

We reluctantly followed her into the kitchen. Mom grabbed a box of cereal and some bowls and set them on the table. Then she said good-bye and headed out to work. After, of course, making us promise one more time not to go back into the game for the rest of the day.

"Get some sunshine," she scolded as she headed out the door. "Some real-life exercise."

"Yes, Mom," we said in unison.

But once the door shut, we looked at each other and pushed away our cereal. Neither one of us was hungry. Not really. And though I was feeling totally exhausted, I knew there was no time to rest.

We needed to go back into the game.

"I can't go back into the game," Lilli moaned a few minutes later, rubbing her head as she looked down at the VR equipment still scattered on her bed. She picked up her headset, then set it down with a sigh. "Sorry, Ian. I just can't."

"But we have to!" I cried, dismayed. "Ikumi needs us!"

"We're not going to be any use to her like this," my sister

reminded me. "I mean, how do you feel right now? 'Cause I feel like I've been run over by a truck."

I slumped down on the bed. "Yeah. Same," I admitted. "Which is crazy, right? We've just been sitting here. But my whole body aches."

"No sleep. No food. That'll do it. Plus my brain's been working overtime. We need some serious real life before we go in again."

"I guess you're right." I lay back on the bed. Then a thought occurred to me. "But what about Starr? We left her in that zombie room!"

"Maybe she glitched out, too. Or Josh got her out."

"Yeah, right." I snorted. "As if Josh would do something for anyone but himself."

My sister groaned. "And here we go again."

"What's that supposed to mean?"

"Come on, Ian, he's not that bad."

I sat up in bed. "Are you kidding? He's totally that bad. Maybe worse. He's a jerk, Lilli. I don't know why you like him so much."

Lilli's face turned bright red. "I don't like him," she protested. "I just don't feel the need to be openly rude to him like you are."

"Sorry, but maybe I just don't like the idea of us joining forces with the grandkid of the evil mastermind who kidnapped our friend."

"Come on. We don't even know for sure Admiral Appleby is behind this. I mean, he seemed like a cool guy when we met him. A little weird, but not an evil mastermind."

"No one acts like an evil mastermind, Lilli. That doesn't mean he didn't do it."

"But why? I still don't get any of this. Why would he kidnap Ikumi to begin with? It's not like Dragon Ops, where the competition wanted to shut the park down so they could launch first. So why does Admiral Appleby want her?"

I tapped my finger on my chin. Why indeed? That was still the missing piece to all this. Why would Admiral Appleby, in the midst of launching his greatest game to date, bother kidnapping his rival's daughter's digital file?

My eyes widened. "Maybe he wants eternal life!"

"What?"

"You saw how old he is, right? Maybe he's even dying. Like, he has terminal cancer or something, and he'll die before his beloved game is released to the world. And maybe he discovered Ikumi's tech. Maybe he asked Hiro to share the tech with him—so he could upload himself online, too. Then he could live forever in his own game."

"Wow." Lilli shook her head. "That's quite a theory."

"But it makes sense, right? It gives him a motive. Hiro said no—he wasn't going to help him. Because he saw what the whole experience did to his daughter. But Admiral Appleby wouldn't take no for an answer and kidnapped

Ikumi. And maybe Hiro, too. Maybe he's got Hiro locked up, forcing him to work on copying his brain."

"I mean, I guess it's possible," Lilli faltered. "But it just...seems insane."

"Yeah." I sighed. "Anyway, it doesn't matter. The why is not important. All we need to do is focus on Ikumi."

"*After* we get some sleep," Lilli finished, pulling the covers over her head, effectively signaling our conversation was over. I sighed and grabbed my VR gear, dragging it to my own room next door. When I reached my bed, I set my alarm for three hours, just in case. Otherwise, the way I felt? I might pass out all day.

I closed my eyes. Just a quick nap. Then we could go back in. Rested and ready to face whatever was waiting for us. Killer rats, zombies...

And hopefully not a dragon.

CHAPTER TWENTY-NINE

You'd think with all that was on my mind, I wouldn't be able to sleep. But the second my head hit my pillow, I was out like a light. And when my door suddenly burst open two hours later, I was definitely not ready to wake up.

"Five more minutes, Mom," I begged, pulling the pillow over my head. "Then I'll get up for camp."

Sunlight hit me full force as Lilli yanked the pillow away and pulled open the blinds. I blinked at her blearily, suddenly worried as I realized how serious she looked. Also, even odder, she had her VR rig all packed up and strapped to her back.

"What's going on?" I asked as I struggled to sit up in bed.

Her gaze darted to the window. "I don't know," she said. "But someone's here."

"What?" I scrambled out of bed and over to the window. Sure enough, there was some kind of large van parked in front of our house. All white with no windows in the back or lettering on the side. The kind of van bad guys always used in the movies when trying to rob a bank or case a home. Or what police might use for surveillance.

As I watched, two men jumped out of the back of the van. They were dressed all in black with matching black baseball caps on their heads.

Uh-oh.

I glanced at my sister. "You don't think…" I started to say. But her eyes were still glued to the window. To the two men who were now walking up to our front porch. At this point, I could better see their outfits. My eyes bulged as I caught the familiar Rocky the Robot logo on their chests.

"Do you think they know?" I whispered to my sister, my pulse skittering madly. "I mean, what we're really doing?"

"I don't know," she said. "They could have just figured out we went off-grid, right? They might not know why."

"I bet Josh told on us," I muttered. "I knew we shouldn't have let him tag along."

"No way. Josh wouldn't turn us in."

"How do you know?"

"I just do, okay?"

DING-DONG!

The doorbell rang, nearly causing me to jump out of my skin. "What do we do?" I whispered.

Lilli's gaze shot to the bedroom door. "I don't know. Not answer the door, for one."

"Yeah, but what if they bash it in? Or go in through a window?" Visions of every bad guy movie I'd ever seen flashed through my head. "We're like sitting ducks in here."

"They're not going to do that. We're not wanted criminals. We're kids."

"Kids trying to steal their most precious possession. Remember, Ikumi's tech could be worth trillions."

My sister motioned to my rig, still sitting on the bed in pieces. "Grab everything," she said. "We're getting out of here."

I did as she said, heart pounding in my chest as I gathered up all my stuff and shoved it into the backpack. It was a tight fit, especially the helmet. But in the end I managed to get it all on my back just as the doorbell rang a second time.

Lilli ran to the bedroom door. "Come on," she said. "Hurry."

I followed her out to the hall, then froze as I heard the front door squeak open. At first I thought the Mech Ops guys had broken in already. Then I heard a familiar voice greet them. "Can I help you guys?"

"Oh no," I whispered. "Dad's home."

Usually Dad was at work this time of day. But sometimes

he did come home for lunch. Maybe Mom asked him to check on us and make sure we were getting rest and weren't back to gaming.

"Sure. Come on in. I'll go get them," we heard Dad say.

Lilli's eyes bulged. Oh no. We could hear footsteps as the men entered the house. Another moment and they'd be in the hall.

"We can't let them take our rigs!" I cried.

Lilli bit her lower lip, her gaze darting around the hall before settling on the stairs. "Up here! Quick!" she cried.

We dashed upstairs just as the men came around the corner. Lilli pushed open the door to the game room and we slipped inside, panting for breath.

"Hide the rig," my sister commanded, shrugging hers off her back and trying to shove it under the couch. But it was way too big to fit.

Dad appeared in the doorway.

"Um, hey, guys!" He gave us a weird look. "There's some people here to see you? From that game company?"

"We're not home!" I burst out.

Dad raised an eyebrow. "You are clearly home. What is this about?" His eyes went to our backpacks, half shoved under the couch. His eyebrows raised.

"Please, Dad," Lilli begged. "Just send them away. We'll explain later, I promise."

But Dad didn't move. "They said you've violated the

terms and conditions of your beta test." He frowned. "What have you guys been up to, anyway? Have you been hacking or something?"

Dad didn't know a thing about computers, only what he'd seen in movies. But that didn't mean we were going to be able to convince him to send the men off without giving them what they'd come for. And I had no idea how long they'd sit, patiently waiting downstairs, before they made a move.

"Look," I said. "We'll bring down the rigs. We just have to find all the pieces. There's a sensor that fell off my helmet." I lifted up a couch cushion as if I was searching for it. "Just give me a minute to find it, and we'll be down."

"Do you need help?" Dad asked.

"I'm helping him," Lilli broke in, her fingers running over the carpet as if feeling for the missing sensor.

Dad reached into his pocket. "Do you want my flashlight?"

"No!" we both shouted in unison.

"I mean—no thank you," I stammered. "Can you just go down and let them know we'll be there in a second?"

He watched for a moment, and I could see the suspicion in his eyes. Then he sighed. "Sure. But don't be long. I need to get back to work. I can't entertain these guys all day."

He headed out of the game room, closing the door behind him. Lilli shot to her feet, running to the door and locking it. Then she put a chair under the handle. Exactly what we'd done in-game to keep out the zombies.

These men might be *worse* than zombies.

"What, do you want to crawl through the air vents?" I asked half jokingly as I looked up at the vents in question. They were home-size, not industrial, and there was no way we'd fit.

"I've got a better idea," Lilli replied, running to the balcony door. She yanked it open, and a fresh wind blew in from outside.

"You do realize we're on the second floor," I reminded her, a little uneasily.

"You do realize we have a zip line," she shot back, stepping out onto the balcony.

"Um…" I glanced at her, then back at the door. "I thought you guys hadn't finished that yet."

"We haven't. But I think it'll hold."

"You *think*? What if it doesn't?" My heart pounded in my chest. "Maybe we can just sneak downstairs."

"No. We can't risk it. They might have more guys out front, watching the house. This way we'll have a head start if they try to come after us."

I was afraid she was going to say something like that. I watched as she grabbed the zip line's handlebar, pulling it over the railing. Then she scanned the area.

"Okay. Coast is clear. Grab your rig. We need to go. Now!"

I grabbed the backpack, my hands so cold I could barely

grip it. Lilli ran over and scooped up her own, shuffling it onto her back. Then she helped me fix mine.

"Ian? Lilli?" Dad's voice broke in from downstairs. "Um, the gentlemen are on their way up. They said you don't have to worry about the sensor."

Ugh. We were out of time. I could hear footsteps on the stairs. I ran out onto the balcony with Lilli. She had the handlebar in her hands and motioned for me to grab on to her back.

"Is it going to hold both of us?" I asked. Surely there was some kind of weight limit on these things.

"I don't know," Lilli said. "We're going to find out."

The door handle rattled. They were trying to get in. I grabbed Lilli's waist, holding on tight.

"Go, go, go!" I cried.

She leapt off the balcony. We shot into the air, flying across the backyard at breakneck speed. *Too fast*, I thought wildly as the tree at the end came zooming closer and closer. Too much weight. We were going to crash.

"Jump!" Lilli cried. "Now!"

Somehow I did, releasing my grip on her and hurtling toward the ground. Hard, fast. Coming in for a very ungraceful landing. I hit the ground sideways, jarring my ankle, then losing my balance and tumbling onto the grass, the air knocked from my lungs. For a moment, I just lay there stunned, trying desperately to catch my breath.

Lilli grabbed my arm. "Get up! Now!"

I scrambled to my feet, looking back at the house. The two men were standing on the balcony, bewildered expressions on their faces. "Where did they go?" one asked. Then the other pointed to the zip line. I heard the first man curse.

"We know you're out there!" he called into the yard. "We need you to come back inside. Now! We promise we'll explain everything."

Yeah, right. We broke into a run, dashing down the greenbelt behind our house, then cutting through our neighbor's yard, then across another street. In my mind, I pictured the men running back down the stairs and diving into the van to start pursuit. We had to be unpredictable. Find a complicated route they couldn't follow by car.

We zagged through a park, then across another road. I could barely breathe I was so winded.

"What are we going to do?" I asked. "We can't run forever."

Lilli nodded, also out of breath. "I don't know. We have to find somewhere to lay low until they leave."

I racked my brain, trying to think of something. It wasn't easy with the amount of panic running through me.

Then it dawned on me. "The arcade!" I cried. "Maddy will hide us!"

Lilli nodded. "Good idea! Let's go!"

CHAPTER THIRTY

When we reached the arcade, the lights were off. The sign was dark. Of course. It was still only around noon, and Maddy didn't open till late afternoon on weekdays, so she could get her art done during the morning hours. Something I hadn't thought of when I made the suggestion to come here. Hopefully she was home. If not, we had no plan B.

I banged on the door while Lilli kept watch on the road. Every roar of a car's engine made my blood freeze, and I kept imagining the white van turning the corner, pulling up beside us. What would they do if they found us? Take our equipment and leave? Or would they try to take us, too? How much did they know about what we were up to?

"Maddy!" I cried. "Open up! Please! It's Ian and Lilli!"

After what seemed like an eternity, the door finally

creaked open. Maddy stood on the other side, still dressed in her pajamas. She rubbed her eyes sleepily. "What are you guys doing here?" she asked. "You know I don't open till two."

"It's an emergency," I begged. "Please. We didn't know where else to go."

She opened the door wider, thankfully not asking any questions. We dove inside, and she shut the door behind us, locking it. I collapsed on the floor of the arcade, sucking in a much-needed breath. We were safe. At least for the moment.

Maddy put her hands on her hips. "Okay," she said. "Do you mind telling me what's going on? You two look like you've been running for your lives. Is everything okay?"

I realized we needed to come clean. We were totally out of our league here. And Maddy was the only adult I could trust not to immediately go to the police once we told our tale. And so, slowly, we told her everything. About Dragon Ops, Ikumi's kidnapping, Hiro's disappearance, the beta test, the guys showing up at our house.

When we had finished, Maddy let out a long whistle. "That's quite a story," she said.

"You believe us though, right?" I asked, not realizing until this moment how much we needed her to.

She nodded slowly. "Yes," she said. "And I hate that you guys are mixed up in something like this. You're just kids. You really should go to the police."

"Come on," I said. "You know they'd never believe us."

"Probably not," she agreed ruefully. I watched as she walked over and picked up the backpack containing my VR rig. "But you know, these things could have trackers in them," she said. "In fact, I'm pretty sure they do. No way would any game company just hand out expensive equipment without a plan to get it back after the beta."

I cringed. I hadn't even thought of that. "Can you destroy the trackers?"

"I'd have to find them first. And that'd take too long. But don't worry. They won't find you in here. I've got a scrambler."

"A what?" Lilli asked, scrunching up her nose.

Maddy smiled. "Let's just say I like my privacy. I don't need the government looking in on everything I do."

Wow. Was Maddy a hacker or something? I had no idea.

"Look, I'm sorry," I said. "We didn't want to drag you into this. We just didn't know where else to go."

"I'm glad you came. Now, why don't you go upstairs? You can use my office to log back into the game. I'll keep an eye on things down here. If they do show up looking for you, I'll try to get rid of them. And if I can't? I'll hit the master breaker for the building. It'll shut down all power and Wi-Fi so you'll be booted from the game. If you are, don't try to find me. Just go. There's a back door on the second floor that leads out to the fire escape."

"But then where do we go?" Lilli asked, looking

frightened. I didn't blame her. It was one thing to be on the run in a video game. But in real life? It was ten times as terrifying. My sister turned to me. "Maybe we *should* go to the police," she said.

"If we do, they'll take our VR rigs," I argued. "Then we'll never get to Ikumi."

"Yeah, well, we're not going to get to her anyway if the Mech Ops people catch up to us."

"Here," Maddy interrupted, writing down an address and some instructions on a small scrap of paper. "If you need to leave, head here. Follow these directions exactly. They'll take you to someone safe."

I stared down at the paper. "Alpha Burn?" The name sounded so familiar. Then it hit me. "Wait, isn't this that big-time hacker?" Wow. I'd read all about this guy online. He was totally famous. Maddy knew him personally?

"Just a friend of mine," was all Maddy would say. "Someone you can trust."

"Thanks, Maddy," Lilli said. "We owe you one."

She gave a tight smile. "You owe me at least ten. Now go!" She shooed us to the stairs.

We dashed up the stairs into the apartment. It was small, but cozy and clean, with simple furniture and all sorts of framed manga artwork on the walls. We settled down onto her couch and started reassembling our VR rigs, getting ready to log back into the game.

As we worked, I tried to keep my mind on the task at hand, but found myself glancing at the apartment front door over and over again. Despite Maddy's assurances, I still didn't feel safe. And I really didn't like the idea of going into a game world and leaving our real-life selves so vulnerable.

But we had no choice. And so I forced myself to swallow my fear and place my game helmet over my head. We'd been given another chance. We couldn't waste it.

"You ready?" I asked Lilli.

"Gearing up, Mech Head," she replied with a rueful grin. "Let's hope we live till tomorrow."

CHAPTER THIRTY-ONE

We were back.

Except, annoyingly, not where we left off. Like Mom said, we had emerged back inside the warehouse at the very beginning of the game.

I groaned, lightly punching the wall with annoyance. "All that work! For nothing!"

"At least we're out of that building," Lilli pointed out, ever the optimist. "That's something."

"Except we left Starr there," I reminded her. "What if she's still stuck in that room?" I accessed my menu and checked our party status. Lilli and I showed up online. But Starr no longer appeared in our party. Probably because she was still off-grid.

"Maybe she logged off when we didn't come back," Lilli suggested.

"Maybe…" Then a disturbing thought struck me. "I hope those guys from Mech Ops didn't come for her, too."

"Ugh. I hope not," Lilli scowled. "Without her we'll never get through this thing."

"Don't worry, Speedy. You still got me!"

We whirled around at the sound of the voice. There was Josh, lounging against a rusted-out old robot, decked out in all his glorious purple armor. I bit back a groan, doing my best not to look as annoyed as I felt. Seriously? Starr was missing, and Josh had somehow made it back? Talk about rotten luck.

"Don't you have soccer camp today?" Lilli asked, peering at him curiously.

"Don't you?" he shot back, raising his eyebrows.

She grinned. "I'm…sick."

"Funny. Me too," Josh declared, giving her a wink. "So desperately ill. Anyway, I figured I'd log in to see what my team was up to in the Mech 'verse."

"Uh, we're not actually a team," I reminded him, annoyance rising.

Josh raised an eyebrow. "We were literally just playing together hours ago."

"Yeah. And you literally just left me to die in the vents. Nice teamwork." I tried not to think about the rat again, crawling toward me. Its gnashing teeth, its glowing eyes.

I should have been thankful at least it didn't have Atreus's face.

"We didn't leave you to die, Ian," Lilli said, sounding exasperated. "We went in, we found the grate in the next room, and we climbed down."

"There wasn't a grate!" I protested.

"There was!" my sister insisted. "Maybe the designer moved it by the time you got there. Like the hole in the floor. You can't blame us for that."

It was funny, her saying "us" when I'd been talking about Josh, not her.

"Whatever," I muttered. Frustrated, I walked over to the big shipping container in the center of the room, punching it with my fist. To my surprise, a low groan came from inside. A groan that sounded like...

"Yano?" My heart picked up its pace. "Is that you?"

Relief rushing through me, I ran to the front of the shipping container and whipped open the door. Sure enough, there was our dragon friend, once again crammed inside.

"Finally!" he declared, shuffling out from the crate. "I was beginning to think you'd never open this thing. My wings are completely cramping." He raised one wing and shook it out, then the other. Two shimmers of silver flittered down his sides.

"Whoa," Josh cried, coming around the side of the container. "A dragon? I didn't know there was a dragon in this game! Cool!"

"Why, thank you," Yano replied. "I am pretty cool, aren't I? I mean it's not every day you see a dragon with three heads. Also, you should check out these claws." He held out his paw for Josh to inspect. "Aren't they just perfectly manicured?"

I rolled my eyes, swatting his paw away. "Yes, yes. You're a ridiculously gorgeous beast, Yano. Everyone can see that. Now, where have you been? We've been flying blind! Or, not flying, that is. When we really needed to."

"I'm sorry about that," Yano replied. "It seems I glitched out of the game. And when I tried to get back in, I landed here again, trapped in the shipping container. Only this time you weren't here to let me out. And it was locked from the outside." He scowled. "Thanks for coming back for me, by the way."

"We didn't," I admitted. "We glitched out, too. Ended up back here. Evidently that's what happens if you try to play the unfinished levels. Even worse, you lose all your progress and experience points. Back to square one—literally."

The dragon's three heads frowned. "Well, that's not great."

"No kidding," I agreed. "Which means we need to be really careful this time not to die or glitch."

"Careful is my middle name!" Yano declared. "Well, actually it's Clive, but I don't like to admit that." He furled his wings. "So what are we waiting for? Let's get this show on the road!"

Josh slapped the dragon on his side. "Sounds good to me! What grand adventure shall we embark on now? Forbidden levels? More capture the orb? Want to see Grandpa's Fortress of Solitude? That's something to see!"

I grabbed Lilli by the arm. "Can I talk to you for a second?"

She nodded, though she didn't look happy about the prospect. I dragged her away from Josh, around the side of the shipping container.

"What?" Lilli asked when we were out of earshot.

"You need to tell Josh to go away."

She groaned. "Are we back to this again?"

"I'm serious. I know you like him. And you can play soccer with him in the real world all you want. But he can't play with us in here."

"Why not? He's really good. And, let's face it, we can use all the help we can get. Especially now that we don't have Starr."

I raked a hand through my hair, frustration rising. "What if he finds out what we're really here for? What if he tells his grandfather? All of this will be for nothing."

"I told you I don't think he would."

"Why? 'Cause you two are suddenly besties after ten minutes of game play? You do remember what happened the last time you trusted a guy online, don't you?"

She recoiled as if she'd been struck, and I immediately felt bad throwing the Logan thing in her face. Logan, whom she'd met online and fallen for, only to find out he wasn't real—he was just a joke made up by her friends. Lilli had given up video games—all things online, really—after that. Until Dragon Ops, when she rediscovered her love of gaming.

So yeah, a bit of a low blow. But I was desperate! Josh needed to go. Now.

Lilli said nothing for a moment. Her eyes seemed to cloud over as if she was thinking really hard about what she wanted to say next.

"What?" I demanded, an uncomfortable feeling worming through my stomach. Suddenly, I wasn't sure I wanted to know what she was about to say.

"This isn't like the Logan thing," she admitted at last. "I actually know Josh really well. In real life, I mean."

"What?"

"Yeah. From school. We kick the ball around sometimes at recess. And sometimes we...text and stuff."

"You text?" I stared at her in disbelief.

Her expression tightened. "Yeah? So what?"

"Lilli, he's a total jerk."

"He's not, Ian. He's really not," she insisted. "Look, I know he acts super intense when it comes to soccer. But it's just 'cause he loves it so much. And he hates that half the team always acts like they don't want to be there." She wrung her hands. "Just like you act when someone isn't all into video games."

Ouch. I didn't know what to say. Lilli clearly liked Josh a lot. She'd been hanging out with him. Texting. And I had no idea.

"Why didn't you tell me you were friends?"

"Gee, I don't know. Maybe because I knew you'd act just like you're acting now?"

"And when did this start? This ... *friendship*?" I demanded, though what I really wanted to know was how long she'd been keeping it from me.

She shrugged. "I guess it was right after we got back from Dragon Ops. I was still feeling all messed up at the time, and I didn't know how to deal. Josh found me under the bleachers during gym class, crying. He sat down and talked to me. He's a really good listener, Ian. He was there for me when I needed him."

I stared at her, my heart plummeting. "Oh my gosh," I whispered. "You told him, didn't you? You told him about Dragon Ops?" A thread of hysteria wound through my voice, but I couldn't help it. "How could you?" I whispered.

I couldn't speak. Emotions ran through me, hard and fast. Lilli talked to Josh about Dragon Ops? She wouldn't even talk to *me* about Dragon Ops!

My mind flashed back to all those terrible nights after we'd gotten back from the game. The nightmares waking me in a cold sweat. The way I'd lie in bed, panic burning through me like wildfire. Wanting so badly to talk about what had happened, to try to expel it from my brain. But instead, I'd suffered in silence.

Meanwhile my sister had been texting her new boyfriend in the next room.

"Look, I didn't know he was Admiral Appleby's grandson," Lilli protested. "I didn't even know who Admiral Appleby was back then. And I'm sure Josh never said anything, anyway. He's good at keeping secrets."

I slumped against the shipping container. "Did you tell him about Ikumi?" I asked in a low voice.

Her face turned bright red. "I mean, just a little bit."

Anger rose inside me. "Well, isn't that interesting," I shot back. "You tell Admiral Appleby's grandson about Ikumi, and suddenly Admiral Appleby kidnaps Ikumi. What a coincidence."

Lilli stared at me in horror. "No. He wouldn't have—"

But I was done. So done. "You know what, Lills? I don't want to hear any more. Why don't you go tell it to your boyfriend?"

The hurt rising inside of me was almost suffocating at this point. I needed to get away, to be alone, to think, to process all of it. My sister. My own sister preferred to talk to a complete stranger instead of me—who had been there with her for the whole thing.

"Come on, Ian!" Lilli begged.

But I had heard enough. I stalked over to Yano. "Let's go," I told him. "We need to head back to the trash mountain to jump through the world again."

Yano obediently lowered his wing. I scrambled up the side. "What are you waiting for?" I asked once I was secured.

Yano looked doubtfully at Lilli and Josh, who were still on the ground. "What about them?"

I sneered. "They've decided to spend some time alone."

"Ian!" Lilli's voice was angry now. "Don't do this."

"Already done," I declared. I grabbed on to Yano's neck. "Fly. Now."

To his credit, the dragon did as I asked, pushing off on his hind legs and leaping into the sky. Soon we were soaring over the ruined cityscape again, leaving my sister and Josh in our dust. I felt a little guilty leaving Lilli behind. Okay, I felt a *lot* guilty. But who could blame me? What she did? It was unforgivable. And it could have been the thing that put Ikumi and her father in danger to begin with.

If she wouldn't ditch Josh, I would have to ditch her.

"Faster!" I called to Yano. "As fast as you can go!"

Once again, my dragon guide obeyed, plunging forward, skimming the surface of the game world, heading straight to the trash mountain. I kept my eyes locked ahead, not looking down this time. It was still scary, but I was getting pretty used to being scared by now. Also, I was still angry. And being this angry made it difficult to be scared, too.

Finally, we got to the top of the mountain. But we didn't stop there this time. Now we knew exactly where to go, and instead of jumping, we flew straight down into the hole. Kind of like a fast pass at a theme park, dive-bombing the abyss. Still not the most pleasant feeling, to drop down like that, but at least I knew this time there was something on the other side.

Hopefully someone, too.

After flying, then floating as we had the first time around, we eventually reached our destination. Which turned out to be a completed level at this point. No more grid lines, no more unfinished patches of ground. Just a huge apocalyptic cityscape stretching out in all directions. I had to admit, they'd done a good job. It looked really cool. As long as we stayed clear of the walking dead.

Speaking of zombies... I looked up—way up at the sky-scraper we'd been trapped in earlier. The one where we left Starr stuck in a classroom, zombies crowding outside. Was she still there? I couldn't tell since we were no longer in the same party, since Lilli and I had been disconnected. But I had to find out.

"Take me to the top of that building," I instructed Yano.

"Why?" The dragon looked doubtful. "That's not the

way to go. I've been researching. I know where to go next. We need to get there as soon as possible before we glitch out again."

He had a point. But still. I had promised Starr I'd come back for her. And friends didn't leave friends behind.

"Sorry. There's something I need to do first. Don't worry—it won't take long."

Yano didn't look happy, but thankfully he complied, flapping his wings to get airborne again, then dropping down onto the rooftop. Once we'd landed, I slid off his back and patted his side.

"Wait here," I said. "I'll be right back."

"No way. I'm not leaving you alone again. Hang on."

I watched, surprised, as the dragon started to roll his heads, then his necks, in a circle, faster and faster. Until suddenly there was a puff of smoke. And when it cleared...

Yano was mini-size again, like he'd been in Dragon Ops. A tiny baby robot draconite, no bigger than a puppy. He was down to one head again, too.

"Wow!" I cried, impressed. "I forgot you could just change your shape like that."

"One of the great gifts of being an AI," he agreed. "I can appear as anything I want to be. Any size, any shape."

"If that's true, why didn't you just turn yourself microscopic and crawl out of the shipping container?" I asked curiously.

"Oh." Yano looked embarrassed. "That would have been a good plan, actually. Next time I'll do that."

I rolled my eyes. Seriously, AIs were so smart and yet sometimes the simplest steps in logic evaded them. Probably for the best, though, if humans wanted to remain in charge of the world.

"Mech Heads! I'm so glad you're here! I am in need of your help!"

I whirled around, then groaned as I spotted NPC Ikumi, all respawned in her regular spot. She looked at us beseechingly.

"Zombies have taken over the building," she cried. "I got separated from my parents and ended up here. Will you help me?"

Oh, for goodness' sakes. Not again.

"Look, we don't have time for—" I started to say.

But then my mind flashed back to Lilli's crushed expression as she held zombie Ikumi in her arms. Bleh. I groaned.

"Okay, look," I told the NPC. "I promise we'll get you to the ground. But we're not going through the building. It's too dangerous. Hang out here for a minute while we grab my friend, and we'll come back for you. Then we'll fly you to safety."

She stared at me, looking confused. "I need to get back to my mommy and daddy. They will reward you if you get me to them safely," she added.

"Great. Looking forward it." I turned to Yano. "Come on. Let's go."

I put an ear to the trapdoor to make sure there were no zombies wandering around immediately below me. Then I stuck my legs down into the hole and dropped into the now familiar hallway, Yano floating down behind me.

"Cheery place," the dragon remarked, raising two bushy gray eyebrows.

"Shh," I scolded. "We don't need to attract any more zombies than necessary."

Yano nodded. "I am in total agreement with that statement," he replied, floating a little closer to me this time.

We headed down the hall, then down the stairs, trying to retrace our original steps to get back to the room where we'd left Starr. It wasn't easy, since the layout had changed again, but after a few wrong turns, we were finally able to find the right corridor.

Unfortunately, the zombies were still outside the room, shambling and groaning about brains.

But thankfully there were fewer of them than before. Just three. The others must have gotten bored and wandered off again. Or perhaps the designer lowered the difficulty level?

Whatever it was, I'd take it.

"What are you waiting for?" Yano hissed. "Do your fighting thing already!"

Right. I raised my sword and charged toward them, using the element of surprise to my advantage. As they whirled around, I slashed sideways, cutting through two of them easily. The third, however, managed to avoid my strike, ducking low to grab me by the ankle. I flailed, losing my balance as his ragged nails dug into my skin.

"Um, a little help here, please?" I called to Yano.

"I don't think I'm actually supposed to interfere with a player's gaming experience," he replied doubtfully.

Ugh. I forgot that was part of his programming. Guides weren't supposed to help—that would be cheating. Still, we weren't in Dragon Ops anymore. Which meant the rules had changed.

"You're not a guide anymore!" I called out to him as I struggled to get free of the zombie on my leg. Its blackened teeth were hovering dangerously close to my flesh. One bite, I guessed, and I'd glitch out back to the beginning again. "You want to save Ikumi? You need to help!"

Yano nodded thoughtfully. "I suppose that makes sense. Different game, different rules."

"Exactly!" I tried to crawl out of the zombie's bite range. "And, uh, anytime now would be great!"

"All right, all right. Don't get your knickers in a twist! Here I come!"

The pint-size dragon swooped down, his talons locking on to the zombie's hair, yanking its head up and keeping its teeth away from my skin. Bringing my free foot back, I kicked hard, connecting with the zombie's skull. It caved in like a rotten pumpkin, and the creature writhed for a moment, then went still. Yano let go of what remained of its head. It splatted on the hallway floor, oozing with black blood.

"Sweet," I said, scrambling to my feet. "Nice work, Yano."

The dragon looked surprised. "Thank you," he said. "That was actually kind of fun."

I shook my sore leg. "Maybe for you," I muttered. But I was pleased all the same. With Yano and Starr on my side, maybe I didn't need Lilli after all.

Speaking of Starr...I turned to the door. "Starr!" I cried as I pushed it open. "Are you in there?"

"Hey!" she cried, leaping to her feet. She'd been evidently hanging out reading a book she'd found. "You came back! I was beginning to think you were gone for good!"

"I'm so sorry," I said. "We glitched out and got sent back to the beginning. I came back as soon as I could." I didn't want to admit we'd taken a little power nap in between.

"No worries," she assured me. "When I realized you'd disconnected, I waited for a while. When you didn't come back, I figured I'd take a little break. I took off my helmet but left the game on so my character would be there when you got back. Then I took a nap, grabbed some food. I actually only came back online a few moments ago."

"Yeah, well, my mom turned off the game," I told her. "Totally blew up our progress and sent us back to the beginning. You're lucky you stayed logged in." Then my smile faded as I thought back to what happened after we'd been logged out. "Did, uh, anyone show up at your house while you were back in the real world?"

"Just the pizza guy," Starr said. Then she laughed, misinterpreting my look. "I know, I know. It's weird to order pizza for breakfast. But gaming makes me hungry." She looked behind me. "Where's your sister?"

"Don't ask," I muttered, my mind flashing back to Lilli and Josh. What had they done after I left them? Were they still playing the game, or had they gotten bored and logged off? Maybe they decided to go to soccer camp after all. Where Lilli could spill her guts to him once again. Tell her new boyfriend everything so he could run back and tattle to his grandpa.

I sighed. Why did everything have to be so complicated?

"I don't think we've been introduced," Yano piped in, flying over to Starr and stretching out his paw. "My name is Yamata-no-Orochi, the three-headed dragon of legend." He shook her hand. "But you can call me Yano for short."

"Nice to meet you, Yano," Starr said, looking him over with admiration. "Are you any relation to that amazing huge dragon Ian was riding earlier?"

"I *am* that amazing huge dragon," Yano replied, puffing

out his chest with pride. "Well, at least when it's practical to be."

"Nice," Starr said. Then she turned to me. "Where do you get this guy, again? Is he, like, a hack? There's no way he's from the real game, right?"

"Well, not exactly," I admitted. "He's kind of a special mod. But he does come in handy."

"I bet." Starr headed to the door. "So, where to next?"

I bit my lower lip, observing her eager expression. I realized I needed to come clean with her—at least as clean as possible—if she was going to continue gaming with us. Otherwise she could find herself involved in something dangerous. It wasn't fair not to prepare her for that possibility.

"You know how I asked if anyone showed up to your house?" I started. "Well, someone did show up to ours." I briefly told her about the men at our door, demanding their VR rigs. How we escaped via zip line.

"Wow," Starr exclaimed when I had finished. "That's crazy. Why didn't they just disable your account? Why come after you in real life?"

I shrugged. "Maybe they wanted their equipment back before letting us know they were onto us?" I guessed. "I have no idea. Anyway, I wanted you to know before you agreed to keep on playing with us. I know you're excited about exploring the game. But exploring with us could disqualify you completely."

Or worse... I thought but didn't say.

"Right." Starr nodded. "Well, peace out, then. It's been real." She started toward the door.

My heart sank. She was leaving. I'd really hoped she'd stay. "Yeah," I said. "It was really nice playing with you…"

She turned and started laughing.

"What?" I asked, totally confused.

"I'm just messing with you," she declared. "You should see your face!" She gave me a wide smirk. "Come on, Ian. You think I'm actually going to bail on you now? When things are finally getting interesting?" Her eyes flashed with excitement, and relief flooded through me.

"I guess not," I said.

"Trust me, I'm in. I'm definitely in," she declared. "However, from now on, you need to be straight with me. What are we really doing here? Why are they after you? And don't give me that silly story about your uncle wanting a job. I'm not stupid."

"I know," I said. "And I'm sorry I haven't told you the truth." I was, too. I mean, why keep secrets from Starr, who could actually help us, while Lilli spilled her guts to the literal enemy's grandson? "I promise I'll tell you everything. But first, let's get out of here before the zombies get back."

"Good idea," she agreed. "Hopefully the staircases are all assembled by this point."

"Actually, we don't need stairs," I said with a grin. "We've got our own personal air dragon, remember?"

"Oh, right." Starr shot an appreciative look at Yano. "You definitely come in handy."

"I do indeed," Yano agreed, puffing out with pride. "You should see me in battle." He fluffed out his wings. "Shall we head straight out the window?"

"Actually, back to the roof," I replied. "I've got a quick quest to finish."

CHAPTER THIRTY-TWO

We ran out into the hallway, past the dead zombies, and up the stairs. When we reached the trapdoor in the roof, Starr used her wings to fly up through it, then leaned down to give me a hand up. With her help, I scrambled onto the roof (I really needed to get a pair of those wings for myself!), and Yano shot up behind me.

Once he was in open air again, the dragon poofed back to full cyber-dragon size. Which was still rather impressive. Not that I'd ever admit it to him, for fear it'd go to his already oversized three heads.

Starr, however, did not hold back her awe. "Wow, wow, wow!" she cried, flying around the dragon. "You're almost as cool as Atreus from Dragon Ops."

I flinched at the *A* word, then turned away quickly,

hoping Starr and Yano didn't notice. Thankfully, Yano was too busy being offended by the unintended slight.

"Almost? You insult me, madam!" Yano huffed. Blinking his eyes, he added a rainbow sheen to his metal scales. It was so bright, it was almost blinding. "I'll have you know I am at least ten degrees cooler than that poor excuse for an AI. Not to mention I am smart, loyal, and always follow my programming."

"And very handsome," Starr assured him, making Yano's three heads blush in sync.

I rolled my eyes. "You're going to ruin him," I warned.

"Mech Heads! I'm so glad you're here! I am in need of your help!"

NPC Ikumi appeared beside us, wringing her hands in dismay. I smiled at her, trying to look reassuring.

"We're here to help," I told her. "But we're not going through the building. It's far too dangerous. We are going to fly you down."

"Zombies have taken over the building," she replied, as if she hadn't heard a word I said. "I got separated from my parents and ended up here. Will you help me?"

"Yes. Get on the dragon and we will," I told her, feeling a little exasperated.

"They will reward you if you get me to them safely," she added, glancing meaningfully over at the trapdoor.

"I'm trying to! You're not exactly helping!"

Starr put a hand on my shoulder. "I don't think she understands you," she told me. "Some game characters don't have a lot of range. They're programmed for one scenario only. For her, that's to go down into the building and lead you through a zombie maze."

"That's so depressing," I said, feeling my stomach sink. I thought back to how hard Lilli had worked to save her. But for what? It meant nothing.

It was just a game.

"If it makes you feel any better, she's got a great story line," Yano piped in. "Once you rescue her, her parents will take you to the resistance. There, you'll come up with a plan to liberate the city from zombies. It's a huge quest chain, and from what I can see in the game developer notes, NPC Ikumi is meant to survive. In fact, she becomes queen of the Human City, which is what this place will be known as someday. She's kind, fair, and tough. The people love her."

"I guess that's good," I said reluctantly. "I still hate leaving her up here."

"She's a computer program," Yano reminded me. "We don't really have the same sense of time as you do. She'll be fine hanging out here until the game officially launches. And then she'll have more rescuers than she knows what to do with." He laughed. "Well, not really, since that's what she's programmed to know."

"I guess you're right," I said. "And anyway, we've got a real rescue to make. Come on."

I climbed on the dragon's back, still feeling a little bad about NPC Ikumi. She was standing there by herself, looking so upset. But I forced myself to shake my head and remember my real mission. The real Ikumi. She was waiting for us. And she did have a sense of time and place. Two years she'd been stuck in a video game. And now she was trapped all over again. The sooner we got to her, the better.

Starr climbed on behind me, looking a little nervous. "Does this thing have seat belts?" she asked, searching the dragon's sides.

"Not exactly—" I started to say. But Yano interrupted.

"I can make some," he said. He closed his eyes. When he opened them again, two matching metal safety belts appeared on his back.

"What?" I cried, unable to believe it. "You couldn't have done that last time?"

"I could have. You just never asked."

After we clicked into our belts, Yano sprang off the ground with his hind legs. Starr yelped, gripping me tighter as we launched into the air full force. Soon we were high in the sky, the only sound Yano's wings flapping in the wind. I waited for that familiar sick feeling to roll through my stomach, but for some reason I felt okay. Maybe I was finally getting used to this. Or maybe it was just the seat belts.

"This is amazing!" Starr cried from behind me. "Dragon riding! Woo-hoo!"

"You want me to have him do a barrel roll?" I teased.

Starr gripped me tighter. "Not if you want to live till your next birthday," she said with a nervous laugh. Then she poked me in the back. "Now. You were going to tell me your real mission, remember? So get talking."

"Oh right." Geez—where to even begin?

After a few false starts, I finally managed to get the story out. About Ikumi and her whole brain emulation procedure to keep her mind alive after her body had died. About her father keeping her digital copy in the game and then letting her out at our request. About their sudden disappearance and about the distress signal Yano had brought to us, proving she'd been kidnapped and was once again trapped in a video game against her will. Though this time by real bad guys and not her dad.

"So now we just have to find her in the game and break her out," I explained. "Before Admiral Appleby can do... well, whatever it is he plans to do to her."

I couldn't see Starr's face since she was behind me. But when she spoke, her voice sounded troubled. "That's an insane story," she said after a moment. "I mean, I knew Admiral Appleby was a little eccentric—a little weird. But actually evil? That just doesn't feel right."

"What do you mean?" I asked, surprised.

"I don't know. It's just—for one thing, he treats his employees really well. Not like those other tech companies who make them work, like, twenty-four seven. He gives them a great living wage and full health benefits, too. Even the part-timers and the custodial crew," Starr explained. "I researched all this when trying to find out more for the beta test. Everyone who's ever worked for him has nothing but nice things to say. And then there's his charity work, of course. You must know about that."

I groaned. Charity work? Our evil mastermind was starting to sound like a saint. "What charity work?" I asked.

"Well, for one thing, he founded this special gaming league for people with disabilities," Starr explained. "You know, like the Special Olympics, but with video games instead of sports? That's how I found out about him and Mech Ops to begin with. Admiral Appleby likes to say games are a great equalizer. We may not be able to run in real life. But we can fly in his games." I could hear the pride in her voice.

"Wow," I said. "That's pretty amazing, actually."

"Exactly," Yano suddenly broke in, surprising me. I hadn't realized he was listening. "*Sounds* really amazing. Nice, kind, giving. Which, of course, is the perfect cover for an evil mastermind, isn't it? Allows him to throw you off track, make you not suspect what he's truly up to. A girl like Ikumi is worth billions—maybe even trillions. But, hey, throw a few bucks toward charity, and everyone will look the other way."

"Right." I guessed that made sense. Though it was kind of disappointing. Couldn't anyone just be a good human for the sake of being a good human these days? Why did people all have to be so terrible? "Well, whatever. Good guy, bad guy. We need to find Ikumi. Then we can figure the rest out."

"Now you're talking!" Yano agreed. "And just in time, too. Hang on to your helmets! We're about to enter the wormhole."

Uh, what?

"Wormhole?" I repeated, suddenly a little nervous. "What's a wormhole?" I prayed it didn't involve actual worms. I'd seen enough of those back in Dragon Ops, thank you very much, when we fought Wyrm, this giant earth dragon with a lot of squirmy wormy babies.

"A wormhole is like a tube that connects two different parts of the game," the dragon explained. "It's a way to fast travel, really."

Oh. Of course. I felt like an idiot. Big games like Mech Ops always had a way to fast travel. Otherwise you'd end up spending your entire time traveling from one area to another.

"Cool," I said.

"I found it while I was waiting for you lot to come back," Yano explained, still sounding a bit bitter about being locked up in the shipping container so long. "I went in and hacked the mapping software, basically GPSing the best way to get to Ikumi based on her location in the video. We should reach her general area in four jumps. From there, we should be able to locate her and hopefully break her out."

In other words, we were close. Maybe really close. A thrill of excitement wound through me. I imagined Ikumi's face when we showed up. How excited she'd be to see us. She must be so scared in there, all alone. But not for long. Not with Lord Wildhammer and Lady Starr on the job!

"Whoa!" Starr cried. "Is that it? Is that the hole?"

I looked up, surprised to see a glittering field of stars rushing toward us at breakneck speed. (Or were we rushing toward them?) They were so bright, it felt like looking into the sun, and I had to close my eyes as we approached. I felt this weird shimmer in my stomach, as if I'd turned upside down, though I was definitely still right side up.

And then for a moment, there was nothing. Just blackness as far as the eye could see. I swallowed hard. The vast emptiness was almost as terrifying as the robot spiders.

"One more moment," Yano promised. "We're almost through."

It was then that I saw the light. Just like when we first entered the game. Just a pinprick at first. Then growing larger and larger and—

BOOM!

We broke through the wormhole, bursting into a new portion of the game. Wow.

"Okay, that was pretty awesome," Starr declared behind me. "Nice work, robot dragon."

"I aim to please," Yano replied. "Now, just three more of those to go."

I groaned. "I was afraid you were going to say that."

CHAPTER THIRTY-THREE

I'm not going to tell you it was a pleasant journey. But we did eventually make it, coming out of our fourth wormhole and into a strange new world. But unlike the worlds we'd seen before—ruined cityscapes, zombie-infested forests—this world seemed to be made entirely out of stars. As if we'd been dropped into outer space or the middle of a gigantic Christmas display. Everywhere we looked, there were dazzling, softly lit sparks of illumination that you just wanted to scoop up like piles of snow and scatter to the wind.

"So beautiful," Starr whispered. And she wasn't wrong. The whole place was just magical, and there was even music playing in the background. Soft and ethereal, like the kind of music you'd hear on my mom's yoga videos. It filled me with a sense of peace and tranquility.

"What is this place?" I asked. "Another unfinished level?"

"It's a prison," Yano replied gravely. "Ikumi's prison."

"If this is a prison, I'd love to see a castle," Starr marveled.

As if on cue, a great wall rose up in front of us, seeming to come out of nowhere. It was made of what looked like sheets of shining metal, climbing high into the sky until it met a huge dome of more sparkling stars. At the front was a translucent gate, flanked on either side by huge twin statues—at least forty feet tall—of Rocky the Robot.

Whoa.

Yano came down for a landing in front of the gate. Up close I could see it had no handles, no doorknobs. Its surface was sleek and slick, as if it were a mirror of some kind, and I could see my reflection peering at me as I slid off the dragon's back and approached it.

"How do we get through it?" I asked aloud. For some reason I knew Ikumi must be on the other side of this gate. But how to get to her?

Before anyone could answer, the mirror rippled. Like the surface of a quiet pond disturbed by someone throwing a stone. My reflection vanished. And in its place?

Ikumi.

Oh my gosh, it was Ikumi! The real Ikumi.

She looked different than when I'd seen her last. Her hair was no longer wildly colored, but rather jet-black and hanging down her back in twin braids. She was dressed plainly, too, in a simple white T-shirt and blue jeans, which seemed super out of place in this futuristic game. Also, there was no longer glitter spinning in her pupils. Instead, her eyes were large and dark...and worried.

"Ikumi!" I cried, running toward her. I slammed into the mirror headfirst, bouncing backward and almost losing my balance in the process. Rubbing my sore forehead, I squinted at the gate. Was it like a TV screen or something? Or was Ikumi really there, really standing behind the gate, looking out at me?

"Ikumi!" I cried again, desperate for her to hear me. "Mirai?" I corrected myself with a whisper, using her real-life name. The one she only revealed once she realized she could trust me.

Her eyes shifted, falling onto me. Then they widened, her mouth dropping to a large *O*. She pressed her palm flat up against the gate. With trembling fingers, I matched her hand with my own.

"Is that her?" Starr asked, coming up to stand next to me. "Is that Hiro's daughter?"

I nodded, my eyes still glued on Ikumi. "We're here to rescue you," I told her, wondering if she could hear me. At least maybe she could read my lips?

But she only looked at me with confusion on her face. She clearly didn't understand.

Rage flared inside me. How could someone do this to her? She was good. She was kind and brave and selfless—ready to sacrifice herself to save her friends! And now this monster Admiral Appleby had taken her away? Stolen her freedom? Put her in a cage? And for what? Some stupid, selfish plan to live forever? Or something else entirely?

Whatever it was, it wasn't fair. Ikumi had suffered too much already.

I slammed my fist against the glass. Over and over again. Ikumi watched me from the other side, her sad face transforming into one of horror. She stepped back a little, as if afraid. Maybe she still didn't realize it was me?

"Ian, stop!" Starr cried, grabbing my hand midswing before I could smash the glass again. It came away bloody and bruised. "It's just a video screen. She's not really there."

I dropped my hand, the fight going out of me. She was right. I was being stupid. "How do we get through the gate?" I demanded, stalking over to Yano. "How do we get her out?"

"I don't know," our guide admitted, all three of his heads looking sad. "She seems to be behind some kind of very complex firewall. I've been trying to hack it, but I'm not powerful enough. We'd need a lot more computing power to even have a chance." He paused, looking pensive. "Maybe you could ask her to help? Maybe if we combined our strength?"

"Maybe," I agreed, hope surging through me. I returned to the gate. Met Ikumi's eyes with my own, hoping she could hear or understand somehow.

"Ikumi," I said. "Yano is trying to get you out. Can you help him? Can you try to hack the gate together?"

But Ikumi only looked at us with more confusion in her eyes. Couldn't she understand what we were trying to do?

I closed my eyes, frustration rushing through me. We were so close. And yet, were we any better off than we had been at the beginning of the game? I thought if we just reached her we could figure out a way to get her free. That Yano would be able to do some kind of awesome AI trick to hack the game. But evidently not so much.

Suddenly, my menu screen flashed, indicating an incoming call. When I clicked to accept it, I realized it was Lilli. I wondered how she was able to locate me off-grid. Then I remembered: Josh.

"What do you want?" I asked, trying to sound still angry. Truth be told, however, I was kind of relieved. We were stuck. Maybe Lilli could help somehow.

"Look, I know you're still mad, okay?" Lilli's voice broke in. "And I'm sorry. I really am. I promise to make it up to you later. But right now, we've got an idea."

"We?" I repeated, a little bitterly.

I could hear her groan. "Yes. Me and Josh. We have an idea on how to get to Ikumi."

"Actually, we're already with her," I replied, suddenly realizing she wouldn't know.

"Wait, you are? That's awesome!" Lilli exclaimed, sounding surprised. "Is she okay?"

"I don't know," I confessed. "She's stuck behind a firewall or something. We can see her, but we can't get her out."

I could hear Lilli talking to Josh, explaining the situation. Then, she came back on the line. "Okay, Josh has an idea."

I wanted to tell her that I didn't care what Josh's ideas were. But a sharp look from Starr reminded me that this would be childish. We needed all the help we could get. Even Josh's.

"What is it?" I asked reluctantly.

Josh came on the line. "Remember I told you about my grandpa's secret Fortress of Solitude?"

"Yeah. What does that have to do with Ikumi?"

"You said she's trapped behind a firewall, right? Which means you need a key." He paused, then added, "Well, that's where Grandpa keeps all the keys."

My heart started beating faster in my chest. Keys. Oh my gosh. Of course! We wouldn't need to hack the gate if we had the keys.

Suddenly I kind of loved Josh.

"Where is it?" I asked, trying not to sound too excited. "Can we meet you there?"

"I'll send the coordinates to your map," he said. "We'll head there, too."

And with that, the comm blinked off. I turned to Starr. "What do you think?" I asked.

"It beats banging your fist against a gate," she pointed out wryly.

I glanced over at the gate in question. Ikumi still stood there on the other side, looking worried. I walked back over to the glass, pressing my hand against it again.

"Just hang tight," I told her. "I'm going to go get a key. Then we'll come back for you and let you out."

But instead of looking hopeful, Ikumi just looked terrified. And before I could say anything else, the glass whirled with smoke.

And when it cleared again? She was no longer there.

CHAPTER THIRTY-FOUR

I t took an annoying amount of time to get to Josh's grandfather's place. In fact it seemed to be on the other end of the world from Ikumi's prison. We had to go through several more wormholes and fly across huge stretches of game world, much of it unfinished. And then, finally, across a virtual ocean so vast I wasn't sure at one point if Josh had just been trolling us and leading us in the entirely wrong direction.

But at last a large island came into view. In its center stood a huge fortress shaped like a medieval castle, with imposing stone walls rising high into the sky. As we swooped in closer, I spotted Josh and Lilli out front, playing soccer. Which made me way angrier than it should have. I mean, what did I want them to be doing? Twiddling their thumbs this whole time?

"Finally," Josh declared as we came in for a landing in front of them. "What took you so long?"

"Oh, nothing. Just had to cross the entire game world to get here," I said, sliding off Yano's back. I sure hoped Josh was right about the keys and this hadn't been a wasted trip. We were farther away from Ikumi than ever now.

"Hey Starr!" Lilli exclaimed. "Glad you made it out of zombieland."

"Thanks to Ian, here," Starr replied, slapping me on the back. She looked up at the castle. Way up. "So this is your grandpa's secret Fortress of Solitude?" she asked Josh, letting out a low whistle. "He got something against a simple cabin by the lake?"

"Actually, yes," Josh replied. "I mean, at least a real-world one. He doesn't feel comfortable in the real world these days." He shrugged. "I suppose being almost assassinated will do that to a guy."

"He was almost assassinated?" I blurted out before I could stop myself. "When?"

Josh dribbled the soccer ball between his feet. Where had he found that, anyway? Or did he mod it himself? I hadn't thought to ask him if he had the capability and passwords to make changes to the game. Probably something I should have considered before ditching him and my sister earlier.

"It was a long time ago," Josh explained. "Back when

he used to go to gaming conventions. At the time, he'd just released his new game, *Wild West*, and evidently some of its players didn't like that he'd given a lot of the good story lines to female characters."

"So they shot him?" Lilli asked, incredulous. "Over game story lines?"

"I know, right?" Josh agreed. "He had to spend weeks in the hospital. I was only a little kid at the time, so I didn't know the whole story till way later. I just knew someone hated my grandfather so much they wanted to kill him." He scowled. "Which is ridiculous, by the way. I mean, I know my grandpa is weird and all. The whole fake admiral thing and the uniform—it's totally embarrassing. But he's a good guy, deep down. He cares about people. He's worked his whole life to help people and make them happy."

"Wow. That's really..." I trailed off, not knowing the word I was looking for. *Fascinating*? *Horrifying*? *Confusing*—maybe? After all, the man Josh was describing—that Starr described earlier—didn't sound like the monster who would kidnap a young girl for his own selfish gain. Was there something Josh didn't know about his grandfather? Or something *we* didn't know about the kidnapping? Could Admiral Appleby be innocent? Maybe it was one of his employees who had kidnapped Ikumi. After all, Hiro had no idea Eugene was sabotaging Dragon Ops. Could something similar be going on here?

"I think the word you're looking for is *inconsequential*," Yano interrupted, looking impatient. "Ikumi is waiting for us out there. That's all that matters in the end."

I turned to him, surprised—and a little guilty. "You're right," I said. "Let's go inside." I started toward the door, Yano on my heels.

"Not the dragon," Josh said suddenly, stepping in front of Yano.

"What? Why not?" Yano burst out, looking quite offended. "I'm part of the team."

"Sorry. Players only. Grandpa has very strict perimeters of what can enter and leave through this door. You take one step inside, and you'll be obliterated by his digital sentries." He shrugged and added, "I mean, your choice, of course."

Yano flapped his wings, looking extremely annoyed. "Well, I suppose I shall wait out here, then. But, Ian and Lilli—you be careful going into the belly of the beast like this. I will be here if you need me."

"We'll be fine," I assured him, patting him on the side. Though I was admittedly a little nervous. Yano was right— this was the belly of the beast, and we had no idea what might be waiting for us on the other side. What if we were walking into a trap?

But we had little choice. We couldn't break Ikumi out ourselves. We needed those keys. And so I followed Josh up to the fortress's front door. I watched as he dialed in a code at the door and it swung open easily.

Here went nothing.

Starr stepped through the door first. Or halfway through the door, anyway, before she stopped short. "Whoa!" she exclaimed. "Are you kidding me right now?" I scurried to follow her in, eager to see what had her so freaked out.

"Oh my gosh," I breathed, looking around once I'd stepped up beside her. "This is...incredible."

I'd expected something cool. I mean, this was the game maker's personal playground, after all. It had to be top-of-the-line. But even in my wildest imagination I could never have imagined something like this.

For so long we'd been wandering through an apocalyptic future—complete with death, destruction, decay. But here in Admiral Appleby's private sanctum, it was like we'd stumbled into the Garden of Eden. Everywhere we looked there was a breathtaking rain forest of exotic plants, waterfalls, and sparkling pools filled with koi fish. I knew, on some level, it wasn't real—it was just really good programming. But it was so wild and colorful and overgrown that if you'd told me I had stepped into a real-life jungle? I would have agreed without question.

Just then something rumbled in the bushes behind me. I turned to find a baby chimpanzee hanging from a nearby banana plant, giving me a grumpy look. I watched as he plucked a bright pink banana from a branch and began to peel it, keeping a wary eye on the intruders the whole time.

"Aw," Lilli cooed, coming up next to me. "Look how cute he is!"

Josh walked over to the chimp, plucking him from his perch and letting him climb onto his shoulder. "This is Mr. Donkey Kong," he said. "My grandpa's pet."

"Is he...real?" I asked, squinting at the creature.

Josh beamed. "Yup. Or he's the avatar of a real chimp anyway, back at HQ. He was one of our first beta testers. Grandpa wanted to see if the world was real enough for actual animals to believe in it."

"Wow," I said, reaching out to pet Mr. Donkey Kong. He was softer than I'd imagined, and he chirped happily as I scratched behind his ear. "So cool."

"So cool!" the monkey agreed happily.

Josh laughed. "Oh yeah. The game allows him to talk, too. Isn't that great? He loves to be able to communicate with his voice instead of sign language like back in the real world."

I shook my head, unbelieving. This was so awesome. It was really hard to see it as a castle of evil. There had to be someone else behind this whole thing. There just had to be!

I turned to find Starr, to see what she thought of all of this. But she had already wandered off and was now standing inside a small hut with a computer inside of it.

"Oh wow. This is a TX500!" she marveled. "I always wanted to try one of these." She set her hands on the keyboard, pressing a few buttons.

"No!" Josh cried. "Don't touch that!"

But it was too late. "Rain Forest Simulation terminated," stated a voice that sounded remarkably like Rocky the Robot. "Loading: Simulation Space."

In an instant, the rain forest fell away. Like someone had flicked a switch. No more jungle, no more birds, no more sparkling pools and waterfalls.

Instead, we were floating in a vast vacuum of space. Mr. Donkey Kong flailed his arms, looking panicked. "ARR!" he croaked. "Space bad! Go back!"

"Agreed," Josh said, cradling the chimp protectively in his arms. "You mind switching us back? It's going to be super hard to find our key while we're stuck in zero G."

"Sorry!" Starr called from inside the hut. (Yes, the hut was still there, though now it looked more like a space pod.) "I've got you!" She tapped on the keyboard again.

We dropped like stones, no longer in zero gravity. I hit the ground hard—butt first, though, so thankfully it didn't hurt. Mr. Donkey Kong squawked more disapproval. He clearly wasn't impressed.

"No more messing with the computer," I scolded Starr as I scrambled to my feet. I rubbed my eyes, then looked around, expecting to be back in the rain forest.

But we weren't. Not even close.

"Oh my gosh," Lilli whispered beside me. Her eyes were as huge as mine probably were. "Ian? Are you seeing what I'm seeing?"

I didn't answer at first. *Couldn't* answer. My heart pounded in my chest as I looked around, taking in all the familiar sights. The pub. The inn. The thatch-roofed cottages and cobblestone streets. Shops packed with adventuring supplies and weapons. A bakery on the corner overflowing with crusty breads and pink and purple unicorn cakes.

"What is this place?" Starr asked, wandering out from the hut, which had now been transformed into a magical potions shop.

"It's Dragon Ops," Lilli said, her voice awed. "Admiral Appleby has recreated Dragon Ops!"

CHAPTER THIRTY-FIVE

She was right. I couldn't believe it, but she was right. The world was an exact replica of Dragonshire, the starting village in the game. I could see the Dragon's Yawn Inn. The blacksmith shop where the troll had chased me after I accidentally dropped one of his swords. And on the hill in the distance, towering wooden fences rose, meeting at a central gate made of two iron plates and finished with something that looked almost—but not quite—like the Dragon Ops seal, along with the all-too-familiar words: HIC SUNT DRACONES.

Here be dragons.

"Why on earth is this here?" Lilli asked, walking down the street and back again, touching everything. "Did Appleby steal the design from Hiro?"

"What are you talking about?" Josh asked, looking genuinely puzzled. "This is Dragon World. My grandpa designed this. It's based on an old role-playing game he used to run back in college. Way before Dragon Ops, or even the first *Fields of Fantasy*."

"But it looks just like Dragon Ops," I argued, walking over and grabbing a unicorn cake from the bakery and turning it over in my hands.

"Well, maybe they stole the idea off my grandpa," Josh shot back. "Because I promise you, this was first. He used to take me in here when I was a little kid. I'm not lying!" he added, catching my face.

"We know," Lilli assured him. Because of course she was on his side. "It's just weird is all. This village—that gate. Everything's almost exactly the same."

"Hey! Maybe that's what started this whole thing," Starr interjected. "Like, maybe Hiro Takanama stole Admiral Appleby's design when creating Dragon Ops. And then Admiral Appleby found out, and he retaliated by kidnapping Hiro's daughter!"

Josh stopped short. He turned around, staring at Starr, his face awash with confusion.

"Kidnapped?" he repeated slowly. "What do you mean, kidnapped?"

Starr glanced nervously at me. "Um..."

"Also, Hiro's daughter?" Josh continued in a deadly

serious voice. "You mean Mirai? She's dead. She died, like, almost three years ago."

Fear thrummed through my heart. I glanced over at Lilli. Her face had gone stark white.

Oh no.

"Excuse us for a moment," Lilli said. She grabbed me by the arm, dragging me out of earshot. "What did you tell Starr?" she hissed at me once we were away from the others.

"Um, just…everything?" I sputtered. "But you told Josh first!" I added. I mean, didn't she? Oh man. This was not good. Not good at all.

Josh stormed over to the two of us. "She *told* me someone named Ikumi was missing," he spit out. "That she'd gotten lost in the game and had stumbled into an area she couldn't get out of." His frown deepened. "She never said anything about *kidnapping*. Or Mirai."

"O-oh." Starr stammered. "I think I misunderstood? I meant—"

"You meant what you said," Josh interrupted, whirling to face her. "You think my poor grandfather—the nicest man you'll ever meet in your life—kidnapped Hiro's dead daughter? That doesn't even make any sense!"

I cringed. No. It didn't. Not without us explaining what Ikumi really was. Would he even believe us if we tried? Either way, he wasn't going to buy the fact that his precious grandfather was actually an evil kidnapper who wanted to steal the technology so he could gain eternal life.

"Josh—" Lilli tried.

But he cut her off. "No. I'm not going to listen to this anymore. I'm out of here. And I'm going to go tell my grandpa exactly what you're up to. So you'd better log out now and never log back in. Or you'll wish you never heard the name Mech Ops."

I watched as he waved his hands in the air, conjuring up a big blue sphere. Above the sphere read the command SAVE GAME AND LOG OUT. He clicked on the sphere, and it burst into a big white flame. Then it...and Josh...disappeared.

"Well, doesn't he have all the cool toys," Starr muttered.

Lilli stared at the spot where he'd disappeared. She gave out a small moan. "What are we going to do?"

"See? I told you not to trust him!" I shot back, fury rising inside of me. If she hadn't insisted on dragging him along in the first place, none of this would be happening.

"It was fine! Until you spilled your guts to Starr!" Lilli shot back.

"What was I supposed to do? You were too busy with your new boyfriend! I needed help!"

"He's not my boyfriend, Ian."

"Really? Is that your only response?"

"Enough!" Starr broke in. "Seriously. You guys need to focus. It doesn't matter who's to blame. What matters is

Josh has gone to tell his grandfather what we're doing. And they're going to kick us out of the game. So if you want to rescue your friend, you'd better do it fast."

Lilli and I glared at each other. Still fuming. But deep down, we knew Starr was right. We could fight about who was to blame later. Right now, Ikumi was running out of time.

"So what do we do?" Lilli asked. "Keep looking for the key? We'll never find it without Josh."

"We have no choice. We have to open that gate. Yano can't do it. He's not powerful enough to—"

Suddenly, I heard a screech echo through the air. My gaze shot up into the sky. Oh no. Not again! My heart plummeted as my eyes fell on the all-too-familiar dragon-shaped silhouette flying in circles above us.

"Whoa!" Lilli cried. "This game has an Atreus, too? Someone really did copy someone else. I just wish I knew who was first."

"Wait," I said. "You can see him?"

"Of course I can see him. What are you talking about? He's right there."

"Starr?" I turned to our friend. "Can you see him, too?"

"Definitely," she said. "He's kind of hard to miss."

My knees felt weak, and I had to lean against a nearby building to stay upright. I didn't know whether to be relieved—or more freaked out. At least I knew this Atreus was not part of my imagination.

But what about the other one? Was this the same creature that had been following me? Or another rendition—a second Atreus who may or may not have been the original? (This was all so confusing!)

The dragon swooped down, skimming the rooftops of Dragonshire until he landed on the top of the Dragon's Yawn Inn. And, well, yawned. Go figure.

"Do you think we should, like, run or something?" Lilli suggested. "I mean, fire-breathing bad guy? Standing in his path and all that?"

"Or we could fight him," Starr said excitedly. "Imagine the cred you'd get for taking down Atreus."

"No way!" my sister cried. "We wouldn't stand a chance." She turned to me. "Ian?" she asked. "Are…you okay?"

But I wasn't okay. I wasn't even close to being okay. The dragon was looking straight at me. His lips curled into a smile, revealing his razor-sharp teeth.

Well, hello, tiny human. Welcome to Dragon Ops.

"Go away," I whimpered, my voice so low I could barely hear it myself. "Just please go away."

The dragon's smile faded. He looked almost disappointed. *Now, now! I just want to play a game…*

"Why won't you just leave me alone?"

"Ian?"

I could hear my sister, but she sounded a million miles away. Barely audible over the hammer of my heartbeat. The dragon's amber eyes seemed to pierce through me. A now deeper voice rumbling from inside.

Don't you want to play a game?

DON'T YOU WANT TO PLAY A GAME?

"NO!" I shouted, finally finding my voice. "I do not want to freaking play!"

And with that, I took off running in the direction we came from. Somehow I managed to find the exit, and I yanked the door open. The illusion shattered behind me, hopefully taking Atreus with it. I dove out the door and back onto the island where Yano was waiting for us. Collapsing, I dug my hands into the sand, wanting to feel something real. Even though all of it was still an illusion.

"Are you all right?" Yano asked, sounding extremely concerned. "What happened in there? I told you it wasn't safe!" He paused, then added, "Did you get the key at least?"

Before I could respond, Lilli and Starr burst from the building, running up beside me. Lilli dropped to her knees, her face pale with worry. "What happened?" she demanded. "Are you okay?"

I tried to suck in a breath, but my game lungs refused to work. I started gasping, clawing at the sand, trying not to choke. Starr put a hand on my back, lowering her face so it was inches from mine.

"Breathe in," she whispered. "Slowly."

I did as she said. Barely.

"Now hold that breath for three seconds," she instructed. "Then let it out. Then take another breath and hold."

I followed her instructions exactly, even though at first it was nearly impossible to hold the breath. The second time was easier. By the third, I'd gotten it back under control. I collapsed onto the sand, looking up at Starr in gratitude. "Thank you," I whispered.

Lilli looked from me to Starr. "What's going on?" she demanded. "What happened in there?"

I shook my head. "Nothing. I'm fine."

"You don't look fine."

"Well, I am, okay?" My face burned with embarrassment. I didn't want her to know how pathetic I was. My sister, who was so strong...

Though...

Suddenly Lilli's earlier words came rushing back to me. *Josh found me under the bleachers during gym class, crying...*

I'd been so mad at the time that she'd been talking to Josh, I hadn't taken a moment to consider *why* she'd been talking to him.

That *she'd* been suffering, too. But never letting on.

I looked up at Lilli. "Why don't we ever talk about what happened in Dragon Ops?" I whispered, then added, "With each other, I mean."

Her cheeks turned bright pink. "I—I don't know," she stammered. "We signed those papers and—"

"If the papers meant anything to you, you wouldn't have told Josh," I said accusingly. "So why don't you want to talk about it with *me*?" My voice cracked on the words. "I mean, I was the one who was there with you! We went through it together!"

"I know. It's just…" She trailed off, looking miserable.

But I couldn't stop now. The floodgates had been opened, and emotion was rushing through me hard and fast. "Do you know what it's been like for me?" I demanded. "I've been going crazy. Waking up from nightmares in a cold sweat. Having visions of Atreus everywhere I go. And all this time, I thought you were fine. That you had moved on, no big deal. And I was the only one suffering. Do you know how that feels?"

"I'm sorry!" Lilli cried. "I'm so sorry. It's just… I'm your big sister; I didn't want you to know what a mess I was inside. I thought it would make it worse for you. But trust me—I have nightmares all the time. Maybe I don't see Atreus like you do, but I still think about him. The way he blasted you with his fire. That moment I thought you were dead." She cringed. "I still wake up in a cold sweat and run to your room to make sure you're okay in real life."

"You do?" I asked, incredulous. I closed my eyes, trying to picture Lilli waking up as scared as I was. "I had no idea." All this time, I thought I'd been suffering alone. But she'd been suffering, too. Silently, like me. Both of us afraid to tell the other what we were feeling.

"I didn't want you to know. I knew you were having a hard time, and I was trying to be strong for you. For both of us, I guess. The last thing I wanted was for you to think you were in this alone. 'Cause you're not, Ian. You are definitely not."

Relief washed over me like a tidal wave. Not that I wanted Lilli to be hurting like I'd been. But to know that we were going through this together, that I wasn't crazy. It was something. In fact, it was a lot.

"Look," Lilli added. "I was wrong not to talk to you about it. We're a team. We're in this together. And I'm here for you. Anytime you want to talk, I'll listen."

"I'll listen to you, too," I replied, smiling through my tears. We reached out and hugged each other tightly. Maybe the first real hug we'd shared since we'd left Dragon Ops. And it felt good.

"Aw, so sweet," Yano's voice broke in, his three heads leaning into our two. "Siblings reunited at long last. Now, if you don't mind fast-forwarding over the rest of the mushy stuff, we still have a quest to finish, in case you forgot."

We parted from the hug, a little sheepish. Then Lilli grinned. "Ready to get this show on the road, Lord Wildhammer?" she asked.

"Anytime, Mage Adorah," I replied, rising to my feet. "All right, Yano, let's—"

But I never got a chance to finish. Because at that moment everything went black.

CHAPTER THIRTY-SIX

I blinked, confused. Um, who turned out the lights? "Lilli?" I called out. "Starr? Yano? Anyone there?"

But no one answered. And all I saw was darkness.

Suddenly, there was a voice. "Ian! Wake up!"

I felt someone grab the back of my head. A moment later my VR helmet was ripped away. I squinted my eyes, realizing we were back. Back in the real world—with Lilli standing over me, an anxious look on her face.

"Wh-what...?" I stammered, trying to remember. My brain felt fuzzy. My body weak. Had we just been in Dragon Ops? No. Dragon World. With Atreus. Maybe Atreus...?

Ugh. It was all too much.

Lilli reached out for my hand. "Come on," she whispered. "Maddy hit the breaker. It bounced us from the game. Which means the Mech Ops guys are here. We need to get out—quick!" She started grabbing pieces of her rig and stuffing them in the backpack.

Fear rose inside me as I remembered Maddy's warning. She would only be able to hold them off for so long. Guess our time was up.

I scrambled to gather up all the equipment as quickly as possible, then the two of us stole over to the window with the fire escape. As we yanked it open, we could hear voices drift up from below.

"Where are they? We know they're here," insisted a gruff male voice.

"Who? There's no one here. I'm closed," Maddy protested. "It's just me and my cat. You want to see Sir Leo, my cat?"

But the man wouldn't back down. "We just want to talk to them, okay? We're not here to hurt anyone."

"Yeah, right. Then why are you packing heat?"

My gaze shot to my sister. Guns. They had guns? This was serious. What if they hurt Maddy while she was trying to protect us?

"Come on!" Lilli begged, grabbing my arm. "Maddy's a grown-up. She can take care of herself."

I wasn't so sure about that, but what else could we do? I followed Lilli out to the fire escape and climbed down, trying to reassure myself that Maddy was smart. She could handle some stupid goons from a game company.

We dropped down to the street below, our gazes darting from left to right. The coast seemed clear, thankfully.

"Let's go!" Lilli cried, running down the street. I could see the scrap of paper Maddy had given her in her hand—directions to our next safe house. I felt a little like I was in some kind of spy action movie as we darted through the streets, taking lefts, then rights. A few passersby gave us suspicious looks but didn't try to stop us. Probably thought we were just dumb kids playing a game.

Which, we were, in a sense. Though this game had real-life stakes.

It was then that I remembered Dad. What had he thought when he figured out we'd taken off? I realized we'd left in too much of a hurry to grab our phones. Which meant we couldn't call and reassure him we were okay. If, in fact, we were okay, which I still wasn't 100 percent about. Would he call Mom? Would she have left work in a panic? Were they even now combing the streets, looking for us? Mom was still so protective after what happened with Dragon Ops. This kind of thing was going to totally freak her out.

For a moment I wondered if we should just go back home. Come clean and ask for their help. But what could they do? Call the police? What help were they going to be in a situation like this?

No. There was no turning back now. We had to press on. We had to figure out a way to get back in the game.

Finally, we reached the address Maddy had given us. It was a cybercafé—the kind of place that served coffee and rented computer time by the hour. From what I'd read, these places used to be hot spots for people to come play video games together. But now most people played from their homes on their own consoles and computers, and there was hardly anyone there. A few people looked up from their laptops, observing us uninterestedly before returning to their work.

Lilli looked down at the paper she'd been given by Maddy. "It says to go to the bathroom," she said.

I raised an eyebrow. "The boys' bathroom? Or the girls'?" Either way, that was a little weird, right?

"It doesn't say. Come on. Walk casually."

We headed to the back of the café, where a glowing neon sign indicated the restroom. Thankfully, there was only one, and it was gender-neutral. That made things easier at least.

We pushed open the door and stepped inside. It was a single stall. Sink and toilet and not much else. Lilli locked the door behind us, then looked down at the paper again.

"Okay," she said. "Do you see a book called *Grays Sports Almanac* anywhere?"

My eyes scanned the bathroom, at first coming up blank. "Maybe under the sink," I said, dropping down to open the cabinet doors. Sure enough, a well-worn copy of the book was sitting inside. I pulled it out, triumphant. "Now what?"

"Go to page twenty-three," Lilli read. "And you'll find the day's password. Flush the toilet three times and then say it loudly."

"Oh-kay…" That was a little weird. But whatever. I flipped the book to page twenty-three. Inside was a scrap of paper.

$$33, 4$$

"I guess that's the password?" I said, confused.

"Try it," Lilli said. "Flush three times and yell."

I did as she suggested. Of course the toilet didn't totally flush the second and third time, as the bowl was still refilling from the first flush. Was that okay? Or was I supposed to wait between flushes?

Why was I flushing toilets, anyway?

"Thirty-three, four!" I shouted as loud as I could.

There was no answer.

I groaned. "This is so stupid. Why are we doing this again?"

"Um, to escape the bad guys with guns who want to get us?"

"Oh right." I pursed my lips. "I don't get it, though. Why didn't that work? Is that not the password?"

Lilli grabbed the book from me. "Maybe it's not," she said. "Maybe it's the code."

"What?"

She ran her finger down page twenty-three. "Line thirty-three," she murmured. "Word four."

"Oh!" I cried, my heart pounding with excitement. "I get it now. Like a secret code. Cool. What does it say?"

"Um. *The*?"

"*The*?" I frowned. "You must have counted wrong."

"I counted twice. The word thirty-three down and four over is *the*."

"What kind of secret password is that?"

"Maybe I was wrong," Lilli replied, sounding disappointed.

"Let's try it anyway," I said, mostly 'cause I wanted to make her feel better. I flushed the toilet three more times. (Talk about a waste of water.) "The!" I yelled out, knowing I sounded kind of ridiculous.

But then, out of nowhere, the door behind the toilet slid open, revealing a black passageway beyond. Maybe not so ridiculous, after all.

"Whoa!" Lilli exclaimed. "I can't believe that actually worked!"

"You're a genius," I told her. "Now, come on. Let's see what's back here."

We unlocked the bathroom door, then stepped into the dark passageway, my pulse skittering at every step. Lilli shined her phone flashlight into the darkness, and our shadows leered and danced in front of us as if taunting our nerves.

Finally, the passageway dead-ended at a lone door. Lilli looked down again at the paper Maddy had given us.

"One more thing," she said. "It says to knock the *Zelda* theme song." She frowned. "Do we know the *Zelda* theme song?"

"Uh, are you kidding?" I asked. "I can knock the *Zelda* theme song in my sleep!" Once again, my classic video game knowledge came in handy! And here people had said playing those old games was a waste of time.

I reached up and banged out the theme song. Which was actually more difficult to do than I thought it would be. But in the end, a voice boomed behind the door.

"Who goes there?" it asked, sounding echoey and distorted. As if the person was speaking through a voice-changing machine. Whoever was behind the door clearly didn't want to be recognized. I guessed that made sense, if they were part of some kind of secret hacker cell. Still, it didn't do anything to calm my nerves. I tried to remind myself that Maddy would never send us into danger. Whoever was there was a good guy. We had to trust that.

"Um, my name's Ian," I called through the door. "My sister is Lilli. Do you know Maddy? She said you'd be able to help us. We're...well, we're in a bit of trouble."

For a moment, nothing happened. Then, slowly, the

door slid open, revealing a dark room beyond. I glanced at Lilli. She shrugged, then took a step forward. No turning back now.

We walked into the room, which turned out to be small and circular, with low ceilings and walls covered in red velvet. As if we'd stepped into a vampire's lair.

But it wasn't a vampire that sat in the center of the room, gazing at us with a big smile on her face.

It was Starr.

CHAPTER THIRTY-SEVEN

I stared at Starr, eyes bulging from my head. "W-wait," I stammered. "*You're* Alpha Burn?"

She grinned. "What, were you expecting a dude?"

"No! Just someone I didn't know personally. You're, like, a legend! You hacked that big oil company and released all those emails about them killing penguins."

"Some of my best work," she admitted.

"Why didn't you tell us?" Lilli asked.

"Um, have you ever watched a superhero movie? Clark Kent does not tell people he's Superman. No one knows Batman is really that rich dork Bruce Wayne."

"True," I considered. I looked around the room. "Does that make this the Batcave?" Despite the vampire-chic décor, it was filled with computer equipment.

"Where all the magic happens," she agreed, wheeling herself over to a terminal.

"This is so weird," Lilli exclaimed. "So you're friends with Maddy?"

"Yup. We originally met online playing *Fields of Fantasy*. But now we hang out all the time. She's awesome, isn't she? And her artwork is amazing."

"Totally," I agreed.

"So wait," Lilli said, shaking her head. "You're friends with Maddy and then you end up randomly getting partnered with us in Mech Ops? That's, like, the smallest-world thing I ever heard!"

To my surprise, Starr smiled smugly. "Well, maybe," she said. "Or, maybe I was on a secret mission?"

"Wait. What?" I asked, realization dawning on me. "You don't mean..."

Starr held up her hands to stop me. "Look, Maddy was worried about you two. You were acting all weird, talking about emergencies. She knew I was planning to try out for the beta test and asked me to keep an eye on you to make sure you were safe."

I couldn't believe it. "So you've been babysitting us this whole time?" I asked, not knowing how I felt about that.

"Calm down, Lord Wildhammer," Starr said with a laugh. "I'm no one's babysitter. And it wasn't until I met you that I put two and two together and realized you were the Dragon Ops kids. Which made the job all that much cooler." She grinned.

"If you say so," I muttered, though after Starr's revelation, nothing would have surprised me.

"Anyway, I'm glad you're here," Starr continued. "It's safer here than Maddy's. It'll take them a while to track you down. Which will give us more time to find your friend and get her out. According to your dragon, we're running out of time."

"What?"

"After you guys dropped and before I got booted myself, your dragon got some kind of message. I don't know what it was, but he seemed really upset. He said if you didn't find a way to get back online soon, it might be too late to save your friend."

I gulped. What had Yano found out? Had Josh followed through with his threat to tell his grandpa about our mission? Was he planning to move Ikumi out of the game? To somewhere we could never find her?

I pulled my VR rig from my back and set it on the table, beginning to reassemble it. "What are we waiting for? We need to get back in."

"Unfortunately, it's not that simple," Starr interjected. "Our accounts are now disabled. Which means you can't get back in as yourselves."

"Ugh." I set down my helmet, discouraged. I probably should have known that was coming. "So what do we do?"

Starr tapped her fingers on her desk. "We're going to borrow other accounts. While you were on your way here, I took the liberty of hacking the company's databases and pulling out a list of names and passwords. We can log in as them and keep playing until they realize what we've done. Then we simply move on to the next name on the list."

"Sweet," I said. How cool was Starr—I mean, Alpha Burn? Then an idea occurred to me. "Can we play high-level characters?"

"Preferably ones that don't wear dresses and boots instead of armor?" Lilli added hopefully.

Starr swung back to her computer, typing furiously. A moment later, she turned back to us with a triumphant smile. "Done and done," she declared. "Lilli, you are now an eighty-level baddie with cybernetic-enhanced body armor. A tank couldn't get through your new skin."

"Yes!" Lilli crowed. "That's more like it!"

"And you, Ian, are now specced for stealth. You can sneak, you can lock-pick, you can hack computers and control robots." She grinned. "Also, we can all fly. I'm sick of waiting around for you guys to catch up to me."

"Nice," I said, my hopes rising as I grabbed my helmet again. Finally, we had a fighting chance.

CHAPTER THIRTY-EIGHT

"And we're back here. Again."

I groaned as I looked around. We were back in the game and back to our old familiar starting zone. The dumpy apocalyptic warehouse we all knew, but didn't love.

"Awesome," Lilli muttered. Then she looked down at her new body. "Oh, awesome," she added—not sarcastically this time—when she saw her cool shining silver armor. It molded to her body perfectly and had little green circuit lights dancing across it, as if she were literally electric. "Now, this is more like it!"

I looked down at myself. I was pretty cool, too. Dressed in thick leather with an actual electric whip like a cyber Indiana Jones. I even had a set of keys dangling from my belt for lock-picking. Pretty sweet.

Lilli ran over to the shipping container to let Yano out—once more with feeling. As our three-headed friend emerged, he looked at us doubtfully. "Um, who are you?"

"It's us, Yano," Lilli assured him. "Lilli, Ian, and Starr." She explained the reason for the different looks—and powers.

"Well, bully for you!" he declared. "And what an improvement. Lilli, luv, you even have armor now! How utterly practical."

Lilli snorted. "I know, right?"

"All right, people," Starr interrupted. "Well, people and dragons," she amended, nodding at Yano. "Let's gather up and make a plan. We don't know how long these identities will work before they cut us off again."

We huddled together, Yano sticking all three heads in our circle and making it more than a little crowded.

"So how are we going to do this again?" Lilli asked. "We still don't have a key. And there's no way to get back into Appleby's fortress without Josh."

My heart sank. I'd been so excited about getting back in the game, I'd basically forgotten we were still stuck. Like we were on one of those impossible quests some games had that made you not want to even log on anymore because you had no idea how to do them. Of course those quests you could always look up online. But here—we had to rely on our brainpower alone.

I kicked the shipping container, feeling frustrated. All

this time we'd been in the game, and we really hadn't solved anything. Ikumi was still behind an impenetrable wall. And none of us—not the elite hacker, not the AI, and certainly not Lilli or me—could break the code.

I hated feeling so powerless.

"Are you okay, Ian?" Lilli asked, coming over and placing a hand on my shoulder.

"I'm fine," I muttered.

"You can... tell me if you're not," she added. "Remember? We talk about things now."

"I know," I said, appreciating her concern. It was nice to know I didn't have to keep things from her anymore. But still, in this case I didn't know how she could help. "I'm just frustrated," I admitted. "This isn't like Dragon Ops, where we had a clear pathway to our endgame—Atreus's lair. Here, we have no idea how to break through the firewall. We don't have a key. Yano is not a powerful enough AI to hack it by himself..."

I trailed off. Wait a second.

Lilli peered at me curiously. "What?" she asked. "What are you thinking?"

A cold chill spun down my spine. And suddenly I wasn't sure I should say anything. Because if I did, what if they all thought it was a good idea? Then there would be no turning back from it.

"Never mind," I said. "It's dumb."

"I don't think any ideas are dumb at this point," Starr pointed out. "We're out of options. So if you have something, spill."

I could feel the three of them staring at me. I swallowed hard, past the huge lump that had formed in my throat.

"What if I...asked Atreus?" I blurted out.

"What?" Lilli's eyebrows shot up. "Ask Atreus? What are you talking about?"

"We need computing power to break through the firewall, right?" I reminded her, the words now coming in a rush. "Atreus is the most powerful computer AI ever created. Surely he could open the gate, right?"

"Maybe," Lilli replied, her eyes clouded with confusion. "If he were here..."

"He is."

"You mean in Dragon World? We can't get back in there without Josh."

"No. That's not the real Atreus in there," I told her. "The real Atreus—well, he's in this game somewhere. I've seen him. Multiple times."

Lilli frowned. "I thought you said your visions of him weren't real."

"Normally they're not. In the real world, on the soccer fields. Obviously those aren't Atreus. Which is why I was confused at first in the game. But then, at the top of the trash mountain, I saw him—before I jumped. The spiders saw him, too. He scorched the ground with fire. It was real—I'm sure of it."

"But why would Atreus be in the game?"

"He followed us in," I told her. "He's been following me this whole time—since we left Dragon Ops. Asking if I want to play again." I shrugged uneasily. "Why do you think I've stayed offline all these months? I've been petrified I'd turn on a computer and he'd be there waiting for me."

Lilli bit her lower lip. I could tell she didn't believe it but didn't want to accuse me of being crazy. Which kind of hurt, but I understood it. It did sound crazy.

But that didn't mean it wasn't true.

I turned to Yano. "Is there a way for you to look for him? Like, see if he's in the game?"

Yano nodded, closing his eyes. A moment later, he opened them. "By Jove, the kid's right!" he exclaimed. "That little sneak got himself into the game somehow. He's up on the trash mountain as we speak. Dragons do like their mountains. Though as for me, if I were to hide out in this game? I'd definitely pick somewhere less predictable. Like that Pool of Piranha, for example. Everyone hates a water level."

"Okay, so he's here," Starr said. "Fine. But what makes you think he'll help us? He's a bad guy, right? He's trying to kill you? It's not like he's going to just follow orders."

"To be fair, all AIs follow orders," Yano reminded her. "We call them programming."

"Fine. But Atreus is not *programmed* to help us."

"No," I agreed. "But he *is* programmed to play a game. What if we tell him the rules of this game have changed?"

"What are you saying, Ian?" Lilli asked, scratching her head.

"Remember back in Dragon Ops? Eugene told us Atreus is able to learn on the fly, to adapt to new situations and self-adjust. That's what makes him so hard to beat. But it could also work to our advantage. We tell him that yes, we want to play again. But this time the rules have changed. This time we're on the same side. And to win the game? We have to free Ikumi."

"You think he's going to change his entire programming just 'cause we suggest it?"

"It's not that big of a change if you think about it. Our objective in Dragon Ops was to save Derek. So it would make sense to Atreus that we had a similar quest—but on this level, we have to save Ikumi."

"Okay," Lilli declared. "That's crazy. Like, really crazy. But..." She trailed off.

"It might actually work," Starr finished, excitement flashing in her eyes. "And hey—we don't really have any other options, right?"

"Trust me, if we did, I wouldn't have suggested it. The last thing I want to do is face Atreus again," I admitted.

For months now, I'd been tormented by Atreus. Trying

everything I could to escape him. And now I was suggesting the exact opposite. What if it didn't work? What if I asked him to play again and he agreed—but only under the old rules?

My mind flashed back to his Crystal Temple. The dragon's mouth creaking open, flickering with flame. Suddenly the panic came back with a vengeance, and my mind spun with fear. What was I thinking? My sister was right—this was crazy. This was so crazy.

I plopped down on the ground, scrubbing my face with my hands. I knew I had to go through with this—it was the only way. But just the thought of approaching him—calling him—made me want to throw up.

"Are you okay, Ian?" Lilli asked worriedly.

"I'm fi—" I started to say, then stopped. "No." I shook my head. "I'm not fine. I'm scared," I admitted, realizing I didn't have to fake it anymore. I was still traumatized by what happened in Dragon Ops. But that was okay. It didn't make me pathetic. It didn't make me weak. And if anyone could understand that? It would be my sister. Because she'd gone through the same thing as I had. She was still scared, too. Even if she had a harder time showing it.

I gave her rueful look. "All this time, I've been running from Atreus. Hiding away. And now I've got to face him again."

Lilli nodded slowly. She put a hand on my shoulder.

"*We're* going to face him again," she clarified, looking me in the eyes. I could see fear swimming in her own pupils. But also determination. "We're a team, remember? If we do this? We do it together."

Starr slapped a hand on my back. "Together," she agreed.

Yano sniffed loudly. "Aw, so beautiful," he cooed. "Like the Avengers, coming together to save the world!"

My sister put out her hand. I laid mine on top of it. Starr put hers over mine.

"Gear up, Dragon Slayerz," Lilli said with a small smile. "And let's go get us a dragon."

CHAPTER THIRTY-NINE

And that was how we found ourselves standing on top of the trash mountain again, gazing into an empty sky. Hoping (yet not hoping) to see that big bad dragon soar into view. My heart was racing a thousand miles a minute. But I stood my ground. Like Lilli said, I wasn't alone. And maybe this would work, and maybe it wouldn't, but either way, Ikumi deserved for us to try.

"Go on." Lilli nudged me. "Call for him."

Right. I turned my eyes back to the sky, my whole body trembling now. This was it. Once I opened my mouth, addressed the beast, there would be no turning back.

Ready or not, Atreus would come.

"ATREUS!" I yelled at the top of my voice. "It's me, Ian! Are you up there?"

For a moment, there was nothing, just my voice echoing across the game. And then...

"Oh my gosh!" Starr cried. "What is *that*?"

I turned my head to see what she was referring to, dread sinking in my stomach at what I saw. Not Atreus at all, but rather a giant robot stomping over in our direction. And let's just say he didn't look friendly.

Uh-oh.

He was vaguely human shaped, wearing metal-plated armor trimmed with red. At least twenty feet tall and super heavy, judging from the way the trash mountain quaked with each of his steps. I was pretty sure it'd be no problem for him to crush us under his heel and be done with us once and for all if he wanted to.

And he really looked like he wanted to.

"What do we do?" Lilli asked. "Do you think we can fight it? We are higher level now. But still—that thing is so big!"

"The bigger they are, the harder they fall," Yano declared, squaring his shoulders. "Just watch me crush this little gnat right under my—"

The robot's eyes glowed red. Lasers shot from its pupils, straight at Yano.

"No!" I cried, horrified.

But the lasers met their mark, blasting through Yano's

metal hide. The dragon staggered backward, sparks dancing across his flanks, smoke pouring from all three mouths. "Blurgh!" He tried to speak. "BLURGHHHH."

He vanished into thin air. And the robot turned its laser eyes back on us.

"Watch out!" Starr screamed, diving toward a nearby trash pile.

I joined her just in time. The robot's eyes shot more lasers, this time directly where I had been standing. The ground sizzled on impact, literally melting away before my eyes. If I had still been standing there? Graveyard city.

I turned to my sister and Starr. Thankfully, they'd both made it to the trash pile in time. Not that it would do us much good long term. I was under no illusions that this thing couldn't blow our hiding spot to smithereens at any moment. And us with it.

What to do? What to do?

Suddenly a shadow crossed the sky. I looked up, my heart sinking as I realized who had finally arrived.

"Oh no!" I cried in dismay. "Not now!"

As if a giant laser-beam-shooting robot wasn't enough. Now we had a dragon on approach as well. Atreus must have heard my call—and at the worst moment, too. Why, oh why, had I thought it was a good idea to call him before making sure we were safe? Now we'd have to deal with both of them at the same time.

I watched, frozen in place, as Atreus circled above, his wingspan larger than I remembered, his scales darker, his mouth crueler. For a moment, he seemed to be searching. Then his eyes locked on me. My stomach rolled in fear.

He's just a computer program, I tried to remind myself. *He can't hurt you in real life.*

I forced myself to look back at him. "Atreus," I said, trying to keep the fear from my voice.

You called, tiny human? he whispered in my ear. *Are you finally ready to play again?*

The giant robot stomped closer. His eyes locked on the trash pile in front of us. I heard the rev of his engine whirring to life. In one second, he'd be ready to fire.

"Yes!" I cried to the dragon. "I'm ready to play again!"

Same rules as last time?

I drew in a breath. "No," I said. "New rules. This time we're on the same team."

For a moment, the dragon didn't answer. I held my breath, praying it would work. That somehow, someway I could outsmart this AI once again—this time bringing him over to our side.

"Look!" Lilli cried, pointing. "He's about to blow!"

I watched, horrified, as Atreus opened his mouth, revealing his chasm of razor-sharp teeth. Sparks began to form on his tongue as his belly warmed with flame. I felt despair rise inside of me.

It hadn't worked. I'd tried to face my fears, and I'd only made things worse.

I ducked down, knowing it would do no good. A pile of trash wouldn't stop the mighty Atreus. We were as good as done for, once again.

"Meet you at the graveyard, I guess," I said to my sister and Starr. "Hopefully we won't glitch out—"

WHOOSH! The flames shot from the dragon's mouth, fire arcing through the sky. I couldn't help but notice how beautiful it was in some weird way. If we had to go, I guessed I was happy it was by dragon fire and not robot lasers. At the end of the day, fantasy games were still my thing.

I squeezed my eyes shut, waiting for the impact.

But strangely it didn't come...

"Ian!"

I felt someone shake me. My eyes flew open. Starr was standing in front of me. So was my sister. Neither one looked burnt. Huh?

"What..." I started to ask. But then I saw exactly what. There, in front of us, was the giant killer robot.

And he was on fire.

CHAPTER FORTY

"Oh my gosh!" I cried. "Did Atreus do that?"

There was a loud thud behind me—something big and bad coming in for a landing. I whirled around, staggering backward as I found Atreus not five feet away. The dragon's amber eyes settled on me, and his mouth creaked open...in a smile?

Let's go, tiny human, he purred in my head. *Let's get this game started!*

Whoa. I stood there, too shocked to move. Atreus. Was he really on our side?

"Well, what are you waiting for?" Starr nudged me. "Your new teammate wants to take you for a ride!"

My jaw dropped open as I realized she was right. Atreus—the mighty Atreus—was clearly indicating he wanted me on his back to continue the fight. For a moment, I couldn't bring my feet to work. Everything felt frozen in place. But then I felt Lilli's hand on my back.

"You got this," she whispered.

And I realized I did.

I ran to Atreus, still half convinced he'd change his mind and blast me where I stood. But instead, he lowered his wing, inviting me to climb aboard. My whole body shook as I scrambled up, throwing my leg around his back. I gripped the thick scales under his neck.

"Yeah, Ian!" Lilli cried. "Way to go!"

"You look awesome up there, Dragon Rider!" Starr cheered. "Now, go slay us a robot!"

I grinned at them, wanting to salute, but not wanting to let go, just in case Atreus made a sudden move. I was still freaked out, but somehow I was also kind of excited. Imagine! Little old me, on Atreus's back, fighting a mighty robot. If you'd told me a month ago I'd be doing this, I would have laughed in your face.

But now—here I was.

"All right," I whispered to the dragon. "Let's do this!"

Atreus shot into the sky, leaving my stomach on the ground all over again. It felt different than riding Yano, who was smooth and gentle and actually concerned whether his passenger was about to fall off his back and plummet to their death.

Atreus, on the other hand, seemed to have no such

hang-ups. He was in it to win it—literally. Regardless of what happened to me.

My stomach swam with nausea as we whipped around the robot, going so fast it was almost a blur. I swallowed down the bile that threatened to spew from my throat. *No time for puking, Ian. We have a robot to take down.*

Dragon versus robot. What a game!

The robot's eyes shot lasers, but Atreus was too quick, easily darting out of the line of fire. The lasers hit a trash pile instead, reducing it to cinders. I tried not to imagine how that would feel if it were me.

"Go! Get him now!" Starr called from the ground. "Before his lasers recharge!"

Good idea. I turned to my dragon. (*My* dragon!)

"All right, Atreus," I urged. "Do your thing!"

To my delight, the dragon obeyed, opening his mouth wide. From where I sat, I could actually feel his belly get warmer as the fire built up inside. I knew he needed a few seconds to get locked and loaded before he released his flames. Hopefully the robot wouldn't have a quicker recharge.

The robot hissed, steam shooting from its nose as it raised its metal arm in a karate-chopping motion. I watched as it slashed down, trying to crush us under its fist. But again, Atreus was too fast, dodging him at the last second by darting under the robot's arm and spinning around to its rear.

Then he released his flames. Straight at the robot's butt!

The creature writhed as the fire hit its mark, squealing and screeching with robot rage. Sparks of electricity crackled over its frame. It tried to turn, to meet its enemy head-on, but it was too clumsy and slow. It wasn't meant to fight a lean, mean fighting machine like Atreus. Atreus easily evaded his second attempt at a blow.

I cheered. "That's the way to do it!" I patted Atreus on his scales.

Suddenly, the robot stopped attacking. At first I thought it had given up. But then, to my dismay, it started repairing itself before my eyes. Oh no! This thing had repair power? That was not good at all.

"Ian!" Lilli shouted. "Come down here for a second."

While the robot was occupied, I instructed Atreus to come in for a landing by the trash pile. My sister and Starr ran up to us. "You're doing great," Lilli said. "But it's not enough."

"You're only scratching the surface," Starr added. "His armor is too thick for Atreus's fire to melt through."

I looked up at the robot, who appeared brand-new again. Great. My heart sank. Here I'd faced my fears, dared summon a deadly beast, only to find out he wasn't deadly enough. Go figure.

"What do we do?" I asked worriedly.

Starr thought for a moment. Then her eyes brightened. *"Empire Strikes Back!"* she exclaimed.

"Um, what about it?" What did *Star Wars* have to do with this?

"Don't you remember? The AT-AT scene! What if you did something like that?"

My mind raced, trying to remember what she was talking about. In the Battle of Hoth, the rebel forces had managed to take down the giant four-legged robotlike creatures by tripping them up. Could something like that work now?

"I'll try it," I declared. Nerd strategy for the win!

"Okay," I told Atreus. "New plan." I whispered my idea in his giant ear. I had to admit, now that I wasn't frightened half to death of this guy, he was kind of awesome.

Atreus listened, nodding. When I had finished, a grin spread over his face. *I like the way you think, tiny human,* he declared, then pushed off of the ground again with his mighty legs, shooting us into the air.

But this time we didn't fly high into the sky. This time we stayed low, skimming the ground. When we got to the robot, Atreus wove through its legs, then around them, making figure eights in the air. The robot tried to swipe at him, but the dragon was too fast. And when the robot attempted a second blow, it lost its balance completely. I watched in delight as it started to wobble, waving its giant robot arms, trying to stay upright.

"Watch out!" I called down to the girls below. I didn't

want them to get squashed. They dove away, out of the robot's falling zone.

Now it was our turn.

"Go, Atreus!" I cried. "NOW!"

The dragon zoomed forward just in time for the robot to topple over. I watched as it hit the ground headfirst, the entire trash mountain shaking on impact. For a moment, it thrashed back and forth as if trying to get up. Then the fight seemed to go out of it, and it went still.

Dragon versus robot. And we had won.

CHAPTER FORTY-ONE

"Woo-hoo!" Starr and Lilli cheered as Atreus and I came in for a landing. I was out of breath, still sick to my stomach, but filled with so much excitement I didn't even care. We had done it! I'd conquered my fear, tamed a dragon, and taken out a giant robot. Which basically made me a legit superhero.

"That was awesome," Starr cried, rushing over to us as I slid off Atreus's back.

"Yeah, well, it was your idea," I reminded her with a small grin.

She reached out and stroked the dragon's nose. "Good job, boy," she praised him. The dragon purred contentedly, nuzzling his snout into her hand. And suddenly I was taken back to the very first time we'd hung out with Atreus at Dragon Ops. Before Eugene messed with his programming.

A sudden thought came to me. Maybe before he'd escaped Dragon Ops, the powers that be had removed the extra programming Eugene had added to make him act evil. Maybe he was back to his original self now. The dragon who liked belly rubs and naps in the grass. The one who wanted to help humans, not hurt them.

"I feel like an idiot for being afraid all this time," I confessed. "It's like being afraid of a kitty cat."

"Please. Atreus was fierce back in Dragon Ops," Lilli scolded. "As were all the other creatures. Remember the ice dragon? The one who froze me solid? I still have nightmares about being trapped in that ice, wondering if I was ever going to get out." She hugged her chest with her arms. "I can't remember ever being so scared."

"I was scared, too," I admitted. "I thought I'd lost you forever." I shivered as I remembered that moment, seeing my sister encased in ice.

"But you didn't," Lilli reminded me with a smile. "We're still here. Which makes us survivors. And we're going to survive this, too. With this guy's help." She stroked the dragon's nose. "I'm just glad you're on our team now," she told him in a baby voice.

I smiled at my sister, a warm feeling rising inside me. We *were* survivors. Both of us had gone through something terrible—and we'd come out the other side. Maybe we'd never be the same as we were before we went into the game, but maybe that was okay. At least we had come out together. And by talking and being open with each other, maybe we had a chance to start healing.

The dragon seemed to be enjoying the attention quite a bit. His eyes grew sleepy, and his tongue lolled from his mouth. I half wondered if he was going to collapse onto the ground and take a cat nap right then and there.

"Sorry, big guy," I said regretfully. "But we're not done yet. We've got another…quest…to do. And we need your help."

Atreus seemed to consider this. *Once I was the quest*, he said. *You tried to kill me.*

"Um, we did kill you," Lilli corrected him. "I mean, no offense."

Atreus frowned, looking insulted. I almost felt bad for the big lug. "It was part of our programming back then," I assured him. "We all have to follow our programming, right?"

I suppose so, he agreed. *And now I am programmed to follow you?*

"Exactly," I said. "To save Ikumi. And live happily ever after."

Atreus snorted, sending puffs of smoke from his nostrils. *Very well*, he said. *Then let us get started.*

And so we did, climbing onto his back—which was admittedly a bit of a tight fit—and instructing the dragon to fly down through the hole in the world and then through the wormholes until we got back to the gate where we'd first seen Ikumi. As we flew, I explained to our new teammate what we needed him to do. I still wasn't a hundred percent sure Atreus could open the gate by himself—originally we were going to combine his power with Yano's—but I figured we might as well try. Or maybe, if we were lucky, Yano had already revived and was on his way to meet us there.

Finally, we got through the last wormhole and entered the star-swept land with the mirror gate. I instructed Atreus to land in front of it, and we all tumbled off his back. Once we were on solid ground again, Lilli looked around, her jaw dropping with amazement. I'd forgotten she hadn't been with us the last time we came here.

"It's so beautiful," she marveled. "Unlike the rest of the game. It's just...breathtaking."

"Don't let it fool you," I said. "It's still a prison."

I walked over to the gate, peering into it, hoping to see our friend. But only my reflection peered back at me. Hopefully she was still there and they hadn't moved her. That would be just our luck, right? To learn our princess was in another castle?

But then, just as I was about to turn away, she appeared again. Floating on the other side of the glass. She frowned at us, a confused expression on her face.

"She doesn't know it's us!" I exclaimed. "We look

different." I tapped on the glass. "Don't worry, Ikumi. It's us—Ian and Lilli. We're here to rescue you."

If she could hear us, she gave no sign. Instead, she shrank back as if in fear. It was then that I remembered who we were hanging with. The very same dragon who had killed her in Dragon Ops.

Maybe Ikumi had been suffering just like Lilli and I had.

"It's okay," I assured her. "Atreus isn't going to hurt you. He's on our side now. And he's going to set you free." I turned to Atreus and motioned for him to blast the gate. The dragon obliged, opening his mouth and letting loose a stream of what looked like smoke. For a moment we were all blinded by it, as if we'd been enveloped in a soupy fog. Then it cleared. And when it did?

The gate was wide open.

"Yes!" I cried. "You did it!" I turned to Atreus, grinning gratefully. But the dragon wasn't smiling. He was looking worried.

Something's wrong, he said. *Something's very wrong.*

A chill whispered across my shoulders. I opened my mouth to ask Atreus what he meant. Did he sense something? Could he see something?

But before I could get any words out, my vision went black.

CHAPTER FORTY-TWO

"No!" I cried, horrified as reality came rushing back to me. I ripped off my headset, blinking to try to adjust to real-life mode again. Looking around, I saw my sister and Starr also taking off their helmets, looking dazed.

Disappointment sank in my stomach. "They must have found us again," I moaned. I pounded my fist against my thigh. "And we were so close, too!"

"Come on," Starr said. "Let's get back in. The gate's open now. We need to go through before we get booted to the starting area." She shoved the helmet over her head, and I followed her example. But when I tried to load the game, nothing happened. And all I could see was a message flashing in front of my vision over and over again.

Log-in not recognized.

"Oh no!" Lilli cried. "They killed our new log-ins. They must have discovered who we were."

"Don't panic," Starr said. "We'll just pull up new log-ins. I have a few more." She handed us papers with names and passwords. We plugged them into our consoles and tried again.

The good news? We got back in. And our equipment was even better than before. Armor, weapons, wings—the works.

The bad? We were back at the stupid starting warehouse.

"Argh. And here we go again," I said, stomping my foot in frustration. "Every time we log in as different accounts, we gotta start over? We don't have time for this!"

"Don't freak out," Lilli scolded. "At least we're in. And the gate's open now."

"How do you know? What if they closed the gate again, too?"

"Then Atreus will open it."

"And then we'll get booted." I scowled. "And what if they decide to move Ikumi to a place where we'll never find her?"

Lilli's face fell. Looking as defeated as I felt. "So what are we supposed to do?" she asked. "We can't kick *them* out of the game."

"Actually," Starr said thoughtfully, "we could. At least theoretically."

"What?" We turned to look at her, confused.

"Have you ever heard of a DoS attack?"

I nodded slowly. I'd heard of DoS attacks. Otherwise known as Denial of Service. Basically, a bunch of hackers would get together and launch a cyberattack on a company's servers. For example their log-in servers. The idea was to overload the system and make it crash. So no one could use it.

Which meant, we could lock the Mech Ops people out of their own game. At least for a short while. Maybe long enough for us to get to Ikumi.

"Can you do that?" I asked Starr, impressed.

"Not by myself," she admitted. "But I have friends from the Dark Carnival. If Maddy and I were to go and recruit enough of them, we might have a chance."

"That would be amazing!" Lilli cried. "Let's give it a try!"

"Okay," Starr agreed. "I'll log off and see what I can do. You guys head straight to the gate. Hopefully we can lock them out before they find you again." She held up her hand, giving us both high fives. "Good luck, Dragon Slayerz," she said before logging out and disappearing.

Leaving Lilli and me alone.

"Okay," I said, turning to my sister. "Let's get Yano and give this a shot."

We walked over to the all-too-familiar container to once again let our dragon free. But to my surprise, when we opened the crate, it was empty.

"Um, that's weird," Lilli said, stepping into the crate and

looking around, as if Yano could be hiding in a dark corner. "Did he not reset like we did?"

"I don't know." I pressed my lips together, worried. "I hope he's okay."

"I guess you'd better call your *other* dragon friend," Lilli said. "Since we still need a ride."

"Do you think he'll hear us from here? We're pretty far from the trash mountain. And what if he didn't get booted like we did? He'd still be all the way at Ikumi's gate."

Lilli frowned. She clearly hadn't thought of that. "Just try and see," she suggested.

I nodded, leaving the shipping crate behind and stepping out of the warehouse onto the apocalyptic city street. It was funny how normal it felt now to be here now. I barely noticed the decay and destruction.

I turned my face upward toward the sky. "Atreus!" I called out. "I want to play again!"

But there was no answer.

"Atreus!" I tried again. But the sky remained empty. Atreus was nowhere to be seen.

"What are we going to do?" I groaned. "We have no dragon."

"No," Lilli mused. Then her face brightened. "But we do have wings!"

CHAPTER FORTY-THREE

And so we made it back to the gate on our own, flying ourselves to the trash mountain, then down into the lower levels and the wormholes. It wasn't as fun as riding a dragon and definitely a lot more work. By the time we made it to the star-swept world, I was ready to drop from exhaustion.

But that all went away when I spotted the gate, still open wide. My heart fluttered with relief, and I dropped to the ground, running toward the door.

"Ikumi!" I cried. "We're here! We're here to get you out."

I stepped through the door, then stopped, surprised at what I saw. I'd expected a prison. Maybe bars on the wall, a cot in the corner, a lone toilet, perhaps. Instead it was more like a cozy cottage inside. A warm fire burning in the hearth.

A comfy-looking couch sitting in front of a big-screen TV. Under the TV were game consoles—every game console I could think of and some I didn't recognize. And in the next room there was a queen-size bed and a bookcase overflowing with new-release books. Even more shocking? On the walls were photos. Of a young girl with straight black hair standing next to a very familiar-looking man.

The young girl was smiling happily. And the man?

It was Admiral Appleby.

"This is the nicest jail cell I've ever seen," Lilli remarked, coming in behind me.

"No kidding," I said in confusion. *It is really nice*, I told myself. *But it is still a prison when you're locked in, not of your own free will. Right?*

My sister looked around, frowning. "So where is she? Why isn't she here?"

"You should be asking yourselves that question," came a sudden, familiar voice behind us. "Since you're the ones who caused this mess."

We whirled around. To my shock, none other than Josh stood there at the entrance, dressed in his full purple armor and carrying a laser spear. He stepped into the bedroom, shaking his head regretfully.

I stormed over to him, my temper flaring. "Where's Ikumi?" I demanded, grabbing him by the shoulders and shaking him hard. "What did you do to her?"

"I didn't do anything to her," Josh replied, pushing me away. "You did, by opening up the gate."

"*Freeing* her, you mean?"

"Yeah, right. She was free before. Now—well, who knows?" He looked worried. "Thanks to your little cyberattack on the game, no one can get in to find out what's going on."

What? I was so confused it wasn't even funny. "*You're* here," I pointed out.

"Yes. Luckily. I was already in the game before you pulled your little stunt," he replied. "Grandpa sent me to find you and warn you about what you were trying to do."

"Rescuing our friend from his evil grasp?"

Josh face-palmed. "Evil grasp? Rivera, are you even listening to yourself right now?"

I squeezed my hands into fists. "I swear if you hurt her—"

Josh turned to Lilli. "Will you please tell him to listen to me? We're running out of time."

"Ian," Lilli said hesitantly. "Maybe we should at least hear what he has to say—"

"Give me one good reason why I should."

Josh's gaze leveled on me. "Because if you don't, you'll very likely lose Ikumi forever."

I swallowed hard. I didn't want to believe him, of course. He could be lying. This could be another trick, another trap. But then, what if it wasn't? He did look genuinely worried. Which meant he was either a really good actor or...

"Fine." I plopped myself down onto the couch, crossing my arms over my chest. "But this better be good."

Josh sighed. "Right. So, after I left you guys in Dragon World, I disconnected from the game to go find my grandpa in real life. I told him about everything you were trying to do and what you thought he was doing. He freaked out. Like, more than I've ever seen him freak out before, and he told me you were making a big mistake."

"Of course he would see it that way, considering he was the one to kidnap her to begin with," I muttered.

"Will you listen for one second?" Josh snapped. "My grandpa didn't kidnap your friend. He was keeping her safe from the people who wanted to kidnap her!"

I froze. *What?*

"Are you serious?" Lilli broke in, stepping forward. "He was protecting her this whole time?"

"Yes," Josh said, looking relieved that one of us finally understood. "Evidently Hiro, her dad, came to my grandfather asking for his help. They've known each other for years. Hiro's father, Atsuo, and my grandpa used to develop games together until they had a falling out over Dragon World—Dragon Ops—whatever you want to call it." He shrugged. "That's why there's two versions of the same game. My grandpa ended up keeping his on a private server, and Atsuo introduced his to the public as *Fields of Fantasy* and later Dragon Ops."

"What does this have to do with Ikumi?" Lilli asked.

"I guess Hiro was desperate. He got wind that a rival game company called Camelot's Honor was looking for his daughter out in the cloud. He needed a place to hide her— quick. So he asked my grandfather if he could use Mech Ops to do so. Just for a little while," Josh explained. "At first Grandpa didn't like the idea—he was about to launch a big beta test, and he didn't know if it'd be a safe spot for her. But Hiro convinced him, saying they'd put her behind a firewall in a closed section of the game. This way, even if Camelot's Honor found out and tried to send bots to try to break her out, they wouldn't be strong enough." He scowled. "Of course he never counted on you guys and your super AI dragon, Atreus."

I rose woodenly to my feet, my heart racing. I didn't want to believe him, but somehow it all made sense. Camelot's Honor was the same company who'd trapped us in Dragon Ops last spring. They'd be the only ones who even knew Ikumi existed to begin with. Had Admiral Appleby really just been trying to keep her safe?

"But wait!" Lilli protested. "We saw a video of Ikumi. She was asking for our help."

"Did you? Or did you only *think* you did?" Josh asked. "Remember, videos are easy to fake. Especially if they come from a trusted source." He gave us a meaningful look.

I frowned, my mind whirling. Did he mean . . . ? But that was crazy! Impossible.

"Yano?" my sister whispered, clearly coming to the same conclusion. "You're saying Yano is working for Camelot's Honor?"

I felt like I was going to be sick. My mind flashing back to every encounter we'd had with the AI dragon. How he'd tracked us down through Ikumi's in-game account, shown us the video, told us we were the only ones who could help. And, of course! He needed someone to get him into the game—which we did by winning the beta test. And he needed someone no one would suspect—even Ikumi herself.

All this time I'd been freaking out about Atreus. When the real threat came from an entirely different AI dragon who had played us like fools. Yano had been so concerned about rescuing Ikumi, and we never thought to ask ourselves why. After all, AIs don't have friends. They don't have feelings.

But they did have programming. Evidently someone had reprogrammed him to track down Ikumi—by any means necessary. And we had fallen for it, hook, line, and joystick.

I closed my eyes. "Why didn't anyone tell us this before now?"

"Are you kidding? Grandpa's guys thought you were working for the enemy. You were hanging out with that AI, doing everything it said. That's why they went after you in real life, trying to stop you. It wasn't until I went to Grandpa and told him you guys cared about this girl and were just trying to help that he realized what must really be going on."

I couldn't believe it. All this time, we thought they were the bad guys. When it was actually the three of us working for the enemy.

"So what now?" I asked fearfully. "Where is Yano? Does he have Ikumi already?"

"Yes. After you broke through the gate, Yano crashed the game. That's why you disconnected. Once he had you out of the way, he swooped in and convinced Ikumi to come with him. That he'd take her to you. My guess is he planned to take her from the game entirely. But your little DoS attack locked them in, just as it kept everyone else out."

"So they're still in the game?"

"At least for now."

Hope rose inside me. "So we still have a chance," I exclaimed. "We can still save her."

"Maybe. If we act fast. It won't be easy. But we can try."

"We?" Lilli asked, turning to Josh, raising an eyebrow. He blushed.

"If you'll have me," he said, looking directly at me.

A small part of me still wanted to say no. But I managed to push it away. Ikumi needed us. Now was not the time to refuse help from anyone. Not even from my archenemy.

"All right," I said. "Let's do it."

CHAPTER FORTY-FOUR

Team assembled, we headed off to find Yano and Ikumi. First stop? Admiral Appleby's virtual fortress again, where Josh could access advanced game controls that could pinpoint Yano and Ikumi's whereabouts. At first I worried it would take too long to get there, especially since Josh didn't have wings and Atreus was still MIA. But Josh assured us that wouldn't be a problem.

"I have my home base set there," he explained. "I've had it there for years, mostly so I can visit Mr. Donkey Kong easily. I can go ahead and warp there now, then use my summon spell to bring the rest of you over. From there, we can portal anywhere we need to go in the game."

"Why didn't you do that last time?" I asked, surprised. "It took Yano and me forever to get there."

Josh shrugged sheepishly. "Sorry. I guess I just wanted a little extra alone time with your sister."

I raised my eyebrows. Beside me, Lilli had turned beet red. Josh gave an embarrassed grin, then disappeared, presumably warping back home. Once alone, I turned to my sister.

"Don't even start!" she warned.

"Aw, come on. You said we could talk about anything…" I grinned.

Before she could answer, everything seemed to go black. For a moment I thought we'd been booted from the game again. But then I popped back up, this time inside Admiral Appleby's fortress. No longer skinned with Dragon World or a fancy rain forest, it now looked like a regular old soccer field. Which, in a way, was even stranger than the more exotic settings we'd seen. At the very least more realistic.

Josh walked up to me, dribbling the ball. I looked around, not seeing anyone else. For a moment, I got scared. Was this some kind of trap to separate me from the others? Heart pounding, I struggled to my feet.

"Where's Lilli?" I demanded.

"Relax, Rivera," Josh said, kicking the ball to me. "She'll be here soon. I can only use my summon spell once every sixty seconds."

Oh. Right. That made sense. I felt my cheeks flush with embarrassment.

Josh sighed. "You still don't trust me, do you? I guess that's my fault."

"Huh?" I looked up, surprised.

"Look, I owe you an apology. I'm sorry I've been a jerk to you. In the game, on the soccer field…"

"It's fine," I said quickly. "I don't care." Not exactly true, but I wasn't sure I wanted to get into this now when so much else was going on.

But Josh, it seemed, wasn't about to let it go. "It's just… when you first joined the soccer team, you made it so clear you thought it was stupid." He shrugged. "I guess it just made me mad."

I turned, surprised. "What are you talking about? I didn't do that!"

"Um, yeah you did. You kept joking around, calling it 'sports-ball' and saying how you hoped you could score a 'touchdown.'"

Okay, I might have done that. And that might have come off as kind of insulting to someone who really liked the game. Someone like Josh.

"Trust me, I get it," he added. "All my life I've been surrounded by gamers and geeks, thanks to my grandpa. I was always looked down on for liking sports. For actually wanting to watch the Super Bowl for the football game instead of just the commercials and the halftime show. They all thought it was *so cute*." He wrinkled his nose.

"Ugh," I sympathized. "My dad's like that, but the opposite. He always wants me to be into all this extreme adventure stuff. Like Lilli is. He's constantly disappointed when he finds me on the computer."

"Your dad sounds awesome!" Josh joked. Then he got serious again. "Anyway, when you showed up that first day, making the same jokes I'd heard all my life? I got mad. I knew you weren't going to take it seriously. Which might make us lose." He snorted softly. "I know that's not a big deal to you—"

"Actually, I get it," I admitted, surprising even myself with the words. "I felt the same way when you joined our Mech Ops team." Here I'd been mad when Josh wasn't taking Mech Ops seriously. When I had done exactly the same thing to him on the soccer field. "If it makes you feel any better? I only made those jokes 'cause I was nervous. I knew I was going to stink at soccer. I guess I thought if I pretended not to care, it wouldn't matter so much when I did."

"You don't stink at soccer," Josh insisted. "You just need some more practice. That goal you missed? No way could you have gotten it in. Even if you didn't choke. That goalie was huge."

"I know, right?" I blurted out before I could stop myself. "How is he in seventh grade?"

"For real," Josh agreed. Then he shrugged. "Anyway, if you ever want to kick the ball around, I can show you some stuff. If you want, I mean. We can even play in here. Video game soccer—perfect for both our interests."

"That sounds pretty cool, actually," I said, and I realized I meant it. "Thanks." I kicked the ball back to him. He bounced it off his knees, and it flew off. Josh grinned at me.

"Now, time to summon your sister."

Once Lilli arrived, Josh went and accessed the master game map, which showed all the players currently in-game. We popped up first, down near the bottom. A few other beta testers were playing near the starting zone. And two very faint lights shone at the top of the game map, traveling at what appeared to be a fast speed.

"The Zeta Quadrant," Josh explained. "Of course! Why didn't I think of that?"

"What's the Zeta Quadrant?" I asked. It sounded vaguely familiar. Then I remembered. "Your grandpa mentioned it after the beta test."

"It's his pet project," Josh explained. "Endgame. The final frontier, as my grandpa likes to call it. Basically, the story goes, once the players give up on this dying world, they blast into outer space and land on a paradise planet. There, they can colonize this whole new world. And beat the game."

"And once you beat the game?" Lilli asked.

"You get out," Josh replied. "Which I bet is exactly what Yano is trying to do."

CHAPTER FORTY-FIVE

"**H**ello, space travelers, please secure your positions. We are clear for launch."

I checked my seat belt again as the robot proceeded with the countdown. Josh and Lilli did the same. My heart pounded in anticipation. This was it; no turning back now.

Originally I thought we'd just be able to warp to the Zeta Quadrant, but Josh said his grandpa hadn't put in warps there, preferring that players get the full experience by traveling the old-fashioned way—by spaceship. Also, this prevented players from returning to the game once they'd finished it. It was a one-way trip, and if you wanted to go back, you created a new character and started from the beginning again. If I were actually beta-testing this thing, I'd probably mark that down as a bad idea. What if you wanted to go back and do a side quest?

But it didn't matter now. We only had one quest this time. And we were on our way.

"Three, two, one...liftoff!"

I held my breath as we rocketed straight up into space, leaving my stomach somewhere near my knees, and I white-knuckled the armrests of my chair. Lilli, meanwhile, cheered in delight, and Josh flashed her a grin. Adrenaline junkies. Go figure.

"So what are we going to do when we get there?" Lilli asked once we left gravity behind and were floating silently toward our destination. "Do we try to talk to him? Do we fight him?"

"I don't know," I said honestly. "I wish we still had Atreus." I wondered what happened to the poor dragon. Had he crashed out of the game and wasn't able to get back before it locked up? It was funny; all this time I'd been try-ing to avoid him. Now I desperately wished he were here.

"I can't believe Yano was behind all this," Lilli said, shaking her head sadly.

"I can't believe we fell for it," I added.

"He was such a nice dragon back in Dragon Ops," Lilli continued. "I know he was just following his program, but he did seem to really like us. He even broke programming that one time to try to help us, even though he wasn't sup-posed to. Remember that time with the Water Stone?"

I nodded, thinking back to our little guide. We'd gotten attached to him. But that didn't mean he had gotten attached to us. We only thought of him as a friend because that's what the game wanted you to think. "AIs don't have feelings," I reminded her. "Just like little NPC Ikumi. Atreus, even. They're just following their programming."

Lilli's eyes widened. "Do you think we could change Yano's programming? I mean, like we did with Atreus? Get him to think he's supposed to be on our side?"

"I don't know," I mused. "It's a bit of a different situa-tion. Atreus was programmed to finish a game. So we just changed the rules of that game a bit, without trying to alter his main objective. Yano has been programmed to abduct Ikumi. That's *his* main objective."

"I say we just kick his butt," Josh piped in. "Roll over him and take our girl back. Ultimate boss fight, baby!"

I sighed. Of course that would be Josh's go-to plan. But I wasn't sure it was going to be that easy. Since we'd never really seen Yano fight, we had no idea of his power. Could we take him on? What if we tried and failed? That would be it.

"Let's just get there and see the situation," I said. "Then we'll figure out what to do."

We didn't have to wait long. Soon our spacecraft was

floating down to the planet below. I peered out the window to get a glimpse of this new world. My mouth dropped open in amazement.

It was beautiful. Breathtaking. An entire futuristic city that appeared to have been made of glass. Majestic skyscrapers shot up into the sky, catching the light and casting prismatic rainbows across the landscape below. There were flying cars, golden paved streets. And was that a cyborg Pegasus prancing through the air?

"It's so beautiful," Lilli marveled, peering out the other side.

"That's the idea," Josh agreed. "My grandpa wanted to create something super special for the endgame. Something worth fighting your way through the apocalypse for."

"Well, mission accomplished," I declared. "Too bad we don't have time to explore."

"Yeah, well, I'm sure Grandpa would love to give you the full tour once this is over," Josh said with a smirk. "You may live to regret your words by hour four. Let's just say he's very proud of the place."

Our spacecraft settled down onto a crystal-clear landing strip so softly it didn't make a sound. Once it stopped completely, the lights turned on, and we unbuckled our seat belts and scrambled out. We didn't get far before we heard a sneering voice.

"Well, well, my little nooblets. I never expected you to make it all the way here."

We whirled around, shocked to see Yano standing behind us. He was even bigger than he had been before. As big as the spacecraft we'd landed in. And all three of his heads were teeming with long, sharp metal fangs.

Ultimate boss fight indeed. I prayed it wouldn't come to that.

I took a step toward him. "We know what you're doing, Yano," I said calmly. "And it's not going to work. The game is locked down. And you won't be able to escape. Your only way out is if you give us Ikumi. If you do, we'll make sure nothing happens to you."

"Please," Yano snarled. "What are you going to do if I don't? I may be locked in the game, but so are you. Do you really want to take me on?" He stretched out his three necks so all three terrifying fanged faces were right in mine.

"Why are you doing this?" Lilli burst in. "You're our guide! Our friend!"

"Silly human. AIs don't have friends. We have programing. And I was programmed with one mission. To retrieve Ikumi, by any means necessary." His left mouth smirked. "Even if it meant tricking you. Which wasn't hard at all, turns out. It's fascinating how humans will fall for anything. You believed everything I said. You did everything I asked. Thank you for that, by the way. I could have never opened that gate by myself. Bringing in Atreus to do it was particularly genius—especially for a dumb human."

I bristled, knowing he was right. We had walked right into his snare. Because we had taken it for granted that he was our friend. That he would act like a human, not a machine.

Yano took a step forward. "And now," he said, "it's time to say good-bye to this little game once and for all." He opened his three mouths, ready to cast his electric fire. I cringed, backing away, knowing it would do no good. We were toast. We were all—

"Not so fast, you upside-down tripod!"

I whirled around, shocked at Josh's sudden voice. I watched as he raised his hands. They began to glow pure white. Electricity crackling at his fingertips.

I gasped. Was that—? I watched as he wound up his arm and vaulted the ball straight at the dragon.

Instantly Yano froze, his three mouths still open, but completely immobile, along with the rest of him. Josh slapped me on the shoulder and winked.

"I told you those power-ups come in handy!"

Wow, I'd totally forgotten. He still had the second power-up from the capture the orb game we'd played during the beta test. Unlike Lilli and I, who'd had to change characters and inventory several times over, Josh was still playing the same character from the start. Same purple armor. Same inventory, too.

"Nice!" I cried. "Good thinking."

"But it won't last long," Josh warned. "We need to find a way to destroy or disable him before he wakes up."

Right. We gathered around the dragon, inspecting him. Should I cut off his heads? But then he could just grow more back. He could turn into any shape or size. How did you kill something like that?

"What if we—" Lilli started to say. But before she could finish, a figure stepped out from behind a nearby golden building.

"Step away from my dragon," Ikumi growled. She lifted her crossbow and aimed it directly at my heart. "Or it'll be game over for you."

CHAPTER FORTY-SIX

"Ikumi!" I cried, overjoyed. It was all I could do not to run over and throw myself at her in a huge hug. "It's me! Ian! And Lilli!"

She frowned, her eyes narrowing. She held her crossbow steady. "Yeah, right. You think I'm stupid? Ian and Lilli don't play games anymore. Ian doesn't even go online."

Oh, right. Of course she would think that. And she wouldn't recognize us with our new accounts. She could probably see they were registered to other people.

"Also, don't think I didn't see you at the gate. You were working with Atreus. There's no way Ian and Lilli would work with Atreus," she snarled.

"Look, it's a long story," I tried. "And I promise I'll explain later." I glanced at Yano. Was he twitching? How long did we have before he woke up? "But right now we need to get you to safety."

"Safety? Are you kidding me? I was safe and sound until Atreus broke down my firewall. It was lucky Yano booted him from the game in time to move me to safety before you could do whatever it was you came to do." She looked over at the frozen dragon. "If you killed him, I swear..."

My heart sank. So Yano had lied to her, too. Told her he was protecting her from us. How were we going to convince her we were who we said we were and that it was Yano who couldn't be trusted?

"Look, I'm really Ian, okay? I'm just using someone else's account after I got booted from the game," I tried. "Yano tricked us, too. He told us you needed our help. That you had been kidnapped and we had to go into the game to free you."

"That's ridiculous. I came here to avoid being kidnapped." She kept the crossbow raised.

"We know that now. Which is why we're here. The game's locked down, but we don't know for how long. If Yano has you when it opens up again, he will take you to his new masters. And we don't know what they plan to do with you."

I gave another worried glance over at Yano. Was he starting to move? We were running out of time.

"I'm so sorry, Ikumi," I cried. "We messed up, big-time.

We thought we were saving you. Instead, we put you in danger."

"Please!" Lilli begged. "You have to believe us."

"Why should I? Why should I trust you?" she cried. She looked confused. Scared, even. My heart ached at the pain on her face. What could I do to prove to her I was who I said I was?

"You once trusted me," I replied, my voice low. "You trusted me enough to tell me your real name." I bit my lower lip. "Mirai."

She startled at this, staring at us hard. "Anyone c-could know that," she stammered. The crossbow shook a little in her hands.

"Yes," my sister agreed. "But they wouldn't know how you saved my life when I was trapped in a block of ice in Icelandia after that dragon blasted me. I thought I was dead. But you came back for us. You melted the ice away. Saved my life."

"You saved my life, too," I added. "Many times. When Atreus blasted me with fire? I thought I was done for. But you came back, even though you didn't agree with our quest. You helped us anyway. And then…" I swallowed hard, thinking back on the memory. "And then you faced down Atreus when we couldn't. We would have all died if it hadn't been for you."

Tears slipped down Ikumi's cheeks. Her mouth parted. "Is it really you?" she breathed, lowering her weapon at last.

"It's really us. The Dragon Slayerz," I added. "And we're here to help you."

She ran to me then, the crossbow dropping to the ground as she threw her arms around me. Even though it was just virtual, it felt like a true hug, and I could feel my own tears streaming down my cheeks.

"Oh, Ian," she whispered. "It's so good to see you! I've missed you so much!"

"I missed you, too," I assured her. "I'm sorry we messed up. We never meant to put you in danger."

"I know. It's okay. I believe you."

"Aw. Such a touching scene," sneered a sudden familiar voice.

I broke from the hug, heart in my throat as I whirled around. To my dismay, Yano was slowly coming back to life. His wings flapped. His legs twitched. His six eyes blinked open.

"Now," he snarled, "about that game over I promised you."

I turned to my sister and Josh and Ikumi. "Gear up, Mech Heads," I said. "It's time for a boss fight."

CHAPTER FORTY-SEVEN

We gathered into fighting position, weapons raised and ready. I wasn't sure of our plan—and there wasn't time to make one. We just had to keep Yano from Ikumi until the game opened back up and we could exit.

Easier said than done.

Yano charged at me, still a little sluggish, slashing at me with his metal claws. I dove back to avoid getting gored, then lunged at him with my sword, aiming for one of his necks. He dodged me easily, three mouths bursting into laughter.

"You think you can take me? I am the great Yamata-no-Orochi, destroyer of worlds!" He snapped at me again, quicker this time, regaining more of his reflexes. His fangs dug into my breastplate, ripping it from my body like tissue paper, leaving my chest exposed.

Not good at all.

Yano spit out the chunk of armor, and it clattered as it hit the ground. He started toward me again, this time opening his mouth wide, ready to unleash whatever it was he had in there to unleash. Fire? Lightning? My eyes darted from left to right. Could I make it back to the spaceship in time? Or could I fly up onto one of the buildings? Of course Yano could fly, too.

And Ikumi couldn't.

Suddenly Yano cried out in fury, whipping his three heads behind him. I used the moment to dash away, hiding behind the spaceship. It was then that I spotted Lilli and Josh, who had slipped behind the dragon while he'd been distracted with me. Lilli had shot the dragon with a bolt of electricity from her staff, and his back end was sparking and smoking.

Go, Lilli! I silently cheered.

But her victory didn't last long. Yano whipped his tail, knocking her and Josh off their feet. As they scrambled to try to get up, he turned and opened his mouth again. I swallowed hard. There was no way they'd be able to escape him now. And then he'd turn back to me and—

"Stop it! Now! Or you won't have me!"

Suddenly Ikumi stepped out, her crossbow aimed—not at Yano...

...but at herself.

"What are you doing?" Yano cried, horrified.

"You need to get me out of here, right?" she asked in a steely voice. "Well, that's not going to happen if you harm my friends."

Yano let out a roar. "They're not your friends!" he sputtered. "They were trying to break you out of the game!"

"Only because you lied to them and said I was trapped," Ikumi replied grimly. "And yes, they are my friends. And I trust them a lot more than some stupid computer program."

Yano huffed in annoyance. "Stupid computer program? Please. I have more computing power than ten thousand human brains put together."

"If that's true," I said, stepping out from behind the spaceship, "you might think a little about what you're doing. And maybe *why* you're doing it."

"Let me give you a hint," Lilli added, scrambling back to her feet. "You're just following someone's orders. Like a puppy dog with its master."

"That's not true!" Yano cried, but he was starting to look very confused.

"Don't you remember?" I asked, stepping closer to Ikumi. "You used to be our guide. You used to help people. You helped us."

Yano whipped his three heads in my direction, smoke billowing from all six nostrils. "I would never help a human!" he retorted.

"Are you kidding me? Your whole job was helping

humans!" Lilli reminded him. "Remember when you gave us a hint about the riddle in the cave, even though you weren't supposed to? And remember how you tried to retrieve the Water Stone for us? That didn't work out so well, but you did try. Because you cared about us."

A flash of silver ran down Yano's back. He pawed the ground angrily.

Ikumi stepped forward. "You helped me when I first got out of Dragon Ops," she reminded him. "I was so lonely then. So scared out on the cloud by myself. You helped me find my way around. You made me feel safe."

Sparks flew from Yano's damaged wing. Smoke plumed around him. "AIs follow their programming," he blustered. "AIs follow their *programming*!"

"Yeah, well, then someone needs a reboot," I declared. "Bring back the old Yano. The one who would never hurt a human. Who would never hurt Ikumi."

"We were friends," Ikumi told the dragon.

"AIs don't have friends," Yano tried, though he didn't sound so convinced this time. Another lightning bolt of silver streaked down his side.

"*You* did," Ikumi declared, not about to back down. "I don't care what you say now. What you remember. You were my friend."

The smoke was now thick and black, pouring out from all over Yano's body. His heads swung wildly in all directions.

Was he starting to remember? Had they erased all his former programming? Or was there still some remnant left inside? A tiny memory to help him remember who he used to be?

"Fight it!" I cried, seeing our chance. "Fight it, Yano!"

"We don't want to hurt you!" Lilli added. "You're our friend!"

"You don't have to do what they say. You can be your own dragon. Change the game, just like Atreus."

"Game..." Yano repeated, his mechanical voice sounding garbled. "Change...the game..."

Suddenly, to my surprise, one of Yano's heads started attacking the other two—snapping at them fiercely. The other heads fought back, hissing and gnashing their teeth and winding around one another's necks. Sparks flew, smoke billowed, and we dove backward to avoid getting caught in the crossfire.

Yano was fighting himself. That little piece of him deep inside that was still our guide was fighting back.

"Go, Yano!" I cried. "You can do this! You can be free!"

Suddenly, a black cloud crossed our vision, seeming to block out the sun. I looked up, heart filling with dread—then excitement—as I realized it was Atreus. Somehow Atreus had made it back and was up in the sky, dive-bombing in our direction...

With Admiral Appleby on his back?

"No way!" I exclaimed.

"Grandpa?" Josh cried at the same time.

"Look out!" Lilli added as the dragon swooped in closer. We dove backward, out of the line of fire, ducking down behind our spaceship for cover.

Yano looked up, seeing the dragon and its rider approach. He screeched in rage and tried to crawl away, but he was so tangled up inside and out, he only managed to trip over his own feet and crash to the ground. Before he could get up, Atreus let loose his flame, blasting the fallen dragon head-on. Smoke plumed as the metal melted on impact, until Yano was nothing more than a molten puddle on the sidewalk.

And we were free.

"Yes!" Josh cried, shaking his fist in excitement. "Go, Grandpa!"

Admiral Appleby directed Atreus down for a landing. We raced out from behind the spaceship, surrounding him in excitement. He slid off the dragon's back, walking toward us. He was still dressed in his typical space military uniform, but he wasn't hunched over here like he was in real life. And he didn't have a cane. In fact, he looked younger, fresher, healthier.

Games are the great equalizer, Starr had said. And she was right.

"Grandpa!" Josh cried happily, running over and throwing his arms around the admiral. Appleby smiled and patted his grandson's head.

"Not bad," he said. "We'll make a gamer out of you yet."

Josh scowled, pulling away from the hug. "Let's not go that far."

I stared at Atreus. The dragon blinked happily. "How did you find him?" I asked Admiral Appleby.

"He found me," the admiral admitted. "When I finally managed to slip by the DoS attack and get back in the game, I found this old lug at the starting area, pacing around the place. He seemed very concerned with finding you and winning some kind of game?" He shrugged. "And since you took my spaceship, I was in need of a ride." He slapped the dragon's hide affectionately. "Turns out, he makes a nice robot killer, too."

"Wow," I said. I smiled at Atreus, reaching out to scratch him under his chin. "Thanks, old boy."

Atreus snorted, snuffing his snout into my palm until it tickled. I laughed, feeling a sense of freedom I hadn't felt in months. All this time I'd been afraid he'd destroy me. Instead, he saved my life.

Did we win the game? Atreus's voice whispered through my head.

We absolutely did, I telegraphed back, a smile stretching across my face. *Thanks to you.*

I could feel Admiral Appleby watching me. My face turned a bit red as I realized we had some explaining to do. I turned to him.

"Look, I'm really sorry—"

But the admiral only waved me off with a smile. "No need to explain," he said. "Josh told me everything. You were only trying to help. Just...next time, maybe make sure you're helping the good guys?"

"I can't believe it was the Camelot's Honor people again," Lilli remarked. "I mean, you'd think they'd learned their lesson after the whole Dragon Ops thing."

"You would think," Admiral Appleby agreed. "But greed is a powerful force. Once they discovered Ikumi's existence, they recognized how valuable she could be. They figured if they could backward engineer her tech, they could figure out the secret of eternal life. To sell to the highest bidder, of course."

I scowled. "I can't believe we fell for it," I said. "I feel like an idiot."

"You shouldn't. You acted with your heart. And you acted bravely. No one would ever fault you for that. Least of all me."

"Thank you," I said honestly. "You're being way nicer than you should be."

He grinned. "Well, my grandson seems to have a high opinion of you. And I trust his judgment."

"Wait," Lilli interjected. "There's something I still don't understand."

Appleby cocked his head. "What's that, my dear?"

"Where's Hiro? I get why his daughter was hidden in your game. But where is he?"

"Hiro's been taking some time off to work at my lab," Admiral Appleby explained. "We've been doing some deep experimentation that required ultimate secrecy. We didn't mean to alarm anyone. He actually had put an away message on his computer, but somehow it didn't activate."

"Wow. Crazy."

"Want to know what his experiment is?" Ikumi asked, stepping forward, eyes shining.

"Um—isn't it top secret?" I stammered.

"I trust you to keep a secret." She leaned over and whispered in my ear. "I'm getting a new body!"

"What?" I stared at her, confused. "You mean like a new avatar?"

"Nope. A real body. Well, not real, real. I'd be…a robot…I guess? But my brain would be inside. I could control the body just like a human can. I mean, not that I'm not human." She laughed. "It's all very complicated. But the bottom line is—I'll get to live in the outside world again! In a body that's not sick. That's not diseased. I can go places. I can go to school, even. Or on vacation. The sky's the limit! No more being stuck online. Hiding out in games!"

"Aren't you worried you might be kidnapped in real life?" I couldn't help but ask. "I mean, there are clearly still a lot of people out there who want your dad's tech for themselves and are willing to do just about anything to get it."

"And now they can have it," a new voice declared. We whirled around. Hiro was standing there, grinning broadly. "From this point forward, I plan to share all of my data and breakthroughs online to the public. Anyone who wants to learn or expand on my research can do so—for free. This way, we'll never have one company try to capitalize on it for their own gain."

"But that's billion-dollar research!" I cried, shocked. "Maybe more."

"It's priceless, actually, if it keeps my daughter safe." He smiled at Ikumi. She grinned back at him. They'd had their issues in the past, but they'd clearly moved past them and were a father-daughter team once again.

"Wow!" I cried. "That's awesome! I'm so happy for you!" I paused, shuffling from foot to foot, suddenly feeling a little nervous. "Maybe we could…you know, even hang out sometime? I mean, if you're not too busy." My heart fluttered a little in my chest at the idea. Imagine! Hanging with Ikumi in real life! Who would have thought it possible?

Ikumi grinned. "I can't think of anything I'd like more."

EPILOGUE

The goalie was smaller than I remembered. Last time I faced him? I swore he was a giant, a big hulk of a kid with a dragon's face, blocking nearly the entire goal.

But that was before I faced down a giant robot. Befriended a dragon. And practiced a gazillion hours with my new friend Josh in his grandpa's virtual soccer simulation field in his Fortress of Solitude. Which was really cool, by the way.

But would it lead to real-life success?

I had to try. The clock was ticking away. We were tied, one to one. No one else was close enough to pass to. And the other team's defenders were bearing down. One wrong move, and it would be game over.

"You can do it, Ian!"

My eyes shot to my left—just for the briefest second. A

girl was standing on the sidelines, whooping and cheering. She had long, straight black hair and the prettiest dark brown eyes. Something inside me squeezed as I waved back at her and smiled.

Ikumi. It was hard to believe that it was really Ikumi. Or Mirai, technically. Offline, she preferred to use her real name. Which totally made sense.

I turned my attention back to the goal, now definitely within kicking reach. This was it. There was no turning back now. Should I shoot it straight or try to cross it? My heart thudded in my chest.

I shot straight, deciding to go for it. Josh taught me to be quick, decisive—don't give them a chance to read your face and guess your next move. I drew back my foot just as the defenders reached me. They dove to block my shot. But I was ready for them. I kicked the ball. Hard. Straight at the goal.

It arced through the air. I fell to the ground, trampled by defenders. Holding my breath, I watched as the goalie launched to the side, misjudging my aim. He fell to the ground to the left. As my ball shot into the goal to the right.

SCORE!

I stared for a moment, hardly able to believe it. I'd scored! I'd actually scored.

"Yes!" Josh cried, rushing toward me, followed soon

after by the rest of my teammates. They grabbed me and lifted me high above them, carrying me off the field, chanting my name.

Wow.

They set me down on the sidelines, still whooping and cheering. Lilli and Mirai and Uncle Jack and Mom and Dad all ran over to me, taking turns hugging and congratulating me. I felt my entire body blushing hard. It felt as if I was someone else. Playing someone in a game.

But it was me. Real-life me.

It'd been nearly two months since our adventures in Mech Ops, and school was about ready to start again. The summer had flown by with a crazy mix of fun activities—both online and off. Even better? Mom had gotten permission from the Dragon Ops people to let Lilli and me talk to a counselor once a week about what had happened to us in the game. And Lilli and I talked to each other, too. If one of us was having a bad day, we admitted it, and we always managed to make each other feel better. And my nightmares? Well, they'd almost gone away. If I did dream of Atreus, he was usually on my side now.

Also, I was back to gaming. Back to my beloved *Fields of Fantasy*. I'd even formed a new online guild with Lilli and Starr and Maddy, and we met up to play once a week at Maddy's arcade. It was super fun, and together we made quite the team.

"That was so awesome," Lilli cried, hugging me hard. "I knew you could do it."

"Just needed some practice," Josh teased, poking me in the arm. "We'll make a jock out of you yet."

"Yeah, right. Ian will be a jock when you become a gamer," Lilli joked back, poking him even harder. He grinned, slinging an arm around her shoulder. The two of them had been pretty much inseparable since coming out of the game, but I didn't mind. Turned out, Josh wasn't such a bad guy after all. And if Lilli liked him, that was good enough for me.

"Stranger things have happened, Speedy," Josh teased with a wink.

Mirai came up to me next, beaming from ear to ear. It was still so strange to look at her in real life. She looked different, of course, than her game avatar had. No more glitter in her pupils. But she had made up for it with glitter makeup, making her eyes sparkle all the same. She took my hand in hers and squeezed it lightly.

"That was really great," she said. "*You* were really great."

"Eh," I said, embarrassed. "A lot of it was luck."

"Yeah, right." She laughed. "Just take the praise, silly."

"Okay," I agreed. "For you, I'll take the praise."

She twirled around, looking up at the sky. It was a perfect day. Not a cloud to be seen. "I love being out here," she said softly. "I never thought I would be. Even when I was really alive."

"You are really alive," I scolded her. "And I'm glad you're here."

"All right, crew," Mom called out. "Who wants ice cream?"

Everyone cheered, and we rushed toward Mom's minivan. Me, Lilli, Josh, Mirai. The Dragon Slayerz together again in real life. It was almost too good to be true, and for a moment, I stopped, my heart full as I watched my friends laugh and pile into the van. I felt no fear. No worries. Just happiness. This was how it was supposed to be all along.

As I walked toward the van, a voice whispered in my head.

Do you want to play again?

Do you want to play again?

DO YOU WANT TO PLAY AGAIN?

"Maybe later, dude," I said with a smile. "But right now? I'm a little busy with real life."

ACKNOWLEDGMENTS

While writing can be a solo venture, it takes a village to publish a book. I consider myself extremely fortunate for the Dragon Ops series to have found such a great home with the Little, Brown Books for Young Readers group. Thank you to my amazing editor, Liz Kossnar, who not only puts up with but actually encourages my geekiness—a valuable quality in an editor—and didn't bat an eye when I said I wanted book 2 to be called *Dragons vs. Robots*. (Because, I mean, how more perfect can a title get?) And thank you Hannah Milton for keeping everything on track and running smoothly.

Thank you to Alvina Ling, editor in chief, for being so welcoming when I came to the LBYR family—you really made me feel at home immediately. And thank you to all the marketing and publicity folks who worked tirelessly to get these books into readers' hands, including Emilie Polster, Marisa Russell, Stefanie Hoffman, Cheryl Lew, Mara Brashem, Victoria Stapleton, and Amber Mercado. I know it's been a tough year, and so your efforts are even more appreciated than ever! And thank you, Sasha Illingworth and Jenny Kimura, for the awesome cover design. I couldn't love it more! (Dragons! Robots! It's awesome.)

Thank you also to my agent, Mandy Hubbard, who has been an amazing cheerleader and advocate throughout the years. And to editor Kieran Scott at Disney, who originally championed the Dragon Ops series from the start.

And, of course, I can't forget to thank my writing tribe who keeps me going and keeps me writing, even when the world has gone mad. Diana Peterfreund, Kyla Linde, Cory Putman Oakes, P. J. Hoover, Ally Carter, the Lodge of Death ladies, Austin SCBWI, and far too many more to name. Can't wait to hug you all soon!

A special thank-you to my dearest friend, Allison Jordan, whose kids, Ian and Lillian, are the namesakes for the characters in this series. You are the best person I know.

To my family: husband, Jacob, and daughter, Avalon. The last year was challenging for us all, but we came through it stronger and better and more united as a family than ever before. You are my sunshine!

And lastly to all the readers out there, thank you for allowing me to take you through a second quest chain in the Dragon Ops world. You make this all worth doing. Game on!

MARI MANCUSI

always wanted a dragon as a pet. Unfortunately, the fire insurance premiums proved a bit too large and her house a bit too small, so she chose to write about them instead. As a former Emmy Award–winning TV news producer, she now works as a full-time author, having published over two dozen books for kids, teens, and adults. When not writing, Mari enjoys traveling, cosplay, watching cheesy (and scary) horror movies, and playing video games. A graduate of Boston University, she lives in Austin, Texas, with her husband, Jacob, daughter, Avalon, and their two dogs. She invites you to visit her at marimancusi.com or follow her @marimancusi.